NORTHERN FRIGHTS 4

Edited by
Don Hutchison

Mosaic Press
Oakville, ON. — Buffalo, N.Y.

Canadian Cataloguing in Publication Data

Main entry under title:
Northern frights 4
ISBN 0-88962-639-1
1. Fantastic fiction, Canadian (English).*   2. Fantastic fiction, American.   3. Canadian fiction (English) - 20th Century.*   4. American fiction - 20th century.
I. Hutchison, Don.
PS8323.S3N664 1997   C813;.0876608054   C97-930001-0
PR9197.35.S33N664 1997

Published by MOSAIC PRESS, P.O. Box 1032, Oakville, Ontario, L6J 5E9, Canada. Offices and warehouse at 1252 Speers Road, Units #1&2, Oakville, Ontario, L6L 5N9, Canada and Mosaic Press, 85 River Rock Drive, Suite 202, Buffalo, N.Y., 14207, USA.

MOSAIC PRESS, in Canada:
1252 Speers Road, Units #1&2, Oakville,
Ontario, L6L 5N9
Phone / Fax: (905) 825-2130
E-mail:
cp507@freenet.toronto.on.ca

MOSAIC PRESS, in the USA:
85 River Rock Drive, Suite 202, Buffalo,
N.Y., 14207
Phone / Fax: 1-800-387-8992
E-mail:
cp507@freenet.toronto.on.ca

MOSAIC PRESS in the UK and Europe:

DRAKE INTERNATIONAL SERVICES

Market House, Market Place,

Deddington, Oxford. OX15 OSF

Mosaic Press acknowledges the assistance of the Canada Council, the Ontario Arts Council and the Dept. of Canadian Heritage, Government of Canada, for their support of our publishing programme.

FIRST EDITION
ISBN 0-88962- 639-1
Cover Illustration by: James Kroesen
Cover and book design by: Susan Parker
Printed and bound in Canada

CONTENTS

INTRODUCTION

Of the praise this series has garnered, one comment that we hear frequently is "I don't usually read horror, but Northern Frights is *good*."

Remarks of this kind are both rewarding and at the same time frustrating. They are particularly irksome when voiced by mystery or science fiction enthusiasts, who have themselves endured the condescension of those who believe that little or nothing meritorious can be found in genre fiction.

When we introduced our first volume I made passing reference to such illustrious names as Mary Shelley, Nathaniel Hawthorne, Ambrose Bierce, Edgar Allan Poe, Algernon Blackwood, John Collier, Ray Bradbury, Fritz Leiber, and Shirley Jackson—just a few of the many authors who over the centuries have enriched our literary heritage with classic tales of terror and the supernatural. We were not suggesting that Northern Frights writers should adopt the vintage mannerisms of a Poe or Blackwood or imitate the unique voice of a Bradbury or a Leiber. What we were attempting to point out was that the tradition of literary horror is a long and honorable one.

The reason why so many of the greatest authors have at one time or another turned to writing what is now branded as "horror" fiction is that these kind of stories have a universal appeal—perhaps because fear is a universal emotion. Stories of terror and the supernatural are timeless; they cut across all levels of culture and class and all levels of sophistication. As the late great author and editor Karl Wagner expressed it, "Adulthood erodes our sense of wonder, society bludgeons our intellectuality, life proves tedium the master of adventure. We never forget how to be afraid."

It may just be that dark fantasy has endured because it's the purest form of escapism; after all, none of this stuff is really true...right? On the other hand, one of the fundamental impulses of horror and Gothic literature is to make the forbidden accessible, a way of confronting our own inevitable death and dissolution and our own darkest nightmares within the slightly distancing environment of fiction. Read Poe or Bradbury or Jackson and discover a literature that routinely deals with such themes of unease, yet by virtue of its poetry and exoticism is widely enjoyed as entertainment.

Most of the stories herein work well as both entertainment and commentary. They are strong, intelligent stories written by authors who care about people—real people with all their dreams and fears. Of course, these *are* horror stories (a dark cloud is always moving nearer), but the virtues of a good horror story are the virtues of all fine writing. While a science fiction story may get by on a particularly novel idea and a mystery tale on a clever plot, effective horror fiction must build up suspense and atmosphere with a subtle accretion of style, characterization, balance and narrative energy.

A meaningful theme and subtext are important. Colleen Anderson based her present story, "Consuming Fear," on the effects of an operation that she endured. Using her personal experience as a springboard, she employed her storytelling imagination to bring fresh insights to a problem many of us find too painful to contemplate. As she explains it, "It is unfortunate that there are now so many stories about abuse that we have inured ourselves to the horror and don't wish to read them anymore. Thus, I had to look for a new twist that still reminds us, and at the same time gives us a good read."

A new twist. A good read. Combined with vigorous writing, these are the guidelines for budding Northern Frights writers. When we began this series we announced that our book would be an open market for quality fiction whether the author be a Big Name or a talented unknown. This is more unusual than you might think. Despite claims to the contrary, many anthologies are closed, invitation-only "concept" books open only to well-known writers and possibly the editor's close friends. This makes for a much easier job of editing and presumably a more commercial product—but the results are all too often disappointing.

Foolish or not, we buy stories, not names. Frankly, reading through an ever-mounting pile of hopeful author's entries is not always a lot of fun, nor is the inevitable task of rejecting a dozen stories for each one chosen. But the rewards are there. The feedback on our series has been extremely good. With this, our fourth volume, I feel that we are presenting our strongest collection yet—the only gimmick being that of offering readers seventeen immensely readable stories.

As usual, our thanks to Howard Aster and the folks at Mosaic Press for their confidence in this series. Thanks also to Peter Halasz and Bob Hadji, who helped, and to Jean for her love and patience. Northern Frights would not exist without the support of the many fine writers who honor us with their best work. We hope you enjoy their stories. We sincerely think you will.

VIA INFLUENZA

by
David Annandale

David Annandale was born in Winnipeg in 1967 and, with the exception of a few years in Paris, has lived there most of his life. His stories have appeared in numerous magazines as well as the anthologies *100 Wicked Little Witch Stories* and *A Horror Story a Day: 365 Scary Stories.* He reports that he got the idea for "Via Influenza" from asking himself many of the same questions his protagonist does, wondering about the stories behind disused roads and forgotten buildings.

The meaning of roads is fragile.

Derek had become aware of this some time ago. Initially, he thought it was an urban phenomenon, but that was only because it was in the city that he had first noticed it. He'd been driving through a part of Winnipeg he didn't see often, just northwest of the city centre, when grey brick and concrete had suddenly made him pull over. He got out of the car and began snapping pictures. Of the factory: nameless, windows grimed with years, and had they ever been clean? and was there such a thing as a new factory? Of the shops across the street: named but faded under grey, pawn shop and parts shop and café, indistinguishable, Pepsi signs hung when they still used molasses, and were the shops ever open? And did anyone actually come here? That was the question that took over. Surely not, the answer seemed to be. There was no one around. The factory was silent. The shops were shut in the middle of a weekday afternoon. The only cars Derek could see were in transit. The road could only be for taking people *through* here, not *to* here. But then why come here at all? What did the road mean in this context? What did it mean at all?

He wanted his pictures to ask these questions. He doubted anyone could answer them, nor did he want that. The questions were the important thing. They forced a new look, a new perspective on the viewer. That was no bad thing.

If it worked, that is. But Val said it did. The critics said so too. So he'd continued his study, finding more and more city streets that were irrelevant to the districts they went through.

A week ago, he discovered that rural roads could be just as meaningless, just as easily. It struck him while he and Val were driving back from her sister's farm. The roads gridded off to the horizon, a thin layer, gossamer fragile, overlaying the prairie's implacable monotony. He realized how easy it would be to get lost. Here the roads lost meaning completely. They weren't just rushing past pointless locations on the way to somewhere else. They were going nowhere. Derek made another study.

It was Val who suggested the next step.

"Why not combine the two?" she asked.

"What do you mean?" Derek sipped his sherry. It was Friday. It was spring. They were home from work, and the weekend beckoned.

"You've done the urban series and the rural series. Now do one of both."

"Um, and how precisely—"

"Ghost towns."

Derek sat and blinked at his wife for a few moments. She smiled at him. She twiddled one of her paintbrushes around her fingers, her expression loving, yes, but smug? Oh, that too.

"Ghost towns," Derek repeated. Of course. The perfect combo. The lost web of prairie road plus the city, shut down and back turned for good and all. "Can you give me a single valid reason why I didn't think of that?" he asked.

"Certainly. You're just not as quick as I am, that's all." Her smile became a grin.

He mirrored her. "Is that right?"

"Yes it is."

"So suppose you tell me where I'm going to find just the right town. I would imagine that most former town sites are fields now. Wouldn't look like much."

Her grin turned into something that might have been a leer if it hadn't been both too elegant and too evil. Derek's fingers twitched for a camera. That look, backdropped by a late May's evening window, deserved better preservation than his memory could offer.

"Suppose I do." Val reached behind her easel and produced a folder. She sauntered over to where Derek sat on the couch and tossed the folder into his lap. She sat down next to him as he opened it.

Inside he found a sheaf of photocopies. He picked up the first. It was a newspaper article from 1918. "Influenza Epidemic in Pierton," he read. He glanced at Val. "Never heard of the place."

She sighed. "Of course not. Keep reading."

He turned to the next piece. "Pierton Quarantined." Then the next: "Pierton Decimated." Then there was a map, locating Pierton in Snow Valley, not far from Roseisle. "What happened?" he asked Val.

"What do you think?"

He stared. "They died?"

She nodded.

"*All* of them?"

"So I gather. Any survivors must have moved away."

"A whole town." Derek shook his head. "Doesn't seem possible."

"There was an influenza pandemic at the time, Derek. It killed more people than World War I."

"The flu?"

"The flu."

He whistled. "Glad we licked that charmer. My God, this sounds so *medieval*." He frowned. "You've done a lot of digging. You've *got* to have an ulterior motive."

She rubbed up against him, purring. "Your artistic well-being isn't reason enough?"

"Hardly."

She ran a finger down his cheek. "I'm so transparent."

"I'm so smart."

She chuckled and reached over to turn over the map. There was one more clipping underneath. It was from the July 23, 1968 edition of the *Winnipeg Tribune*. "Artists to Set Up Colony in Ghost Town."

"Ah," Derek smiled. "Now I understand. And did they?"

"If they did, they didn't stick it out for very long. But this is what makes me think the town's worth checking out, if a project like that was doable as recently as '68. Look," she pointed to the third paragraph. "Says here a lot of the buildings were stone."

"Highly unusual."

"Yes it is. But lucky for us, eh? There should be more than just a field."

Derek took her hand and caressed it. "Tell me. Just how much self-interest is behind your sudden inspiration for *my* next career move?"

She leaned in and nibbled his earlobe. "Call it a happy confluence of interests."

"Is that right?"

"That's right."

"Like this one?"

"Like this one."

They headed out to Pierton late Saturday morning. It was sunny when they left, but the horizon was frowning before they'd been on the road for an hour.

The irony of the trip appealed to Derek. They were travelling purposefully, giving a road meaning, in order to find that meaning's loss.

He folded the map. "Know the way?" he asked Val.

"For now." She overtook a dawdling Geo. "I'll probably need you to navigate once we get near Roseisle."

Derek nodded. "Incidentally, why are you so interested in the colony?"

"Well, you know how you've been working on the absence of meaning?"

"Yes."

"I'm playing with the reverse. I want to work with sites with a history. Art history is even better. And if most of the evidence is gone, and I have to bring the history back, then better still."

"I'll bet it's times like this you wish we lived in Europe."

"More history, you mean."

"Of the kind you want."

Val shrugged. "There's probably more around than we might think. It just fades away more easily here."

The clouds were waiting for them when they reached Snow Valley. The shift from prairie was a surprise, but just subtle enough not to be an ambush. Grasslands took over from cultivated fields. Clumps of trees camouflaged some of the early ground rolls. Then the road dipped, quite suddenly, and there were lots of trees, and they were into the valley. There were hills, virtually invisible from outside. Once you were here, though, they made their presence known and final. Rounded and hunched with age, they remembered Pangaca. They crowded around the car and drew the clouds down. The light changed from white to grey, then darker. Derek looked at the hills. He could almost hear them whisper: *History? Oh, we can tell you a thing or two about history. Just wait. Just you wait.* The hiss, he knew, was just the wind. He knew.

"Looks like rain," Val commented. She sounded like she sensed a need for intervention by the mundane, and so had supplied it herself.

"Um," said Derek. He wasn't sure he wanted to break the atmosphere, to interrupt the hills' concentration.

They came to a crossroads. Val stopped the car. "Could you check the map?" she asked.

Derek unfolded it. Lines ran over the land, doubtful as a palimpsest. "Left," he said, and Val turned onto gravel so old and disused it had mostly sunk back into the mud. Derek made a note to take a shot of the road, meaning fading to trace.

The road turned into a clump of trees, then dipped again, and levelled off in a shallow bowl. In it was the corpse of Pierton.

Val slowed the car down to a crawl.

A number of buildings were still standing, or at least were distinct ruins. Most of the roofs had caved in, and some walls had collapsed into cascades of stone. Derek saw a barn, one of the few wood structures still around, leaning at a forty-five degree angle. The scatter of the buildings implied a past presence of other roads, but there was only this one now. It went through the middle of Pierton, but then, coming out the other side, it stopped. Over. Gone beneath the grass.

Val stopped the car. She gestured at the field before them. "End of the road," she said.

Derek was already fumbling for the right lens, thinking Oh perfect, perfect. Perfect. "I have to tell you, honey," he said. "When you pick them, you don't kid around."

"No point in half measures."

"True enough." He got out of the car and stretched. He checked the clouds. They were a very dark grey now, with black in some formations. Definite low-light conditions.

"How long do you think we have?" Val asked.

"Before the rain? I don't know. Could start any moment, I'd say. Do you know what you want to see?"

"I want to look inside some of the buildings."

"Okay," said Derek. "Well I want to get some exterior shots while I still can. I'll come find you or meet you back here if it starts to bucket. Deal?"

"Deal." She picked up her sketching pad and headed off towards the nearest intact house.

Okay, Derek thought, what first? He looked around. The hills were still keeping close track of him. He decided to start with them. These wouldn't be road shots, but they could establish context. He began with focusing on the top of the hills, where the clouds were so low they were a lid over the valley. As he clicked the shutter, the wind came up, as if the hills resented his returning of the gaze. The breath was chill and sharp, a scalpel through his sweater.

He worked the view down, over the trees on the slopes, some leafed, some budding, some still the palsied claws of winter. Down, over the grass, already green, shaded richer yet by the darkly filtered light. And then the road, fading with a whisper into its grave.

When he turned around to take his first shot of Pierton itself, something flickered in the corner of his left eye. He had a sliver impression of a fragment of grey gauze, barely darker than the surrounding air, candleflame dancing. It was gone when he moved his head.

He shrugged, raised his camera— And there it was again: visible through the viewfinder, but not when he looked directly at the corner where it moved. Fatigue, he thought. Has to be. He couldn't feel the lower eyelid twitch he would have expected. But fatigue it must be, and he pushed the shutter release for proof.

He tried to ignore the grey as he blanketed the town with shots. But it was always there, flutter flutter, film ribbon. It didn't stay put either. It skittered to different sections of the frame, and of his vision.

Up left, down right, skating the periphery, sometimes flicking in from the edges, but never upfront, never face to face.

Keep 'em guessing.

Concentrate, Derek told himself. It would be a crime to waste such a perfect location with half-assed shooting. He made his thoughts focus beyond the viewfinder, past the flicker, to the town. He wanted to imagine the life that had been here, so he could better photograph its loss.

He walked slowly up the road, clicking, clicking, stealing souls. And so here: a rounded pile of stone going drowning in the grass, going down for the third time. And here: a store? Yes, could be. A store, bigger than the houses, roofless walls, windows the idiot glare of empty space. And here: the church, spire gone except for a broken molar base, and behind it—

—the cemetery. Derek was almost able to forget the flicker. There were only a couple of graves still visible, and Derek wondered who it had been who had warranted stone markers. The two graves were close enough together that he could keep them both in frame if he wanted to, but far enough apart that the distance, the absences, the loss, could not be missed. This, this was the centre to which his pictures had been moving. Here were the milestones for the end of all roads. Here even the ending was fading. Barely more than trace already, it disappeared from the land as it vanished from memory. In less than a century, there would be nothing left at all. Not even the presence of loss, the signs of death. Just the green, silent and smug in its reclamation.

So what, Derek wondered, was he doing with his photographs? Hardly a resurrection. Preservation? Perhaps. But he liked to think it was a bit more than that. He wasn't exactly keeping memories alive. He hadn't lived here. He didn't know what would be authentic to remember. But he was creating new memories. People could see his pictures. They could think about Pierton and its deaths, and maybe imagine the helplessness as disease spread its wings over your home, slamming down the little piece of history you were trying to make, putting an end to all future stories and erasing the old. But here was Derek, hero of the lens, freezing the closing images of final extinction, keeping at least the end alive a bit longer.

Wasn't that a form of life? If not a resurrection, at least a haunting? He liked to think so.

He raised the camera. One last exterior shot. Then he'd have covered the whole town. He centred on emptiness, but kept one stone at bottom left, isolated and cold under a grim sky, and click—and the flicker vanished and behind him, a fluttering rattle like the wings of a huge moth.

His shoulders spasmed, tension a steel trap. The wind blew colder, the hand of a glacier slowly wrapping its fingers around him, closing into a fist. His chest locked, refusing him breath.

"Derek?"

The moth sound stopped. Derek whirled with a shocked grunt. But it was only Val, who didn't ask him what the hell his problem was, only Val, who was looking pale and rattled and no better off than he was.

"Val?" he asked back, all mixed up with concern for her and relief that he wasn't alone anymore.

She inhaled, deep and shuddering. "Derek, there's something I need you to see." She took his hand with one just as cold. In a numb clasp, she pulled him out of the graveyard.

She led him around the church, across the road, and toward one of the three houses that still stood firm and whole. The roof sagged slightly, but wasn't going anywhere. There was glass over the dark windows, eyes that were not glazed and blank but secretive, brooding. The clouds leaned in closer, putting pressure on the hills. Old gods jostled for a better look.

Derek saw the house come for him, expand and open its mouth wide. Swallow. They were inside. The wind, whining shrill, dug at the windows' weak spots.

"It's downstairs," said Val.

Derek squeezed her hand, giving and seeking reassurance. They moved to the cellar steps, and breath held, went down.

Light oozed in, limp and grey, through narrow rectangles. It was just enough to reveal the secrets. Skeletons spread out over the floor. Derek counted six. Two were laid out neatly, side by side, in one corner. Three others sprawled and jumbled as if tossed. One of them appeared to have fallen down the stairs. The sixth was huddled against the far wall.

"My God," Derek whispered. This wasn't just a reminder of meaning's end. It was the end itself, laid bare and grinning.

"It must be the artists," said Val. She too spoke quietly. You never knew.

Derek nodded. "Must be," he agreed. Decades old as it clearly was, this death had to be more recent than the town's. "But I don't understand. Why wasn't there a follow-up article? Why were they left like this? Didn't anybody know?"

"Maybe not. They might not have been local. Perhaps no one knew to miss them here."

"Maybe," Derek conceded. Val had to be right. One way or another, Pierton had kept this to itself.

Val picked her way over the bones to the crouching skeleton. She knelt beside it. "Come here," she said.

Derek braced himself, stepped off the cellar steps and weaved through death. "What is it?" he asked when he reached Val.

"Look." She pointed.

The skeleton's hands clutched a large stone. Ceramic shards littered the floor. On the wall were the remains of a tile mosaic. Whatever the picture had been, it had been smashed into jigsaw mystery. Some of the pieces showed a faint blue in the gloom. Others were grey, but whether from art or grime, Derek couldn't tell.

"I don't think this was originally part of the house," said Val.

"Meaning?"

"Meaning I think it was made and smashed by the same people. These people."

Derek looked around. Skulls stared back, the darkness of their sockets as deep and full of despair as a final sigh. He decided that it was time to go. His nerves and imagination were taut over barbed wire, and if he heard any strange noises now, he would lose it. Simple as that. He didn't care about the town's mysteries anymore. He didn't care about its construction, or its honored graves, or its life, or its demise. It didn't matter. There were meanings here, dead but lingering, and they could hurt him if he saw them. He didn't want to learn. "What I think we should do," he said, not even trying to keep his voice steady, "is leave. I take some pictures of the scene, and we go to the police and tell them about this, and we show them the pictures. But we leave. Now."

Val stood up, hugging herself against cold breaths. The wind crept downstairs to see them. "Yes," she agreed.

They went back to the stairs. Val waited near the top while Derek mounted the flash and began to record the cellar's memory. Four shots, he thought. Four shots and I'll have it, everything that counts in this place on film. Four shots and we're gone. And so from left to right, panorama, don't worry about the aesthetics, just get it and flash, flash, flash, flash—

Something outside started to bang. It was the sound of solid metal against hollow. Metronomic, twice a second, bang bang bang bang bang. Derek and Val looked at each other, eyes linking their fear directly, and then they scrambled up the steps and out of the house.

Run for that car.

The banging was sourceless. It rode the wind, beating from whatever direction it chose, sometimes from all. It would come closer, but never close enough to show its hand. It called on the clouds. With a rear and a roar, they opened up. Blackness poured down, torrential and drowning. Derek staggered as the rain smashed onto him. It drove the gravel deeper into its grave. The road turned to mud. And bang bang bang bang, all the way to the car, as Val fumbled with the keys, as Derek, rainblind, fell into the passenger seat, as the wheels spun, flinging gumbo. Bang bang bang, as the tires gripped, as Val turned the car around, as she accelerated through the white sheets of water. Bang bang bang—

It stopped the instant Pierton disappeared from view.

Back in Winnipeg. Back in their apartment. Back in dry clothes. Warm. Cozy. Safe. So they talked about it. A little.

"Do you think we were hallucinating?" Derek asked. They had both heard the banging.

"Seems a little unlikely, doesn't it?" Val seemed sorry to have an objection, no matter how reasonable. "I mean, that we would both spontaneously imagine the same thing?"

Derek grimaced. She was right, of course. But that was no comfort. "Then what...?" he asked, not quite in despair, not quite in fear, but helpless just the same.

"I don't know," Val sighed.

They sat and stared at each other for a few minutes, each waiting for the other to solve the dream and wake them up.

"Okay," said Derek, trying for a collaboration. "Well something had to cause it—"

"—it did come right before the storm—"

"—so the weather—"

"—the wind—"

"—caught a door or something on a loose hinge—"

"—and banged it back and forth," Val finished, smiling.

Derek smiled back. There. They had done it. Here was the explanation. It made perfect sense. They were back in the logical again.

Back in the rational.

Warm. Cozy. Safe.

Derek didn't sleep a wink that night.

And on Sunday, Derek went into the darkroom for the reckoning. He was nervous about developing the films, for reasons that he knew were stupid, since it had all been explained. Didn't matter. He was still nervous, and if he was going to be silly about the pictures, he didn't want Val to see.

Anyway, he suspected that she was wrestling with the same jitters. She had moved her easel and paint out of the living room and into the spare bedroom she used as a studio, and closed the door. Derek had felt a nibble of unease when he'd seen a tube of blue paint in her hand.

He got to work. He concentrated on the pure mechanics of developing. He refused to look at negatives or anything else until all the prints were complete. He didn't need to fuel his imagination with small or still-forming images, thanks all the same. He kept his eyes moving, letting them rest on a developing photograph only long enough to make sure he wasn't making any stupid mistakes. He didn't break for lunch. Nerves fought with appetite, and won.

Val's door was still shut when he finally emerged from the darkroom, prints in hand. It was early evening, but the overcast sky made it later. Derek glanced out the living room window and had to shake himself. For a moment he'd thought the clouds were the ones from Pierton. Watch it, he warned himself.

He sat down on the sofa. Took a breath. Ready? he wondered. Not really, he answered. Too bad. Here we go. He looked at the first picture.

The grey was there. Flicker immobilized, it was a faint gauzy wash, smirking in a corner. He'd been braced for it, or so he thought. But the chill still stabbed down to the marrow.

He looked at the next picture. The grey was there too. Different location, different shape, different texture, but there. And on the next one. And the next. And the next. All the way through, up until the last exterior shot, when he had finished covering the town and had heard the rattle of wings. By contrast, the shots of the skeletons were reassuringly normal.

He went through the pictures again, looking for the magic clue that would make everything mundane again. He didn't find it. Instead, he froze, fingers poised, breath arrested. He was looking at the first shot he took, before the grey, of the hills and the sky. The clouds looked out of the picture, straight at him, and even without faces, they were smiling significantly. Derek bit his lip. He turned his head, slowly, slowly, plenty of time for a prayer, and looked out the window.

The clouds were the same. He hadn't imagined it. Every shape, every frown, exactly the same as in the picture. Reality was suddenly a road whose meaning was evaporating, and Derek couldn't get off. He looked away from the window and shoved the prints, snakes, off his lap. They fell, shushing, to the floor.

He got up. He took a step back. He wanted to move around the couch, away from the pictures, away from the window and the sky. He wanted to go to Val. But the pictures weren't quite done yet. He noticed how two of the prints had fallen, how the two fragments of grey connected. He sighed, fatalistic. He should have seen it coming. He went to the kitchen, got some scissors, came back to the living room, and got to work.

It was easier than he thought. Some of the pictures, the ones where the grey was close to a corner, didn't need cutting. The puzzle fit itself together under his hands. He didn't know what to expect, or what to hope for, or even whether he should hope at all. But there was no point in fighting this, he thought. If nothing else, some kind of meaning might emerge to counter the entropy he was feeling.

He slotted the last piece into place and leaned back. He started to shiver. The grey formed a face. It was sheer, contorted, and screaming. Head back, mouth open to tear tendons. Inside the mouth, details collided into a shape he couldn't understand. The town orbited in angled fragments, debris in a tornado. The sense of movement was unmistakable, a vortex, a spiralling in to that shape inside the scream.

What was he looking at? With its agony and its transparencies of flesh, it was what he imagined the picture of a ghost would look like. Ghost town, he thought. Ghost of the town? No, not right. The shape in the mouth, now vaguely familiar, said no. Not of the town. Then what? The town's death?

He started. Where were these thoughts coming from? The grade of this road he was on was getting steeper, aiming for vertical, down into the dark, and the meanings he was hitting were not his, and they were corroding the ones he did own. He needed to get away before free fall. He shuffled back on his knees.

Too late. Wind hit the window, and he knew where he had seen that shape before. In pictures, of course. Grey ones. Ones taken using an electron microscope. It was a virus.

Influenza. The town's killer. His shivers almost prevented him from standing up. Influenza, the defanged plague. Could a pandemic have a ghost?

Then: as he stumbled back, body trying to find an expression for his fear, the picture began to flake. The grey face lifted off the prints like ash in a breeze, twirling, little dust devil, then slinging itself up, over his shoulder, and behind.

Then: the sound came back, the rattle of the moth, the clacking of wings, the the the wracking of phlegm, choking the throat, drowning the lungs.

Derek tried to scream, but his voice, deep in the tunnel, falling and lost, only whispered "Val."

The last of the face flaked away, and this time he spun with it, watched the cinders, followed their road as they drifted right through his wife's closed door.

Denial was too big, a block of concrete expanding in his chest. It burst through when he heard the crash. It came out as *"Val!"*, loud this time, a shredding cry that still, still, could barely compete with the rattle.

Derek threw open the door. The face was waiting for him, staring back in blue and grey from Val's easel. The same face, striated by the reimaged mosaic. Here it rose as a pain cloud from the roofs of the culled town. And as he ran to her, Derek saw. He saw. He saw what had claimed meaning for its own to kill as it saw fit. Not peripheral vision this time, but dead centre, in your face and here I am: a grey figure, no longer flickering fragments, but doubly recreated. Brought back, its death a liberation, its very movement a smile, it danced out the closed window and into the welcoming storm. It spread racketing wings to fly down the new roads opened to it.

"Val," Derek moaned. Third time, last time. He crouched beside her. His shivering was of a different order now, the product of something much more fatal than fear. And Val turned to look at him, her eyes all wrong and shining.

Her skin was already reddening with the first fever flush of the end.

HELLO, JANE, GOOD-BYE

by
Sally McBride

Sally McBride's short stories have appeared in *Asimov's Science Fiction*, *The Magazine of Fantasy and Science Fiction*, *Tesseracts*, *On Spec*, and numerous other publications. She won the Aurora Award in 1995 for her story "The Fragrance of Orchids" (*Asimov's* May '94), and along the way has garnered a few Nebula and Hugo nominations as well. She is currently at work on her second novel.

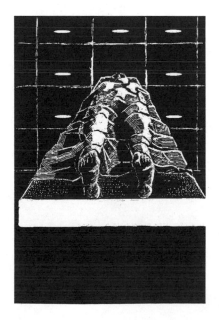

"Count backwards from fifteen, please, Angie."

Angie's brain doesn't just lie placidly in its bone cup, it moves and breathes. Not a lot, just enough so I know it's paying attention.

"Fifteen, fourteen, thirteen, twww..w...wwelve, eleven...ten—"

"Okay Angie, that's fine. Super."

Yes, her brain is paying attention, but it can be fooled.

Angie is a chubby sixteen-year-old with smooth pale skin and small, bright blue eyes, and a nervous mother in the visitors' lounge. Her father is most likely at work; not the type to take time off for something like this.

Angie's straight sandy hair will grow back after we pop the cut-out doorway back onto the top of her head and sew her scalp back up. She'll look like a skinhead for a while, but maybe her boyfriend will like that, maybe the other kids will think she's cool.

Better than epilepsy, isn't it, honey?

"Suction. Thanks, Kim."

I've got a good team. They're quiet, brisk, efficient. Quick on the uptake. At first a couple of them didn't like working for a female doctor, but they came around. I'm good. And my nurses are the best, they're on my side; we've done quite a bit of this sort of thing together.

I love it. God, I love it.

"Angie, can you tell me what you're thinking right now?" I can see her face in the mirror, and she can see mine. The edge of the green plastic dam separates her pasty little face from what's going on in her open skull. She can't move her head at all, but her eyes slide around, looking at me and away, flicking around as much of the operating theatre as is in her view, then back, shyly, to me. She licks her lips. She's scared, but she's doing fine.

"What'm I thinking...?"

Her face goes a little softer. Her eyes look at something, a little memory that's popped to the surface.

Her snub nose crinkles a bit. "I smell french fries," she says. "And vinegar... no, now it's gone."

The rounded tip of the electrode wand moves fractionally, gently padding along the skin of her brain like a tiny finger checking for blemishes, as if it were Angie delicately confronting a nascent pimple, getting ready to deal with it.

Leave it or squeeze it out?

I prefer to think of it as the paw of a cat, padding silently in search of mice in the mind's hidden crevices. The device is the perfect extension of my hand, my eye, my desire. I have tamed electricity to my personal will.

A smile creeps over her face. "It's Trish!" She's giggling. "Oh, God, I can't talk about this... It's just like I'm *there*, wow... Trish, she can't handle booze, right? It's a party for Bruce ...she falls in Bruce's lap, right? Like, she's had too many—" And now her voice changes. She isn't just telling the story, she's living it. "Bruce, take it *easy*! Trish, come on. Let's go to the bathroom. Bruce, you asshole, help her up." Angie is still giggling. I wonder how many beers she's had? It's a fun memory, harmless, though her parents wouldn't like it.

Leave it there. Leave it and go on.

"Suction here, Kim. Time?"

"Nine nineteen, Barb."

We're all on first-name basis here, none of this Doctor Bell shit. My people respect me, I respect them; simple.

Angie's face blanks out for a moment. Her lips slacken. The electrode moves. I do love this, I do love it all so. . .

What we're doing here on this Tuesday morning in Operating Room 6 of Jubilee Hospital is eliminating epilepsy from this girl's life. No more seizures, no more medication. A normal, healthy life for an average young woman, a middle-class white girl with a so-so future, but shouldn't she have a life without disease?

Outside is a cold morning, snow in flurries whipped hard by the Manitoba wind. Inside is a haven of light and warmth and gleaming sterility. My world.

I know where it is, the little bit of brain tissue that must be destroyed. And I'll get to it, I'll get to it and have time for coffee before doing my rounds. But not just yet.

Move the electrode. Move it again, a millimetre at a time would be too much, too gross; I'll not wantonly rampage across Angie's life. But I know I'll find that little something tucked away, something she doesn't realize is still there. Most people have something they don't want to remember.

Angie, in the mirror, suddenly looks alert. Her heart rate leaps, her respiration stops, held in, then off she goes. Yes.

Yes, this is it. This is what I want.

"Hold her down, ladies. Let's find out what's happening."

Kim and Mattie lean into it. Angie's fighting hard; but for the head clamps she'd be off the table and out the door, wires trailing.

"No!" she screams, her voice high and childish. She's trying to pull her knees together, trying to twist her body away from the hands holding her down. "I'll tell Mommy! I'll — ah!" Another scream, cut off. Amazingly, a red patch flares on her cheek as if a phantom hand has slapped her. Then she goes silent, panting, her heart rate sky-high, her lips clamped shut as if a big heavy hand is over them.

I want very much to shut my eyes and take it all now. But the electrode must not move away from this sweet spot, this precious little node locked in Angie's cerebrum. If I'm going to get it I have to concentrate, trust that Mattie and Kim will do their part and trust me in turn. I'll enjoy it later, at home. Angie won't miss it; no, not at all.

She didn't even know it was there.

The buried traumas are the best. When they've been encysted deep and long, aging like brandy in a barrel, they taste the sweetest.

Angie is reliving the rape as we watch. It enters my brain as it exits hers, and I can even catch a little echo of what her father is feeling as he ravages his child. It's a very good session, very exciting. Who would have thought that ordinary little Angie Pitney would contain such delicious buried treasure?

"Well," I say as Angie lapses into unconsciousness and her heart rate levels out, "let's not let that come back. What do you say, ladies? Shall I excise this little bit of nastiness?"

Mattie and Kim, releasing their grip on Angie, nod as one. They see it my way, as always. Mattie must have some idea of what I do, but she doesn't care. She trusts me. Mattie can be elbow-deep in any sort of physical horror, but mental anguish knocks her sideways. To her, I'm purging these children of pain, cleaning them and making them well. How I do it is not her business. She keeps the others in line.

"Sue?"

Sue is my sterile nurse, new to this, and at first she won't look up from her tray of instruments.

"Sue? Are we in agreement?"

She nods then, gulping, and looks up at me. She's crying, her eyes spilling over as she gives me the kind of look I imagine a shepherd would give a burning bush.

"All right then. Probe, please."

The area will be heat-coagulated by the application of a controlled radio frequency current. It will never pop up out of Angie's psyche again. It won't need to: it's safe with me now.

When I was a girl, I'd get impressions from people: vague, shadowy pictures and emotions. They wouldn't stay, they vanished like fish in a lake. It didn't seem like anything special to me, and I never told anyone about it.

I knew I was destined to be a doctor when I grew up, I never wanted to be a nurse like the other little girls. I knew even then that I had to be the one in control, the one with her hands on the very essence of life.

As I learned more and took up neurosurgery, the belief that I was doing much more than empathizing with my patients sank in. I was *living* their memories. The electrical currents generated in connection with my work boosted the signal, as it were; I could capture what I wanted and keep it.

At first it frightened me, just as it does Sue to see me at work; then I learned to love it. I think there may be something wrong with me, something deep inside my own skull's cellar, but I'm functional, aren't I? Successful, in fact—even happy. I know what I'm doing. And what is wrong with that?

I'm the stereotypical image of the lady doctor, driven and love-less, burying herself in her career. Sex is a mundane, tedious exercise. I don't like to be touched. Driving is better, and I love to escape to midnight highways and see how fast my Mercedes will really go. Fast is good. Music is wonderful; the right aria, the right voice.

Drugs are good, and I've developed a fondness for certain uppers I can get in my professional capacity. I like to feel my brain race and burn and send off sparks like a screaming engine, knowing all along that it's different from anyone else's brain—it can do things that defy reason.

But *this* is the best. This quiet, sterile plundering of another's mind. The savoring of sweetness and pain that comes later. It's a pleasure that is all mine.

At home, I strip off my thin leather driving gloves and throw them on the credenza. It's dark out, the early frigid dusk of the north, and the drive was boring and stressful, past interminable petty accidents. Benita has laid a fire as she always does in the winter, after her cleaning and polishing duties. I never see her, she does her work and goes home.

Bending, I touch a match to the paper and watch the flames rise, feel the heat flare. The tension in my thighs as I crouch before the fire triggers something, and the next thing I know I'm on my back on the carpet, groaning as the stolen memory pounds its way into me, just as little Angie's father pounded his way into her. Past the defences, past the helpless, yielding flesh, right to the heart of *self*. For it's happening to me, *I'm* doing it, *I'm* feeling it from both sides, and it's strong, so strong...And it is mine, mine to enjoy as often as I want. How I would love the chance to get *his* brain under my hands, cracked open like an egg. What if I could get my own?

Afterwards, there's the glow of brandy, and as I watch the golden swirling liquid I think of what I do. What it means. If I were to announce this odd phenomenon, try to study it clinically and publish papers, then it wouldn't be mine any more. I'd be the one helpless under the electrodes, and I wouldn't like that, would I? So it's a moot question really. I have no intention of studying it.

I watch the news, then go to bed and enjoy Angie one more time.

"Jane Doe" lies under the sheet on the operating table, her head braced and shaved. She's seven, as near as can be determined. Records of her birth have yet to be found, and she's never been to school. Malnourished, thin, yet wiry as if her muscles have been tempered somehow, in some crucible of pain.

When she was brought in a ripple of shock went through the hospital like a physical thing, a wave of pity and horror. How could anyone treat a child so? How could the poor thing possibly have survived? There was hushed talk in the cafeteria and lots of speculation over the internal e-mail as people compared news broadcasts they'd seen, vied with one another to provide sordid morsels of information.

It got to the point where my initial reaction of pity was swamped under by the gossip. She's just another case, a brain-damaged child exhibiting symptoms that make my attentions necessary. Her cult-member parents, sub-human dregs at best, are beyond reparations now; the adults having taken the coward's way out: suicide.

Sue is readying the drill, Mattie and Kim bustle around. This time all we're going to do is drill some burr-holes in likely spots and pop the electrodes in for preliminary testing.

Jane Doe's charts tell me that she is unable to speak, though not for any organic reason. It has been determined that the epileptic seizures she experiences are probably the result of an infant brain inflammation, probably brought about by abuse, subsequent infection and lack of care. Her body has been brought to the edge of destruction by the tortures she has suffered, but fortunately it has not been permanently disabled. Her mind, though....

Ah, her mind.

"All right, ladies, time to get to work."

Jane Doe has been prepped and sedated already, and since she's to be awake during the procedure there is no need of an attending anesthetist. The brain itself has no pain receptors, so a local to the scalp is all that's needed. Sue can do that. Jane seems relaxed. Her respiration is slow and even, her eyes open and staring dreamily at the ceiling.

Over the past few days in the hospital, many of her injuries have started to heal, and the swelling around her eyes and jaw has gone down. She might even be pretty some day.

Silence reigns as we work, except for monosyllabic orders and observations. We're like a planetary system, myself the sun, my ladies the planets securely in my orbit, little Jane the rogue comet to be studied as she flashes through our space.

The pattern of burr-holes might look random to the uninitiated observer, but it isn't. I'll be dropping my lures into several areas today, the way an Inuit hunter might fish from many holes in the Arctic ice, in hopes of catching a succulent seal. What is swimming under Jane's battered skull?

"Sue," I ask, "when was Jane's last seizure?"

"Oh two fifty-five," she responds. "Just over six hours ago."

"Duration?"

"Twelve minutes, thirty-three seconds."

"Okay. I'm going to insert the electrodes now, but we'll wait till they're all in place before running any current. Mattie, you're all set up? I want copies of the data sent to my office as well."

"No problem, Barb."

The hair-thin wires go in with no resistance. Jane stares at the ceiling, completely unresponsive, seeing who knows what. Telemetry aids the slight adjustments for exact positioning, in the amygdala, the cerebrum, the locus ceruleus and more. I'm casting my net wide.

I'm thankful that no electrocardiogram is monitoring my heart-beat right now. I know that if I spoke, my voice would betray my excitement, my impatience.

But when the current is initiated, there is almost no response at all.

It doesn't make sense. The electrodes are well within the centres of memory and emotion, as well as conscious thought; there must be something. Have her experiences left no impression at all? Is she so far gone that her mind is scrambled?

Now I wish I had gone ahead and opened her skull. I'd have more latitude to hunt with an electrode wand in my hand. For a moment there's a hot, clear image in my mind of my hands thrusting deep into the grey jelly, digging through Jane's brain up to my wrists, but it's nothing new. I always want to do that.

Perhaps, because the child is mute, she can't tell me her memories as they are drawn up, perhaps for that reason they can't come to me. But that doesn't seem likely; I've had other patients whose speech centres have been affected and it's made no difference. In fact, the impressions are invariably more sensual, more detailed in the areas of touch and smell.

Mattie, Kim and Sue exchange looks. I can sense their doubt, just as they can sense my anger and frustration. Sometimes I grow impatient with my role as goddess, and wish my ladies would vanish and leave me alone with my prey.

"Sue, I want sequential pulses. Start with the amygdala and move out."

That got something. "A little more power, if you please."

More, but nothing definite. There was a feeling like the sigh of wind through a high tree, thousands upon thousands of fluttering leaves making a rushing whisper in my head.

I also notice a flutter within Jane's amygdala, as I anticipated; a precursor to an epileptic seizure. "Did we get that? We'll have Jane back in here in a week or so, when she's strong enough, and take care of that."

A general lessening of the tension passes among my nurses. They like to be reminded of why we're here.

"Give me one more, Sue. Up it to point 3."

I see the motion of Sue's hand on the regulator out of the corner of my eye, and almost before it has a chance to register I find myself flat on my back on the white tiled floor.

My ears are ringing and my vision has narrowed to a black point. Mattie's voice wavers in and out as she sits me up and leans me precariously against the gurney leg. I feel her soft strong arm supporting me.

"Barb! Barb, what happened? It's okay, Sue's closing her up, don't worry, just take it easy — "

The blackness expands, sparkling at the edges. My lips are numb, and I feel intensely shaken and dizzy. Mattie has pulled my mask down, I can feel cold air on my face. I feel as though I have been flooded with something, like a rush of black water, or a howl of icy wind. Nothing like this has ever happened before.

In a few minutes I'm able to stand and leave the operating room. Little Jane lies on the table, her eyes turned toward me. She's awake and aware, and she's watching me with interest. Her eyes are bright in their bruised pits. Her lips are moving silently as if she's singing to herself, or repeating a word over and over, opening and closing.

"You want me to call Dr. Thom to look you over?"

I shake my head. It hurts. "No, Mattie, thanks. I'll be all right. I skipped breakfast this morning. I guess I've just been overdoing things." I give her a rueful smile which she seems to take as assurance that I really am all right. "I'm going to head home, though, okay?"

"Yes indeed. Put yourself to bed. Doctor's orders." I can feel her eyes on me as I head for the scrub room to doff my gown and gloves.

Just before I pass out the door, I hear a breathy little whisper from Jane. "Good-bye, good-bye..." She flashes me a tiny smile. It's eerie. It makes her seem *less* pathetic, not more, for some reason I can't fathom.

All the way home I keep well within the speed limit. My head feels as if it is going to explode. What have I got in there? What came over from Jane Doe to me?

I'm reluctant to light the fire that Benita has laid. Not afraid, I don't allow myself to be afraid. I can handle whatever it is; it's just more of the same after all, and like a connoisseur of wines I know how to take a sip and spit the rest out.

First I fix myself a sandwich—I really did skip breakfast—and then I take off all my clothes and lie on my bed. I keep it warm in my bedroom, so I don't need blankets. I don't like the feel of blankets touching me. As my breathing slows I start to feel the familiar tingle between my legs, the yearning that grows until it cannot be denied.

I know I'm in for a fast ride today, a bumpy ride. Maybe a crash. I can feel my lips pull back into a smile as I close my eyes. The possibility of a crash is like adrenalin to me, like the best upper in the world.

"All right. Come and get me."

It's like turning on a radio that is tuned between stations. Static fills my ears, hissing and throbbing as if powered by some vast generator pouring current into my head. There's nothing I can do to stop it now. I'm not afraid. I'm not afraid.

Then it's as if a weight has dropped onto me from a great height. A big heavy *thing*, not a body but a force. I'm quite familiar with the weight of men, the heavy bodies of rapists and pederasts crushing the breath out of their victims—out of me—and this isn't it.

It's grinding down on my chest and abdomen, leaving my legs and arms free. I can barely breathe. My arms fly back over my head, crashing into the headboard before halting locked behind me, as if caught in a very strong hand. My legs spread wide, drawn apart by that same rough force, my feet bent down into a ballerina's *pointe* and secured.

The static increases until I can barely think, but I'm past thinking now. I feel a point of heat come down and singe my breasts, licking along in a pattern, a pentagram sprawling sloppily across my belly. Looking down I can see round red welts on my skin, springing up as I watch. The heat and the pain spiral and stink, burning, and then are overcome by a crooning voice.

I feel my body rock and swing as if someone is dancing me around. The crooning turns into a song, a broken lullaby mumbled by a madwoman.

I swing, and then the arms let go and I'm falling free.

And then they all come in. All the Janes.

She's spent years creating the personalities that inhabit me now. Seventeen of them, and they take their turns with me over the next hours, each one different from the last, each one no preparation for the next. Jane—the core of the Jane personality—has been forced to become very inventive. I stop enjoying it after number five.

My own body is in league with the things inside me, and I'm tearing myself apart. I can feel the muscles rip, the flesh sizzle, the bruises flare and seep under my skin.

"My name is Gregor." He's a forty-something male built like a wrestler. Gregor is who Jane turns into when she's alone with the younger ones. He snaps my knuckles with gleeful force.

"I'm Susie," lisps a shy voice. "Will you play with me?" Susie is an artist who paints things in blood, her own blood. Layer upon layer of Susie's art covers the walls of Jane's room.

There's the screamer, the one who has no name, because all she does is scream. It drowns out everything else for a while. She's pushed aside by Auntie Crissy, who is able to do very nice things indeed with some of the toys in the room.

More follow; none of them listen to me. They are mine now, mine to keep in my head, but they won't listen. They won't stop. They won't let me go.

At last, at the very centre, is Jane. The real Jane who has no name and no identity, only the fearsome intelligence that has built this army of selves around it.

I see her at the end as my eyes give out, just as she was on the operating table, holes drilled in her skull. Wires trailing like reins, like veins, into my hands, my head, my soul.

Her lips are moving, she's saying good-bye, good-bye, good-bye. Thank you, doctor. Very softly, and with a smile on her swollen lips. Good-bye and good riddance.

THE CHILDREN OF GAEL

by
Nancy Kilpatrick and Benoit Bisson

Prolific author Nancy Kilpatrick has had a story published in each of our *Northern Frights* volumes. Of her latest, a collaboration with Montreal writer Benoit Bisson, Nancy writes: "Benoit and I wanted to collaborate on a story, and his description of Grosse-Île intrigued me, so I went there myself. The island is haunting, especially thinking about all the people who traveled there under such harsh conditions, only to die by the thousands from cholera. It seemed a natural setting for a ghost story."

"If they had not made the voyage," the tour guide said, "they would not have died."

And you wouldn't exist.

"What?" Patrick glanced around. Some of the others on the tour smiled indulgently at him. While the tour guide repeated what she had said, a dark cloud passed over the sun, wiping color from the bright day. A gust of cool air crossed Grosse-Île and sent a shiver down his spine, through his legs, his arms, his stomach. His stomach tensed and goosebumps crawled over his skin, as if he'd fallen off the dock and into the chilly waters. He stared into the dark St. Lawrence; the waves pulled hypnotically, like a woman beckoning. He thought he could see faces there, some grinning, some howling, some just staring back at him...

Patrick shook himself, clearing his head of silliness. He had never liked crossing water. Boats made him seasick. And who hadn't envisioned drowning? Obviously, the unexpected wind had made a sound, which he had interpreted—

"Overcrowded ships, lack of food, rough seas, sickness..." The voice of the bilingual tour guide who called herself Francine dragged him away from his thoughts. "The Irish traveled out of desperation, on anything, from rag-tag sailboats to four-masters, trying to escape the potato famine and hoping to find a new Emerald Isle. In the end, for many, their quest drowned in disease and death."

Francine chirped and bounced, managing to convey the facts without too much emotion, which suited Patrick just fine. He hadn't come here for distortions of history or emotional renditions of the past.

Thinking about why he had left Montréal three hours ago, on a business day, and had driven to this island, his jaw tensed. It was just not like him to do such a thing. The death-bed promise to his demented father was ridiculous. The old-man had lost his mind and become a raving lunatic. But despite knowing that, and in spite of the persistent voice that kept telling him that what he had sworn to do was idiotic and a complete waste of time, Patrick knew making pledges to the dying was one of those things that had to be carried out if the living were to have any peace.

And even though he hated to admit it, something else nagged at him as well: fear. Fear that this sickness was hereditary. His father, grandfather and great grandfather had all died agonizing deaths, lost in insanity. Patrick was terrified he would end up the same way, helpless and as out of control as he'd seen his father.

"Before we get started," Francine said brightly, "I'd like to ask each of you what brings you to Grosse-Île."

Patrick listened to the reedy man from Nova Scotia ramble on about his ancestors, whom he didn't know, really, and how they seemed to have come from Ireland, although he wasn't exactly sure of that either.

Then there was a stuttering journalist from Winnipeg doing a travel guide on Canadian parks, then two short, round women with brush-cuts, one from Toronto and one from Montréal, traveling east toward the Gaspé Peninsula, who thought they'd take the island tour.

By the time the frumpy grandmother from Saskatchewan began to claim her astrologer had sent her, Patrick had tuned them out.

To the left, he saw an enormous, imposing cross atop a hill, overlooking the water. To the right, more of the structures, dating from mid-nineteenth to early twentieth century. The wooden buildings scattered amidst the coarse pines and cedars reminded him of summer camp in the Gatineau Hills, which he had always hated. Loneliness, desolation and abandonment settled around his shoulders; a heavy stone, the weight of more than a century... *Nonsense!* he thought, and checked his

watch—the next boat out was loading now. The next one in wouldn't
be for three more hours. He sighed in frustration.

"What about you?" the cheery Francine asked. He glanced up to
see the others waiting for his response, and cringed inwardly. He was
not about to divulge why he had come here; telling them who he was
would just have to suffice.

"My great grandfather took his fortune and left Ireland. He was
clever enough to jump ship before it docked here, or I suppose he would
have died of cholera."

"Oh, that would be Patrick Lynch," the guide said brightly.

"No, it would not be."

Francine looked confused and intimidated, which suited him just
fine. His lineage was nobody's business. "Oh," she finally managed,
"you're not related to Patrick Lynch? He's the man who jumped ship at
the height of the cholera epidemic and swam to the mainland, where a
French family took him in. He married one of their daughters. I think
his descendants still live in the area. Isn't he your great grandfather?"

She must be a college student at Laval University, as her t-shirt
claimed, and couldn't have been more than fifteen years younger than
him, but Patrick didn't believe he had ever been so stupid. And although the circumstances were similar—his grandfather *had* married a
French Canadian woman—that's where it stopped. "My great grandfather was Patrick O'Mallory. I was named for him."

"Really?"

"Yes, really. I think I know my own ancestor."

That gave her pause, but only for a split second. She blinked, then
continued on, as though Patrick hadn't said anything at all, especially
in a crisp tone. "We'll begin with the autoclaves."

They walked a wide dirt road, passing buildings that she called
the "first class hotel", and the "second class hotel". Apparently, most
of the Irish who came to this Canadian version of Ellis Island were poor
and had stayed in barracks or tents, but some immigrants had been
well-heeled enough to pay for decent lodging. If his great grandfather
had actually had the misfortune to land on this pathetic island, he would
have stayed at the first class hotel, of that Patrick was convinced. The
long line of money built on property investments that had come into
Patrick's hands had been acquired through business savvy not luck.

From County Cork to his plush offices on St. Jacques Street, his great granddad had been a sharp man, taking advantage of opportunities, as was his grandfather, and his father until the dementia set in, and now Patrick. And if he ever had a son, the boy would be just as sharp. Privilege was in the genes.

Francine pointed out the bakery, the telegraph building, and eventually they arrived at what appeared to be iron boxcars, used to disinfect clothing by employing high-pressure steam. They were huge, rusted remains, stored inside a type of dark warehouse, and reminded him of photographs he'd seen of concentration camps, for some reason.

When the others had had their fill of snapping photos of the train cars, the small group moved along. Patrick, though, hung back for a moment. He walked to the open end of one of the cars and peered inside for a closer look.

You promised me! You promised me!

Instant sweat stuck his shirt to his back. He glanced around nervously. The words were clear, and the voice—was it a woman's voice?—the same as he'd heard at the dock. But how could that be? He was alone.

"Oh! There you are!" Francine sounded wary, as if he might jump down her throat. "We're just up the road." She didn't seem to notice him jolt as she spoke.

She turned, paused to wait for him, then began to move away. It occurred to him that the sheer volume of sickness, disease and germs that had been annihilated here made him uneasy. And it was a very hot day. He loosened his shirt collar a bit more and hurried to join Francine.

They proceeded on, the tour guide rattling off facts about the island. Back then, it seems, the land had been divided into three sections, the gated west wall where the immigrants were brought on arrival, the east wall where the cholera victims were taken, and the center of the island, for staff. Patrick saw it all, much more than he cared to. He needed to get to his destination but leaving the tour at this point would obviously not work, not with the ever-vigilant Francine on guard. Besides, the next boat off the island wouldn't arrive for another two hours, and he might as well get his money's worth.

The island tour lasted far too long. Patrick saw churches—a Protestant and a Catholic version; the carriage that had done triple duty as a taxi, ambulance and hearse; the school and the children's cemetery; and the main graveyard with white crosses, precisely aligned, uninscribed, symbolic of the bones beneath the surface where the disease victims were buried in mass graves. The land of the graveyard rolled and dipped in wave after wave, untouched since the early plows had turned the bodies under. As he stared at the earth, it seemed to pitch like waves on water, making him slightly dizzy. The heat is really getting to me, he thought as he undid another button of his shirt. He wished he'd brought along a hat, and some water... But this would be over soon and he'd cool off in the BMW's air conditioning.

Finally, and just at the point where he was almost ready to forego the reason he had come here, they climbed the hill to the 63-foot Celtic cross.

The dirt path was awkwardly narrow, and as they wound their way up, they met one of the other tours hurrying back down. Eventually they reached the isolated stone monument, woods surrounding it on three sides, a sheer cliff to the rocky water below on the fourth, which Patrick kept well away from.

The cross was impressive, he had to admit, and while the guide chattered on about how the Ancient Order of Hibernians had erected this cross in 1909 in memory of those who had died here, Patrick busied himself reading two of the three inscriptions on the base.

In English, the dedication was in memory of the Irish who had been victims of cholera. Another side, in French, said virtually the same thing, although it also thanked local priests for their work. The third inscription was in Gaelic, which Patrick did not understand, but assumed to be similar to the other two.

"I'll lead you to the cafeteria to wait for the boat," the guide said, "or you can wander around and take pictures. But don't miss the boat! It's the last one of the day."

Finally! Patrick thought as the others drifted, by ones and twos, back down the hill. He was alone.

He stood in the shadow of the cross, staring out across the water at the mainland. Absently, he reached into his pant pocket. The metal against his skin felt cool on this hot day, a rounded shape against his sweaty fingers. He pulled it out and stared at the locket nestled in his palm. Burnished gold, hanging on a gold chain—wealth did not always presume taste, but in his great grandfather's case, it had.

He turned over the piece of jewelry, then turned it back again, and sighed. His father had gone completely nuts at the end, just like his grandfather and probably his great grandfather too. "Patrick," he said, "you must promise me! Promise me you'll go to Grosse-Île. Take the locket. Take it! Bury it there, beneath the cross!" His father had pleaded and begged, exacting a promise from Patrick, ranting the entire time about Celtic demons, and breaking curses. In truth, the intensity of his father's rage had unnerved him, and that's why he'd given his word. Now, he thought himself foolish. He should have just given the locket away, or better yet, sold it—after all, it was 24-carat gold. That he should travel so far, for such an irrational reason—

"Sure and it's a lovely piece."

Patrick spun around. Behind him, between him and the cross, stood a woman, barely five feet tall. She was attractive enough, red hair against a pale face waving down to her shoulders, green eyes liquid and lively. Her Irish accent was thick, though, and he had some trouble understanding her.

"Yes it is," he said, closing his hand, slightly annoyed. He wanted to just bury the locket and get off this island. And now he had this woman to contend with. From her clothing, she wasn't a tourist but must be a park guard, dressed in period costume. "Are you part of some...historical event?" he asked, for lack of anything else to say.

"Oh indeed," she said. "That's why I'm here, you know." And then she said nothing, just folded her hands together prayer fashion and stared at him, a look of rapture on her face, which made him think she was strange. How was he going to get rid of her?

"Look, Miss, I'd like a few minutes alone here. My ancestor..." He left it open ended, hoping she would fill in the blank, making a connection that didn't exist, that he felt some sort of emotion about someone or other who had died on this island, and that she'd respect that and get the hell out of here.

"Have you opened the locket, then?" she asked.

"No." He said it before he could stop himself.

"Ah, but you should. Here, give it to me."

She reached out for it, but he pulled his hand away instinctively.

A look crossed her face that he felt was hostile in some way. But maybe he'd imagined it. After all, he didn't know this woman and her moods.

As if to negate that, she smiled at him, and looked him directly in the eye. It was a suggestive look, and he began to reassess her. A quick glance at his watch told him that if he could bury the damn locket quickly, he might have time for a private tour—

"I've waited for so long," she said softly.

"For?"

"I think you know." She took a step towards him.

The hairs at the back of his neck bristled, but he knew he was being ridiculous. What was there to fear? A small woman, coming on to him. It didn't happen every day, and maybe that's why the situation made him nervous. Despite the nervousness, he felt himself physically responding to her.

"I'm Patrick," he said.

Her smile broadened. "Of course you are!"

"And you?"

A look of complete surprise passed over her face, which shifted first to a pained look, then—again—an angry one. Her voice sharpened. "Sheleagh. Sheleagh McGuire." She said it as if they'd met before, and he had disappointed her by not remembering. Something about this woman was very odd. Patrick decided that he could forego whatever pleasure might have been had with her.

But just when he thought that, she moved very close to him. The sunlight on her crimson strands mesmerized him for a moment, as if her hair was on fire. Those green eyes became mossy pools, soft, vulnerable, deep... Before he realized it, she was standing on her toes, pulling his head down so that his lips could press against hers.

The kiss pulled him in, sweeping aside all thoughts, overwhelming him with sensation, and awareness: of her, of him, of being enclosed together here, in the warmth of the day. He heard water below them. Time felt eternal—the kiss could go on forever...

In the distance, he heard a boat horn and a small voice in the back of his mind whispered he should pay heed, but he no longer possessed the desire to do so. And then he felt sharp coolness against his fingers, pressing in between them, like small icicles, wedging, trying to pry open the hand that held the locket.

He pulled back, barely able to break his mouth away from hers. Only then was he aware that he was short of breath, as if she had drawn all the air from his lungs.

Those eyes! Everchanging...hard jade one second, soft spring moss the next. As he gasped in air, he became aware of a smell. Soil freshly plowed. As when something that has been buried for a long time is brought to the surface!

Patrick shoved her away from him. She crashed back against the cross. He ran down the hill, tripping over fallen branches and rocks until he fell, then stumbling to his feet. Once he reached flat ground, he headed full steam to the dock. It was empty. The last tour boat of the day was halfway across the water, headed for the mainland. He had been left behind!

Patrick yelled and waved frantically, but they were obviously too far away to see him. A quick glance told him there were no rowboats or canoes tied to the shore. Panic set in. Surely he couldn't be alone on this island! They must have staff that stayed overnight! And telephones!

He turned and ran toward the buildings, the first and second class hotels, the bakery, pounding on locked doors, on windows, staring inside at rooms devoid of furniture, yelling, his voice growing louder as the panic deepened. How could they be empty? How could he be alone?

He raced along the path, hoping to encounter someone, anyone, past the autoclaves, and came to an abrupt halt at the graveyard. Now, in the twilight, the wavy soil appeared to be moving. It couldn't be an illusion from the heat: the sun was setting! One of the crosses piercing the earth began to push up out of the ground.

Patrick shook his head and rubbed his eyes. No! This couldn't be happening! Yet the wooden cross tore free of the earth, and toppled. And what was coming from the hole it had left behind he did not want to see!

Instinctively, he took to high ground, and only knew he was back at the stone cross when he saw her, still there, as if waiting for him.

"I knew you'd come back," she said, opening her arms.

Terrified, he grabbed up a rock as a weapon. "Who are you?" he demanded. "What's going on?"

"Ah, but Patrick my love, you promised me."

The voice was the same he'd heard at the dock! And at the autoclaves. Some of the same words, said in the same way. He was sure of it now. But how could that be?

She reached out her hand. "You've what's mine, you know. And you swore to bring it back when you came for me."

"What are you talking about?" But even as he answered, Patrick knew she wanted the locket.

From below, down the hill, he heard sounds, like a thousand voices whispering. He glanced around. The forest on three sides, too dense; the cliff, plunging into the dark water below...

"Are you saying this is yours?" He held up the locket.

"Why, Patrick, I gave it to you, don't you recall? When you left me on the boat, with the others. Left me to come down with the cholera. When you took my life's savings, and those of the others, and the deeds to our homeland, and swore to return one day with the profits you'd make. When you promised you would love me for all eternity, and come back for me. Don't you remember?"

She was insane! Or he was. Not that it mattered now. The whisperings had grown more intense. And closer. Animals moving through the grass and trees and bushes, scrambling, climbing the hill.

"Give it to me," she coaxed.

For some reason, he felt it was crucial that he hold onto the locket, and yet keeping it might spell his doom. Quickly, he snapped the latch, and the spring mechanism opened the jewelry. Inside were a dozen short strands of fiery hair. Hair the color of this Sheleagh's. And beneath that, an inscription: *"Ar ngradh is ar gcinniuint i gcomhar againn go deo deo."*

"It means 'Sharing forever, our love and fate'. A blessing, or a curse. But you understand that, don't you Patrick?"

It was all clear to him now. His great grandfather had made a promise to this woman, to come back for her. He had avowed love and, as a token, she had given him the locket, with her hair inside.

And because the first Patrick O'Mallory had not fulfilled his promise, Patrick was standing here now—the last of his line?—facing what? The ghost of Sheleagh McGuire? A jilted lover, who had died of cholera? It sounded impossible to him. Utterly impossible! But what explanation could there be for the fact that he was seeing her, talking with her, *believing* her, just as she believed him to be his own great grandfather. Had the madness finally passed on to him? Was he as doomed as all the males in his family had been? Curses and spells didn't really exist! They were just things you made up when you were a kid! No, she couldn't be a witch.

Now the whispering and shuffling were accompanied by other sounds: heavy breathing, wheezing, gasping. Sounds that were closer, much closer, crowding the top of the hill.

"If I give you back the locket, will you free me from the curse?"

Sheleagh stared at him for a long moment while his body trembled. He expected the worst: she'd want to get even, to exact from him the commitment made—broken—by his great grandfather. She would either kill him, or curse him with the same insanity.

Patrick felt immense relief wash over him when she said, "If you return that which belongs not to you, I'll release you from my love."

The light had dimmed and the darkness made him see things. The woods were alive with eyes. With flesh. And with a terrible odor that stabbed at his senses. He did not know whether or not to believe her, but there was no choice now.

"Here! Take it back!" he said, shoving the locket at her.

Sheleagh reached out for it. The moment the metal touched her hand, her face altered; deep sadness overwhelmed her features. The sounds in the woods stopped, as if a switch had been thrown.

Patrick stood quivering in the silence, hardly daring to believe that it was over. That he was free.

Sheleagh pressed the locket to her heart. In the darkness he saw now that she was not flesh and blood, but something ethereal, ephemeral, with no substance.

"Patrick O'Mallory," she said, her voice laced with sorrow, "I release you from our love." He breathed a sigh of relief; he was going to get out of this nightmare!

She turned from him and looked at the Gaelic inscribed into the enormous cross. "You know, Pat, though your heart and mind left me behind, you still should have remembered. You should have heeded these words in our mother tongue. They speak to your blood. They speak of our fate: 'Thousands of the children of the Gael were lost on this island while fleeing tyrannical landlords and the artificial famine they caused. God bless them. God save Ireland! And God bring them home.'"

She glanced back. "I can forgive you, Patrick, and release you. But they cannot."

From all around him, corpses emerged from the woods, their bodies torn, decayed. Was it possible that he recognized these skeletons? As if he had known these people when they were living? As if his great grandfather dwelled within him? As if the roots of every cent of his wealth could be traced to each one of them?

Terror permeated his body. He backed up towards the cliff. True to her word, Sheleagh made no move to stop him, or to intervene. But the others. The others! They were coming. Skeletal hands like claws, eye sockets devoid of compassion, jawbones grinding in fury.

At the edge of the cliff, Patrick's foot slipped, but he barely made the effort to catch himself. With gut wrenching certainty, he knew that the end was at hand, at their hands.

The children of Gael would bring one of the lost ones home.

ROSES FROM GRANNY

by
Mary E. Choo

Poet and short story writer Mary Choo appeared in *Northern Frights 2* with her story "Feast of Ghosts," set partly in Southeast Asia and partly in her native British Columbia. While "Roses From Granny" is not specific as to location, the story's ambience suggests the quaintly genteel atmosphere of Victoria, B.C. It's a beautiful city but, if you should plan to visit it, avoid attending any of granny's special tea parties.

I hate it when Granny wakes up.

This morning she's being particularly bad, drumming her heels against the trunk at the foot of her bed. I hear her muttering and complaining in her room next door.

"Robert, she's doing it again ..." I roll over in our double bed, reaching towards the other side. My hand touches the empty pillow before I remember he's gone. I was dreaming of him, a moment ago. It's a terrible way to start the day.

I lurch to my feet and out into the hall. The landing is just beyond, and morning light pours from the colored panes in the main stairwell to the right. It traces bright patterns along the floor, almost hiding the path Granny's worn in the carpet from dragging her foot.

Everything's silent now. I push at her door, and it swings open with the usual creak. I've oiled the hinges countless times, to no avail.

The trunk lid is open—she's broken the lock again—and she's sitting bolt upright inside, the contents strewn all over the floor. She's wearing her maroon silk dress; she must have sneaked it on again after I left her last night. Her silver hair is all rumpled, her owl-like glasses hanging askew over snapping blue eyes.

"Really, Sarah Louise," she says, "it took you long enough!"

"Granny." Intent on helping, I start towards her, trying to keep the exasperation out of my voice. "You know the doctor doesn't want you getting into bed with your clothes and shoes on. I'm sure he wouldn't want you crawling into the trunk and sleeping there, either—"

"Is that so?" All things considered, her agility is remarkable, and she squirms away from me, out of the trunk and onto her feet. She looks almost derelict, with her clothes hanging every-which-way. "That sounds like something your husband might say." The blue eyes are watchful, accusing.

Well, poor Robert tried, but it wasn't easy, looking after a strong-willed old woman after she'd had a stroke. Granny's stubborn as anything, peculiar now, too. We took every precaution we could; locking the trunk so she couldn't get in and hurt herself, putting in special railings on the stairways and in the bathrooms, making sure there was enough light everywhere. She will wander, but we stopped short of strapping her down at night or locking her door; the doctor said it would be bad for her morale, and we took his point.

"Robert's gone, Granny." I'm sure she remembers that I've told her this before. Robert and I quarrelled about her, one night. I woke up next morning and realized he was gone. He called and we talked, but I won't see or speak to him any more; it's too painful, as we'd only argue. He'd have good reason. Things were awful here, and they're getting worse.

I don't want to think about any of that this morning, anyway. I won't think about it.

She gives me a furtive smile and starts for the door. "The ladies of the auxiliary are coming this afternoon," she says. "We'll have to work hard, if we want to be ready ..." I try to straighten her clothes, but she pushes my hand away. "Leave my dress alone!" she snaps. "Honestly, Sarah Louise, people will have to make allowances."

Dragging her foot, she limps across the hall and landing, then turns left down the back stairs, clutching the railing. The abilities she's recovered since her stroke are quite selective. It's amazing how she can move, always just that step ahead of me. There's no chance for me to dress now, and I feel unkempt and resentful. I'm starting to despise this old house, and everything that living here entails ...

I'd leave if I could, but I promised—swore with my hand on the Bible—that she could remain here, that I would stay, with Robert, and look after her. The house has always been in the family, and she was so upset at the thought of giving it up, especially the garden. Of course I had no idea then of the price my promise would exact ...

I follow her downstairs, across the back hall to the kitchen. There's a number of flower pots just outside the hall door, planted with things she's brought in from the kitchen garden. She works out there whenever she can, grafting and crossing certain varieties of plants, and some of the results, like the ones in the pots, look pretty strange. She even had a tub of hawthorn branches, but it's gone now. Hawthorn was my father's favorite, and with that thought comes pain.

"That wretched Naeine! She's late again," Granny grumbles as I enter the kitchen. She's banging pans about, hunting up platters for sandwiches and cakes.

"You let Naeine go, Granny," I remind her, trying to be gentle. She dismissed Naeine outright for something trivial. A pity too, as Naeine was an excellent cook, willing to put up with Granny's growing eccentricities. I try to tie an apron on Granny, but she's ducking and twisting as she reaches for things, and eludes me.

"Well, we'll just have to manage, Sarah Louise." She gives me a sly, provocative smile. "It's unfortunate Naeine's gone. Even a disappointment like her can be useful. I'll tell you what." She brightens. "I'll go and fetch some things from the garden—you carry on here, set things up for tea. We'll use the drawing room, of course ..."

She hurries, limping, out the back, taking her secateurs from the small basket by the door. She keeps them there, to prune the roses that are in bloom all around the house. She's famous for her roses.

I watch as she unlatches the gate and enters the kitchen garden. She busies herself cutting and pruning, singing in that toneless way she has. Granny is obsessive about all her plants, insisting that they grow just so. She's ruthless about weeding out things that don't conform to her ideal. I think her garden is her 'out,' her way of dealing with the disappointments in her life, especially her family. None of us ever quite measured up.

Between the racks of runner beans I can see the small stretch of woods in the back. Woods are unusual near a large city, but the grounds are extensive, and have been intact since this house was built over a century ago, in the time of the early settlers. Granny had a wall put up around the whole property. Among the trees I glimpse, slow-moving, the antlers of a deer she says wandered in when the back gate was open a while back, that she's kept and befriended. He's fenced in, and I've attempted to see him, to feed him a number of times, but he always creeps away into the trees. Granny's off to visit him now, with some of her greens. She must have quite a way with him, as she spends a lot of time back there ...

"At least she won't be underfoot," I mutter, trying to plan for the tea. The stove is impossible, a battered old thing that has served generations of family. She won't hear of getting a new one; in fact she won't change anything, even when it's falling apart. I resent this, as I work like a slave around this place. Baking is out of the question, so I decide on sandwiches, and wheel the tea trolley into the dining room to get the china. I sort the cups and saucers, extricating the plates and linen from the buffet before returning to the kitchen. She's waiting, with a peculiar assortment of greens strewn over the worn counter. There are roses as well, and she pulls one out separately; it's a strange, rusty red.

"Goodness you're slow, Sarah Louise! Time's getting on. I'll have to take things from here, I see. No, now go and change, and do comb your hair!"

I swallow a retort. I'm not going to ask what's on the counter. She can still put together a passable sandwich, so she can feed her friends whatever she wants. I cross the hall and take the back stairs two at a time.

I'm out of breath when I reach the top of the stairway, and I'm getting that uncomfortable sense I always have that nothing in the house—including Granny—is right. I look over at her room with a vague dread. The feeling lingers as I hurry into my bright, familiar bedroom ...

It's hot, so I take my time changing, deciding on the Egyptian cotton dress. Shod in soft sandals, with my hair combed back, I look presentable. I take the main stairway down, pausing by the newel post on the lower landing.

"Come, Sarah Louise, do! I'm almost done—everyone's arriving!" Granny limps past me on her way to the drawing room, pushing a tea trolley. She's got the tea pot, cream and sugar, and a number of tarnished spoons. The napkins don't look too fresh, but her friends will use them and say nothing; their manners are old country, imported, like the china and the tea. She disappears, shadow-like, through the archway. Exasperated, I go to the kitchen and fetch the remaining trolley with its assortment of oddly cut, lumpy sandwiches.

The ladies are arriving in the south garden, where the driveway ends. From there, they mount the steps and cross the conservatory into the drawing room. There's a large bay window to one side where you can see the high trees that bar the view of the city, with the inlet beyond, and the strait. Granny has arranged chairs in a semicircle, facing the front of the vast, bright room.

Mrs. Parker is my favorite, a kind old lady in a pretty, flowered dress and pearls. "Hello, Sarah Louise! Lovely day," she waves and finds herself a chair. Then there's the Misses Smith and MacIntosh, and the others, all dressed in linen and lace, wearing wide-brimmed hats; their dresses are loose-sleeved, the skirts almost ankle-length, in the style that older women wear. Cook or no, it's still considered an honor to have tea in this house, something which I'm certain Granny never lets them forget. She's a pillar of the community, and has done a lot for them all over the years.

It occurs to me that Mrs. Parker looks unwell. She was limping somewhat, and I remind myself to ask about her arthritis. I hate to see her getting so frail. They settle in and begin their discussion. I half-listen to Granny's quiet orations as she persuades them on some point; whatever it is, her opinion always wins the day. I'm bored, between pouring tea and offering up the sandwiches. They smell vile, with off-green bits poking from between the layers, but though some look at them askance, all the women take at least one.

The grand piano is to one side. A picture of my father, with his dark hair and expressive eyes, sits on top. That's enough to set me off, and before long I have a dull headache. I keep thinking of my father, and Robert. Granny's put her roses in several vases around the room, placing them among her recent and grotesque collections of dried branches and knickknacks. Their perfume, mingling with the scent of tea in the heat, is almost overpowering. Displayed this way, the blooms are a striking assortment, but none are familiar—they're the result of her labors, unique, like her. Flashing magenta, livid mustard, one that's almost black ...

Mrs. Parker is talking to me.

"You really must play something, dear," she smiles, gesturing at the piano. "You know I love music—we all do." There's a strange, pained look in her eyes. I stare at her for a moment. The piano was my father's forte. He had genius, was at the top of his profession. Granny drove him half mad with her perfectionist zeal. Hesitant, miserable, I nod. There are times when I despise myself for it, but I was brought up to indulge my elders.

There are polite murmurs as I seat myself at the bench and run my fingers over the keys. I'm out of practice, and the instrument needs tuning. Of course, the headache doesn't help. I finger a few notes and begin ... Chopin, a waltz, and somehow appropriate for the afternoon and my mood. I'm careful, watching my tempo, but the fingering is murder, and I stumble through the last few bars. I'm embarrassed as the ladies clap politely, and slip away, gathering up empty plates and soiled napkins.

"You played very well, dear," Mrs. Parker says as she takes her leave. Her sentiment is echoed by the Misses Smith and MacIntosh. "We're going to stay in the south garden awhile," she adds. She's looking at me in a covert, pleading manner. "Your grandmother is such an exceptional gardener..."

She might as well say that I'm not—exceptional, that is—at gardening or anything else. Granny certainly will. Her eyes are snapping as she looks at me over her glasses. She never fails to point out my shortcomings, and I've just humiliated her with my performance.

"Perhaps we could have a chat, later ...?" Mrs. Parker whispers. Granny overhears, and glares at her, so she troops out into the garden with the other women. Through the bay window I see them in the brilliant sunlight, wandering among the roses, their skirts floating about them. It seems to me a number of them are having difficulty walking. After a moment, Granny joins them, and as she limps in among them they cluster around her. Her silver head dips up and down as she moves from one to the other, rearranging and admiring their dresses ...

Granny bides her time until we are alone in the kitchen. I've done pretty well with the cleaning up until now, when I smashed her favorite tea cup. Worse, it used to be my father's, and she hates to lose anything of his.

"You're determined to make things difficult, aren't you, Sarah Louise?" she sighs. "This house is so important to me. I know it's hard work, but I don't think, considering how I've always stood by you, that I'm asking too much ..."

She goes on as I scrub and sweep and tidy, about how she's supported Robert and me. It isn't a tirade. Granny's too much of a lady for that. But a phrase here, a word there, can be more effective than any outburst. Robert wanted us to have a place of our own, but I was so concerned about Granny that I wouldn't hear of it. Finally I break a glass, and cut my finger, bleeding all over the counter.

"Granny, this can't go on," I speak through clenched teeth, my hands shaking. It's grown dark outside, and there's a high, bright moon at the window. "We can't cope any more, not just the two of us. I know you don't like outsiders, except the ladies of the auxiliary, but we must have help, at least replace Naeine ..."

"You needn't speak to me in that tone." She's upset, in tears. I hate this. Even in conciliation, it seems I fail. Any suggestion I make to ease the workload is met with stubborn refusal, and I've never been this bold before. She's had a hard life, personally, and I don't want to hurt her, but she won't listen to reason. I'm appalled at the resentment I feel, its deep, savage ferocity. I feel trapped, the proverbial animal in a cage, swamped in endless days of backbreaking work with no one to talk to but a demanding old woman.

"You don't understand," she says, trembling. "I'm not a bad person Sarah Louise, not cruel—I love you, I truly do. I worked so hard to keep this house for the family, but I must have the things that matter around me ... "

"No matter what the cost?" For once, I'm not about to back down. I expect more tears, anger, but she surprises me.

"You're right," she says, placating me, mopping at her eyes with the hem of her dress. "We do need some changes. It's hard to lose people; I do need others about me ..."

"I'm sorry about the piano, today, but music was my father's gift, not mine."

Until I say this, I had no idea just how much I miss him. He used to play while I went to sleep, the notes drifting up the stairway and through the house; always my favorite Brahms waltz, then some

Schubert...I can still see his fine-drawn features, the reflective, sensitive mouth that was never lacking a smile when I needed one ...

Granny begins to ramble, as if she can't decide what changes to make. I'm not sure I've won my point, and suddenly I don't care. Her hair stands out in wispy clumps where she's pulled at it in her agitation. In the overhead light, her eyes and mouth appear sunken, her skin ghastly and sallow. She picks up a wilted rose, left on the counter earlier. It's the weird, rust-red one, its edges curled, darkened now, like dried blood.

"Now, let me see...do I, or don't I...and should I tell Sarah Louise tonight?" Granny smiles maliciously. She begins to pluck select petals in her own version of loves-me-not, and the rose is soon a pathetic, plundered thing.

I can't take this. I'm exhausted. I know I'm abandoning my responsibilities; I should see that everything's locked up and she gets safely to bed, but my head is almost bursting, and if I don't leave her and this kitchen and that poor mutilated flower, I'm afraid I'll die.

The light bulb is out on the back stairs so I take the main staircase. I make my way into my room and fling myself face down on the bed. My hand is still bleeding from my cut, but I don't care. I miss Robert with a pain that's almost physical. He escaped what I could not. I'm a coward, pure and simple, bound to a demanding old woman by a sense of family and duty she's ingrained in me since childhood.

I roll over and try to sleep, but the night air is heavy in this old house, mingling with the scent of seasoned wood and wilting roses. I'm haunted by this place, my nagging sense of its malaise. Through the open window I hear the deer in the woods out back, trapped like I am, moaning and battering his antlers in frustration against the trunks of the trees ...

I feel vaguely aware that Robert's somewhere nearby, with his beautiful, patient smile. In the depths of the house, someone is fingering the piano. Brahms, the first few bars, but the left hand is clumsy, as though the player has trouble finding the keys. The right hand has my father's touch, though hesitant and melancholy. In the next room, Granny begins drumming her heels against her trunk again; I'm aware I may be dreaming, but I don't really want to wake up ...

The reality of the room is stark as I open my eyes, all moon-shadow and black silhouettes. At some point, I would have sworn I heard voices in the far garden, making clucking sounds at the deer, calling him. The house is silent.

"I'd better check on Granny," I mutter. I'm loathe to leave this bed, the lingering sense of Robert. But maybe the drumming on the trunk wasn't a dream ...

Panicked, I hurry through the doorway, afraid she's hurt herself, or worse, but a look in Granny's room tells me its empty. I let out a sharp breath. My chest hurts so much, I feel as though my heart's about to stop. I should have seen her to bed. have to find her. God, what if she's wandered away, what if ...?

A rhythmic creaking comes from the far end of the landing: crick ...crick ...crick.

"Granny." My voice hoarse with relief, I turn. The matted silver tufts of her hair catch in a shaft of moonlight as her head tilts back and forth. "You shouldn't have dragged your rocker out here. You could hurt yourself —"

This is it, I decide. It's a small thing in itself, but added to all the other frustrations, the pinpricks, the endless work and worry, it pushes me over the brink. I take a deep breath. "I can't take this any more, Granny—I'll make other arrangements for you, but I'm leaving."

She doesn't answer me at first, just rocks back and forth, crick ... crick...crick. Then:

"It's a little late, don't you think, Sarah Louise?" Her voice is gentle, almost seductive. She leaves the rocker and limps towards me along the rut in the carpet, secateurs in hand. Her eyes and mouth look even more sunken, and her dress is horribly wrinkled, torn. The blue gleam of her gaze is mesmerizing, malevolent in the moonlight from the stairwell. "Do you think I didn't know?"

"I don't understand." My assurance fades.

"Oh, I think you do." She stops.

Her look is so focused, so chilling, unlike the way she's been for what now seems a very long time. She snips her secateurs. The feeling of dread grips me again, stronger this time; it compels me to turn and look in her room, but I resist.

There's a moaning from the back landing, a clattering, followed by shuffling sounds.

"The deer—you brought him in the house?" I manage.

I push past her towards the noise, peering down. The perverse back stair light is on again, and I can see the deer, rounding the stairwell. It's only when he's taken several steps that I recognize him. Mrs. Parker is right behind him, choking him back with a tether. She's still wearing the dress she had on this afternoon.

"No!" I can barely say the word.

He rears, trying to stand upright, but I can see it hurts him, he's so bent. The hawthorn branches that my grandmother has somehow grafted to his head scrape the wall, and there are leaves growing from one side of his mouth so he cannot speak; the other is pulled down into a slit, as if Granny's made a space to feed him. Smaller branches sprout through the rags on his body, from his left hand and arm, his chest; his feet are covered in bark.

"Daddy!" I break, sobbing like a child, as the true horror of this place sinks home. Mrs. Parker moves up the stairs a little, and I see the others behind, with the Misses Smith and MacIntosh.

"Sarah Louise," Mrs. Parker is crying, her eyes sunken and hollow, nightmarish, like Granny's. "I'm so sorry, dear, but I did try to warn you ..."

Slowly, she lifts up her skirt, and I see why she and the others had so much trouble walking, what Granny was doing with them in the garden. Green-stemmed roses sprout from her calves, large florid blooms like something out of a hideous painting. The others want to show me too, lifting their skirts, rolling sleeves, removing hats, but I won't look, I can't.

"Why, Granny?" I'm choking with terror and rage. "What was in those filthy sandwiches this afternoon? Something to help you do *this*?" I gesture at the thing that was once my father, the women, but Granny isn't looking; she hasn't moved. I head back to her, face her.

She just stares at me. The compulsion to turn, to look at her room returns, and this time I yield. I take in the moonlit bed, the trunk. And I know, with an indescribable anguish, that I can't refuse to think about it all, not any more; I must remember.

It got so very bad, especially after Granny's stroke, and no help would stay... We planned, Robert and me, to put her in a nice place, because there was no way that we could cope with her any more ...

But there was that awful night, just before we were to send her away. I was exhausted. I thought I heard a noise, and Granny calling out, complaining, but I didn't get up. I just didn't want to go in to her. Neither did Robert. We didn't know she'd crept out of bed and broken into the trunk, climbed inside, that the lid had slammed shut, trapping her. She almost suffocated before we realized something was terribly wrong. When we finally got her out, there were marks inside where she clawed and kicked to get free. I think she knew what we were planning. The doctor thought she climbed in there to hide from us, to feel safe. It was after that when Robert and I had that bitter quarrel, each blaming the other ...

"Granny..." I turn to her. There's no forgiveness there, none of the occasional gentleness I knew as a child. "Oh Granny, I'm so sorry!"

As for the ladies, they sided with my father, with Robert and me, when we decided to send Granny into care. They soothed and placated her, pretending she could stay at the house. Daddy went along with it all, but the strain destroyed him, drove him away before we ever got around to moving her.

Of course the house isn't right. The place is like a macabre echo of what it was, once, the differences both subtle and sinister. Granny's later touches, the ornaments and branches, the plants, all add to the effect.

"Your father shouldn't have lied to me, Sarah Louise. None of them should." Granny sighs. "It took me some time to find him, but the ladies were more accommodating. The house is the way I want it now, and the garden...it's a pity your father doesn't like roses—I have tried to please everyone."

"What about me, Granny?" I'm bitter now, defiant. All along she's been daring me to face the truth ... like today, when she mentioned the cook—she dismissed Naeine the same day as the accident. "I made the decision to send you away. I broke my promise—mine was the worst deception of all!"

"I know that. It broke my heart, when I found out. And the trunk, what happened to me that night—I called and called you...I was so afraid ..."

I feel sick. She starts to cry, and in some ghastly way I think she's sorry, that she'd like to stop all this, but she can't.

She pulls something from the pocket of her crumpled dress. It's the mangled, rust-and-blood-colored rose she plucked earlier. There's a dark stain on one of the remaining petals; real blood, perhaps, from when I cut my hand.

"My devoted child, " she says. The sunken mouth curves in a trembling smile. "Of all the roses I've created, this is the one for you. I have such special plans. We'll forgive each other, you'll see—we'll have our friends, the family..."

She regards the rose for a moment, then stuffs it back in her pocket. I can't even pity this thing my grandmother has become. I head down the main stairs; anything, at this point, to get away from her. Running, I make my way into the drawing room. I can hear the ladies, and my father the deer, shuffling and clattering around by the back stairs. As I approach the conservatory, I glance out the window. A pale-haired figure nears the edge of the drive, coming up from the south garden.

"Robert!" I cry in joyous recognition. I start for the closed glass doorway into the conservatory. Granny has made it downstairs, and I hear her dragging her foot as she comes up behind me. The limp is more pronounced, when she's really determined.

As I draw near, Robert is at the outside conservatory door, pounding against the glass. The moonlight pouring into the conservatory shines on him, the panes of the door.

"Sarah Louise!" he calls out. His voices sounds muted and distant. "I know you're in there! You have to talk to me!" He takes a backward step or two on the porch, staring at the upper levels of the house. "It's been so long. This can't go on—I mean it—Sarah Louise!"

"Robert!" I cry again, reaching for the door. He doesn't hear, and starts down the stairs, distraught.

"Well, Sarah Louise?" Granny says from behind me. "It's up to you, you know."

Looking back, I see her clearly in the moonlight, hear the snip of the secateurs in her hand, like a lock turning, closing. Some of her hideous roses are stuffed in the top of the copper urn beside me. She makes a slit on her forearm, then moves over to the urn and takes a cutting, inserting the stem in the wound.

"I called Robert, earlier," she says. "I'd like to have him back; he'd be perfect, with his lovely, smooth skin. I think I can manage it, but it would be easier, if you asked him..."

When I look at Robert again, he's scanning the upper windows of the house, starting around it. Frantic, I reach for the door once more, then stop—I just freeze—I want to rush out, to warn him, but so help me, I can't.

I should have spoken up.

If I had, I could have stopped Granny's unspeakable acts, her ruthless, never-ending quest. I should have faced what happened to her that terrible night, my part in it, a long time ago. But if I leave here now, I'll have to do more than that. I'll have to accept everything that followed it, the absolute blame, and I just can't—not even for my beautiful Robert...

I hear her move away, her limp exaggerated, loud, like my own panicked breathing. My elbow knocks against the urn, rocks it. The roses spill out. I didn't think flowers made a sound when they fell, but these do, at least for me; like mounting thunder, the repeated slam of a door, one by one they hit the floor. I kick and claw against the conservatory door, as Granny did on the lid of the trunk, feeling what she must have felt: the terror, the pain. I know there's no way I can open it—not to escape.

Not yet.

And somewhere, lost in the fall of roses, their growing tumult in my ears, are the dark, desperate sounds I make in my struggle to be free.

At Fort Assumption

by
Dale L. Sproule

Dale Sproule's stories have appeared in professional, small press, and literary publications, including *Ellery Queen Mystery*, *Pulphouse*, *Tesseracts 5*, and *Northern Frights 2*. With his wife, Sally McBride, he publishes and co-edits *TransVersions*, an award-nominated magazine of speculative fiction and poetry. He writes: "At Fort Assumption is one of the most autobiographical stories I have written. While the characters have been changed to suit the story, the horror is very real."

In daylight, the flying saucer landing pad looked cartoonish against the bleak brown landscape.But in the eternal twilight of the northern summer, it looked frighteningly alien and Theo loved it. The only thing in High Level he could ever love.

Sitting in the centre of the paintworn, concrete disc, Theo blinked his eyes, which stung from bug repellent splashed on too thickly. The air should be fresh in the middle of nowhere, but instead, smelled like dust filtered through an oily sheet. At least the sky was filled with stars. He took a deep breath and lay back in spread-eagled surrender to the vastness.

"Come and get me."

Betty at the Esso Restaurant told all the tourists it was famous, but Father knew the truth and bequeathed it to his son. The local Rotary Club had built this landing pad as a Canadian Centennial monument in 1967, only to find that it was one of half a dozen such artifacts built by prairie communities vying for media attention. The publicity furor began and ended with a single line in the AMA Guidebooks. "Things to see in High Level: Flying Saucer Landing Pad in Centennial Park."

Now the pad was just the centrepiece of a huge, weedy park in a town on a mudflat in the centre of the muskeg. When dry, the white mud filled the air like filthy talcum powder, when wet it turned to soft slime that painted fences, trees, vehicles and buildings up to human eye-level in a fine spray. It was August in High Level. Nights were cold

and the mosquitoes moved like small thunderheads through the empty
streets.

Father should have returned from Fort Assumption hours ago.
Probably went straight to the Legion Hall after the long drive back;
presidential responsibilities and the magnetism of the liquor more
imperative than the love of a son he'd barely seen in nine years. Theo
was supposed to be on this trip, his last chance to spend time with his
father before going back to school in Edmonton.

Entertainment Options in High Level: Seven Pines Motel, on highway featuring Lounge(which refused to serve Theo), Restaurant (where
all the kids from the trailer park hung out) and Satellite TV; Legion
Hall—Members & Guests Only (his father would not be thrilled to see
him); Esso Restaurant, on highway; High Level Movie Theatre—Main
Street, downtown (a ten minute walk from his father's house on the far
corner of a tiny patch of suburbia in the wilderness).

The only movie theatre for 500 miles in any direction had a blue tiled
facade. On the night his father didn't come home, the poster display
box was empty, so the only indication of what was playing was the
marquee. "EXPOSURE".

"What's the movie about?" Theo shouted through a metal grate.

A plump man with a fringe of wiry gray hair shrugged, "This is a
replacement. It was supposed to be Deathwish 13."

"Can I get some service in here?" shouted a voice from the
lobby. Through the open door, Theo saw a thin man with a beige and
white plaid shirt and a straw cowboy hat standing at the snack counter
as though in a saloon, a young Metis girl standing quietly at his side.

"Are you buying a ticket or not?" the plump man asked Theo.

"Yeah, sorry." Theo paid and as he entered, the ticket man
bustled past him to the snack counter. The popcorn machine was an
empty glass monolith on one side. On the other, stood a rack with two
bags of chips and some peanuts. Lying flat on the counter were a large
box of Goodies and a handful of chocolate bars.

"Got sunflower seeds?" asked the cowboy.

"We don't allow them. No spitting, no smoking...even in the
washroom."

"How old is this candy?"

"Whattdya mean."

"The packaging looks yellow. Could probably sell it as fossil fuel." The cowboy laughed.

While this was happening, the girl stared at Theo with angry eyes. Her date was still laughing as he turned away from the snack counter and grabbed the girl by the waist. With a smirk, she whispered into the cowboy's ear and giggled. Contemptuously, the thin man looked Theo up and down, then turned and walked the girl into the theatre.

As Theo entered with a can of warm, generic-brand cola he saw the couple sitting in the back row. From his threadbare seat near the front, he could hear them snickering and murmuring behind him.

They shut up briefly when the opening credits came on.

"EXPOSURE," said bone white letters on a black field.

As he sat, he glanced back to see the cowboy sitting alone. The girl giggled again, invisible. The cowboy smiled. The music swelled and when Theo looked back up at the screen, a subtitle had appeared. "The Theo Richards Story."

Sitting slack-jawed with wonder, his memory filled in the sensory details that went with the visual images on screen.

Scene 1. Interior. A funeral chapel.

Theo Richards arrived for his mother's funeral wearing mirrored sunglasses and a black tuxedo. Father grabbed his arm and steered him through a doorway into a cool, dark room, tearing the glasses from his son's face.

"Ow, that hurt my ear."

"Is that the suit I gave you the money for? You rented a tuxedo for a hundred and thirty dollars?" Father's complexion looked florid even in the dim electric candlelight. "I guess I'll be getting some money back."

Theo smelled beer.

"You're drunk?"

"Not drunk. I had a drink. There's a difference."

"You promised."

"Did you rent the tux, Ted?"

"Well kind of." But before Theo could go on to explain, it occurred to him that there was an open coffin in the room. "Is that Mom?"

"What do you mean, kind of?" Father said. "How do you 'kind of' rent a tuxedo?"

"Let's not talk about this in front of Mom, okay?"

"That's not your mother any more. It's just a place she once lived. She's gone, I'm your reality now and I'm telling you that you are not going to wear this monkey-suit to her funeral."

Theo turned his head toward the casket, to look at whatever had, in his peripheral vision, just sat up. But his mother lay still and silent in her forever bed of blue silk and mahogany.

Organ music droned from the chapel. Wasn't everyone depressed enough already?

Mom's eyelids flickered infinitesimally. Was that the suggestion of a smile? He stepped closer, she became more real than ever, as though she would sit up at any moment in her crisp white dress and ask him if he'd finished his homework, quiz him in her usual gentle way until he confessed that he was lying to his father.

Her lipstick was the wrong shade.

"Did you hear me, Ted?" Father said.

"It's Theo now. Mom calls...used to...call me Theo." Past tense. In a few days, he'd be living with Father in High Level. Spending the next month with a man he hardly knew anymore.

"Now take off this fucking coat." Grabbing the collar and one of the lapels, Father pulled the garment roughly off Theo's shoulders. "Where's the receipt for the tux rental?"

"Must have lost it." He actually rented the Tux for forty through the Ballroom Dancing Association that his friend Ben's parents belonged to. He and his friends had blown the rest of the money at the arcade. "I'm sorry, I should have been more careful about the receipt."

"I'll go to the rental place with you tomorrow and look at their copy."

Theo nodded because he couldn't think of anything else to do. Besides, Father wouldn't come with him to return the tux. He never followed through with anything.

As his father folded the jacket and tucked it under his arm.

The music stopped.

Father said. "We'd better get in there."

Theo reached out and touched his mom's cheek, recoiling at first from the powdery marshmallow texture of her flesh and the second time from its coolness. The third time, he slid his fingertips lightly across her skin to the corners of her mouth. Wondering if there was some chance it would make her smile and call off the joke, he pushed up the corners of her mouth as though they were made of modelling clay.

"What are you doing?" Father stepped up behind him, face full of anger, gaze locked on Theo's face. "Don't do that."

Looking at Father, Theo suddenly realized the man couldn't even bring himself to *look* at the corpse of his ex-wife. The iron man of his childhood didn't live there anymore.

"Give me the jacket. I'll hang it up."

As his father extended the folded garment, the collar slipped from his fingers and the jacket dangled like the Hanged Man from the Tarot, arms dancing madly. Even as Theo took the jacket his father was walking unsteadily away.

"It's about to start," his words melted into the light. The man Theo saw occasionally on Christmases and birthdays left him with his Mom for the final time.

She didn't look like someone who had died in a car accident. Didn't even look like his mother anymore either. This time when he touched her lips, she moaned. A very sexual sound. Theo jerked his hand away, but discovered the voice wasn't coming from the casket, it was coming from behind him in the movie theatre.

Peering back into the darkness, he saw a woman's naked shoulders rising and falling. He averted his eyes, back to the screen, where the Métis girl was lying naked in the coffin staring at him like she'd done in the lobby. The giggle from the back row had turned into his mother's rich, familiar laughter. Theo swivelled in his seat.

Zoom back for a two shot of boy and coffin; slow fade to black.

In the diminishing light from the screen, Theo could see nothing. Too terrified to walk back for a better look at the lovers, he forced his attention back to the movie, where the scene had changed dramatically.

Scene 2: Interior. Day. The passenger cabin of a small aircraft.

Cut to: Aerial shot - a green monotony of forest, dissected less and less frequently by the grey ribbons of roadways.

Theo pressed his head against the airplane window, watching intently for the occasional black and yellow squares of farmland or glistening blue amoeba-shaped lakes.

"Everything you love goes away in the end..." sang the music track of the movie.

"Everything is going bad all at once," said Father, sounding like another line from the same song. "Julia left me. Your mother died. And you know what started it all? My teeth."

The man in the seat next to Theo, his father, looked impossibly distant, as though seen through the wide end of a telescope.

"Never had a cavity in my life. Then six months ago, the dentist in Peace River told me that they've been rotting from the inside out. They all have to be pulled." As remote and indecipherable as the landscape below them, Father's voice crackled and trailed off into a tinny blur. Covering his face with both hands, he wept.

At the funeral, all he'd talk about was money. Now it was teeth.

Theo put his forehead against the window again and let the vibration take him away from this chattering and weeping about petty things and into the forest far below where the trees grew smaller and sparser and less full, like twigs reaching up out of a lime green sea.

Wondering if his mother was eavesdropping from whatever dimension or time warp she was in, he looked at the streaky, distant clouds, perhaps hoping to glimpse her there, but instead, he saw a light, darting and dodging through layers of sky.

"Hey, what is that?" Theo said. But when he turned back, his father was looking smaller and more faded than ever. Still talking about government dental plans, his voice disappearing into swirls of static. He seemed unaware that Theo had spoken.

The object outside was clearly visible now, less a saucer than a giant hubcap. Colored lights flashed randomly around the rim.

"Don't you see it?" Theo asked aloud. But the seat beside him was empty. And when he looked back outside, the saucer too was gone. All that was left was the drone of the plane and the music.

"Everything you love goes away in the end...."

Scene 3: Interior. Day. Father and son sit at a dining room table, eating breakfast.

As he decapitated the second soft boiled egg of the fifth morning of his northern exile, Theo scowled at Father who unexpectedly looked up from the table.

"Something wrong with the egg?"

"No. Good egg. I'm just bored. You're never home and I don't know anybody."

"I could get you a job."

"There's less than three weeks before school. I'd hardly start before I'd have to quit."

"A lot of casual jobs come through my office. Perfect for Indians. Work two days, get drunk for a week then come back for a couple more days work. Only way to keep them at something longer term is withhold their paycheque until the project's finished. Most are good workers when they're sober. Trick is, keeping them away from the bottle."

Theo knew not to mention Father's drinking problem, however relevant to this conversation it might seem. "Yeah, but...this hasn't been much of a summer holiday, with Mom dying and all. I want to do something interesting for a few days. I mean I think that's cool about the casual jobs and all. I'm definitely interested. I was just kind of hoping to do something...you know...fun?"

Theo's father grinned. "You want to see what I do for a living? I'm flying out to John D'Or Prairie for a meeting this afternoon. Why don't you come along?"

Father's shouted commentary filled the air as warmly as the sunshine slanting in the cockpit window. After a week without company, Theo found his father's redneck philosophies not only palatable but almost profound, "This is a model reserve. The Band Council outlawed drinking. With the money they would have otherwise spent on booze, they built a sawmill. They keep their lawns neat, houses painted. This is what the others reserves have the potential to become."

When they landed, a fat native man was waiting to pick them up.

"This is my translator, Raymond Cardinal, from Fort Vermilion. Nobody at John D'Or speaks English."

Theo's father went into a meeting. The only person left in the office was a secretary who spoke Cree and French. There was no visible English language reading material, so Theo went outside.

Strolling aimlessly down the dusty road, he listened for the absent shouts of children. Occasionally, a saw whined in the distance. The field around him was freshly turned, brown clumps of dirt bristling with yellow stubble. The earth here in the Peace River valley was richer, less dusty than in High Level.

There were no birds chirping, just grasshoppers buzzing up at him from the roadside like little rudderless helicopters, dragonflies whirring past constantly. A chain saw chortled to life nearby, but before Theo could determine which direction it was coming from, it stopped and didn't start back up again. There was no wind. No traffic. No livestock, although the smell of manure hung faintly in the air. Houses were tiny white dots, barely visible at the end of the road he was standing on. But Theo couldn't go anywhere in case the meeting ended. Knowing Father would be pissed if he was gone, he went nowhere. The sun continued to shine. The wind didn't rise.

That was the first hour. The next three were much longer.

When the doors to the meeting room finally opened, they were back on the airplane within five minutes.

"What did you talk about in there?" Theo asked.

"Oh, the meeting? Nothing interesting. Look, I've got to write a report before this all goes out of my head. Sorry, Ted."

"It's okay," Theo said. "Look, Dad, could you please call me Theo?"

"I'll try to remember," his father mumbled, going back to his work, which he didn't manage to finish before getting back to the airport. Dropping Theo at the Esso, he gave him ten dollars and said, "Pick up something to eat while I check in at the office. I'll come round and pick you up."

"Should I get something for you too?"

"No, I'll grab something later at the Legion. It was nice having you along today, Ted. We'll do it again before you leave, when I won't be stuck all day in a meeting."

At first, Theo dreaded the day, but by week's end, he was begging Father to go along with him again before school started.

"The only trip on my calendar is Fort Assumption. "

"Couldn't I come with you?"

"I dunno. It's not as nice out there. When I give them their welfare cheques on Monday, it'll all be gone by the end of the week. Spent on potato chips, cigarettes and booze. Can't tell you how many times we've found babies sitting in their own shit, drinking cola instead of milk because that's all their brother or sister could find to feed them. The kids fend for themselves until the parents sober up. There's lots of abuse. The reserve is squalid. And it's not accessible by plane. Schoolbus only gets up there when the road's passable, a couple months a year. But there's no airport, so I'll be driving, four hours there and four back. There for about an hour, that's all. And there's nothing to see."

"It's better than being cooped up here."

"Well, okay, but we have to be up at the crack of dawn."

The conversation on screen was almost identical to the one they had a few nights earlier, only with a different outcome. In real life, Dad received a Sunday night phone call and returned to the table apologetically, explaining that there had been another suicide on the reserve.

"Under the circumstances, I shouldn't have you along with me. Sorry, son."

"But you promised, Dad."

"It's out of my hands. I'm sorry."

In the movie it all played out quite differently.

Scene 4: Exterior. Day. Father and son getting into a 4 x 4 truck.

From the driver's seat, Father smiled at him, pulling the flat black rifle clip from his coat pocket and sliding it under the seat cover, between his legs.

"Never know when you're going to hit a deer or run into a bear. Had a showdown with a moose last time."

"You killed it?"

He shook his head. "Naw, but it charged the truck."

"You're kidding."

"They do that sometimes."

"Wow."

The enthusiasm on Theo's face wore off as the drive rumbled on and his father wouldn't let him take the wheel despite his learner's licence.

"Mom always let me drive."

Father explained that the "Texas pea gravel" on the highway often shattered windshields and if something like that happened, he'd rather be at the wheel. Prophetic, because an hour later, the driver's side window of the 4x4 was hit by a knuckle-sized rock thrown by an oilfield truck that roared past them out of the tundra. As a sheet of shattered glass avalanched into his father's lap, he managed to steer the vehicle to the side of the road. Father pounded on the horn and shook his fist out the window, but the truck didn't stop.

They cleaned out the broken glass with some hunting magazines from under Father's seat, but they had no way to patch the window. Under the seat, Theo saw seatbelts pushed down through the seat cushions. He'd have pulled his out and used it, if it wasn't coated in grime.

They parked at the side of the road and dove for cover whenever a rooster plume of dust came at them on an intersect course. When vehicles actually passed, the air grew so thick it made Theo gag. The twenty minutes to the turnoff into the forest seemed more like an hour.

"Forest" was a generous description of the countryside. The trees were thin as tentpoles, holding aloft airy webworks of leaves beneath an empty grey sky. "Road" didn't begin to describe the rutted, muddy pathway they were driving on. The worst parts had bridges of freshly felled trees which hammered like angry demons at the 4x4's undercarriage. It might have been exhilarating at a greater speed than Father was driving. At least he was forced to pick up the pace a bit by the mosquitoes which filled the cab whenever they went too slow.

"How do people get out when the road's not passable?"

A shrug. "There's a helicopter for medical emergencies and food drops."

"Why would anybody live in a place like this?"

"Because they're too drunk or too lazy to get off their asses when they can just stay in their broken-down houses and collect welfare."

Just then they hit a bump that almost put Theo through the roof of the cab. He clutched his head.

"You alright?"

The truck was standing still. Mosquitoes almost literally poured into the cab of the truck.

Theo worked up a grin. "I'm fine, let's just get going before we're eaten alive."

A nod. They took off again. Once braced for it, Theo managed not to hurt himself again.

It was well after noon by the time they got there. Unpainted, ramshackle houses rimmed a big field of mud. A crowd was gathered in front of the church that stood in the centre of the open space, its austere black steeple aimed into the sky.

"Wait here," his father said, climbing out of the truck with his briefcase in one hand. He slipped the bullet clip into his pocket with the other. "You can get out and walk around if you like."

Slamming the driver's door, his father went into the church, leaving Theo alone among the crowd of villagers grunting strange monosyllables among themselves. A couple of them looked in the broken window.

"Cheques here?" asked an emaciated looking man with a businessman's haircut, casually brushing mosquitoes from his face and neck.

"Yeah, I think so. They were in his briefcase."

The man nodded and turned, his announcement in Cree eliciting scattered moans.

As the mosquitoes came in, Theo jumped out of the truck and rattled the church doors. But they were locked.

"They're in the basement having a drink," the gaunt man said, "Church had no wine last spring. Somebody stole it. So he always locks the doors."

"The priest locks you out of church?"

"No. God locks us out. 'Cept on Sundays, eh?" He walked away laughing.

"Is there a doorbell, or anything?" But his translator was gone and all Theo got back were vacant stares. A man stepped out of the crowd, came up grinning and shook Theo's hand. His ears stuck on both sides and his head actually got narrower toward the crown. He had buck teeth, no chin and his tongue lolled out of his mouth.

Theo said, "Hi, glad to meet you."

"Lafou," said the ugly native, "Lafou."

"What?" Theo asked.

"Charlie doesn't speak English," the thin man explained as Charlie kept pumping Theo's hand. He wasn't strong, his grip spidery and light. The crazy man's other hand patted Theo's shoulder, "*Je suis un bon homme, n'est-ce pas? Un bon homme! Je m'appel Charlie. Charlie Lafou.*"

Charlie the Fool.

Theo heard his father's voice, shouting names, "Rene Lefevre...Pierre Lefevre..Yves Lefevre....Wilfred, Alice, Daniel, Leslie, Roger, Jean, Rene, Alex...Leopold Sauvage..Anne Sauvage, Pierre, Rene, Wilfred..."

People streamed past, cheques in hand and grim purpose in their downcast eyes. Charlie wouldn't let go of his hand.

"No, I don't want to shake anymore," Theo pulled away. Whereupon Charlie took his *other* hand, shaking almost violently now and laughing.

What was the French word for 'stop'? "*Arret. Arret!*"

Looking him in the eye, Charlie laughed even harder. When the English-speaking man walked past, Theo shouted, "Hey, can you help me."

But it seemed that the fool was the only one who could see or hear him.

The crowd had dispersed. Father had vanished. Alarmed, Theo pushed Lafou away and ran for the church doors, which were already locked. He pounded on them but no one answered.

"Is there a back door?" he asked the fool, who shrugged.

Behind the church, the ground was mossy and wet. There was no back door. Theo hurried back around to the front of the building, just in time to see the pinhead walking away.

"Hey Charlie. Did you see...*excuse moi*...oh, fuck it."

The stained glass wasn't as translucent as it seemed. He could see nothing through yellow, green, red or blue. Theo briefly considered putting a rock through the window, then looked out at the now distant Lafou. Wavering between the fool and the church, he pounded on the door once more before turning and running after the only human being in sight, following him into the woods.

Tree trunks no bigger around than broomsticks created an effect like a vertical slat curtain. Through them, Theo saw a blur of movement.

"Charlie! Wait."

The mud path ended a few steps into the woods, the ground underfoot turning into small hills of thick moss. Spindly pines and birch trees poked up like sidewalk weeds between them. Theo's first close-up look at muskeg.

When Charlie flickered briefly into sight again, Theo forged a bit deeper into the forest. The tussocks of moss grew smaller, the gaps between them bigger. The crevices weren't wet or muddy, but were very deep. When he missed his footing, he occasionally sank in past his knees.

Realizing Charlie wasn't going to wait for him, Theo turned and began threading his way back the way he'd come. When the village and church steeple remained invisible after several minutes, he curved to the left. Was it possible to get turned around in such a short space? Obviously it was. He stopped and thought hard about any unconscious turns he might have taken.

Movement again.

"Charlie?"

Wearing six-pointed antlers and a startled expression, a muledeer buck fled the instant it saw him, bounding deftly through the bog.

The sky was an even, dull grey, shading toward black. He couldn't even hazard a guess where the sun was. It couldn't possibly be as late as it looked. Almost evening.

Picking a direction at random, he walked. The first time he paused, mosquitoes settled on his skin in living sheets. Frantically brushing and swatting at them, he hurried through the woods shouting, "Charlie! Dad! Somebody!" After awhile, his shout turned to, "Help!"

As long as he kept moving, the insectile vampires couldn't land, but his progress slowed as the terrain grew more uneven. Moss hung from the lower tree branches and the ground grew squishy underfoot. He was heading deeper into the muskeg rather than back toward the village, but whenever he turned to retrace his steps, the landscape became more severe. There were no landmarks.

Sweat irritated the bug bites. Beginning to panic, Theo ran and his foot slipped into a crevice. If he had been wearing regular shoes, he'd have lost one, but the running shoe was tied on tightly. He was trapped. A shifting black clowd settled on him thick as dust. Trying to shield his face, Theo sobbed into the crook of his arm.

"Giving up already?" asked a voice and Theo squinted into the darkening forest.

The fool stood in front of him, naked except for some strange headgear, not feathers, but antlers. He spoke English. Puzzled but relieved, Theo reached out to him.

The Indian made no move to help. "Everybody gives up out here," the Indian said. "There's no choice. But you didn't last long at all."

"Can you help me out?"

Lafou shook his head very deliberately. The antlers appeared to be growing out of the man's head. "You have to help yourself. That's what your father always tells my people."

"Please."

"Climb up. Climb up he says. He doesn't know. You don't know. But you're learning." The horned man turned and walked away.

"Wait!" By the time Theo freed his foot, and clambered up his visitor was striding away through the trees, which now trapped him like the bars of a cage.

The next time his foot slipped, it didn't sink in very deep at all. As Theo pulled his foot out, he peered down and saw a human arm, part of a torso, white skin crusted with mud. Resisting his instinct to scream and run, he reached in queasily, checked for a pulse. It was a dead woman, skin puffy and bloodless.

Dangerously close to vomiting, Theo stood up, unable to walk away. Finally, with a grimace, he bent back down, took hold of the hand and pulled, praying that her arm wouldn't separate from her body or something equally obscene.

As he pulled the body out, Theo saw his mother's face and released her with a squawk. He scrambled away, tripped, then lay there watching and hyperventilating, suddenly oblivious to the mosquitoes.

Edging toward her, he reached out and ran his fingertips over the familiar contours of her face. Finding the mole on her collarbone and the vaccination scar on her arm, he wrapped his arms around her and began to cry.

This had to be some sort of hallucination.

No. Now he remembered! It was a movie.

Fade to Black

Scene 5: Interior, night, movie theatre.

Turning, he looked toward the back of the theatre, but where there should have been empty seats, were tussocks of moss. Trees jutted up between them like long, thin bones.

Listening carefully, he heard moaning and laughter.

The couple in the back row!

Then a deep throated chuckle Theo knew was his mother's. The corpse fumbled for his zipper, grabbed his shrivelled little cock. Theo screamed, tried to get away, but she wouldn't let go. She climbed on top of him. Despite his terror and disgust he became erect.

A male voice said, "It's okay. This is Fort Assumption. We have needs but no choices."

Looking over his shoulder, Theo saw Lafou, his skin turned to tawny brown fur, looking more deer than human.

"What's going on? This can't be happening," said Theo.

"That's true," said Lafou. "It can't, but it is. It's just entertainment, white boy. Go with it."

"But this is my mother!" Theo sobbed as she lowered herself on him.

"My mother is my sister and my lover. She's all I ever had. Until we had a son. My little brother. He has less choice than you have right now."

Screaming and gagging and crying, Theo found a rock and pounded it against his mother's skull, which came apart like wet paper maché until she lay limp astride him. When he rolled the body off, he saw that it wasn't really his mother after all, but an Indian boy of nine or ten. Half of his face was crushed, but with a sad little smile he said, "and love them...and hate them and fuck them and kill them..."

"Help me!" screamed Theo.

"You killed my son. Why should I help you?" The horned man fled through the woods.

In blind panic, Theo crashed through the woods after him, not stopping until he was knee deep in icy water, the lake bottom sucking him down as he waded back to the mossy bank. When he was submerged, the cold water soothed his burning skin and kept the mosquitoes away. He swallowed some water, rising up and spitting out the foul tasting stuff.

Darker, colder, the night swirled in around Theo, alive and thirsty for his blood.

In the moonlight, he could see emptiness all around him. His face itched horribly, but when he scratched his cheek, he found something wet and tissue-like, clinging to his skin. He pulled at it, but it oozed out between his fingers. Black streamers hung from his wrists and the backs of his hands. Running his fingers over his face and neck, he felt dozens of leeches on his face and neck. Inside of his clothes too he knew. But he could do nothing to get them off. Couldn't even try.

Curling into a foetal position beside the lake, Theo cried until his throat was raw. He rolled onto his back, staring into the sky, no longer noticing the thousands of mosquitoes that came down to feed. And through those open eyes he saw a light; a flashlight? A search party come looking for him? But no. It was coming from the wrong direction, out over the lake.

As the light came closer, he recognized the flying hubcap shape. Despite the fear that roiled through his insides, he sat up, waving his arms and shouting.

The object zig-zagged toward him across the darkened sky, held aloft by a cylinder of light, illuminating the oily water which rippled beneath it in shattered rainbows. Until finally, it was directly above him, its light warm and cleansing.

Then, it shot back into the sky like a meteor freed from Earth's gravity, leaving Theo weeping, slowly sinking into the wet moss.

Minutes or hours later, Theo saw a form hovering above him. It was the fool, slashing his own wrist, bleeding into a wooden bowl, lifting Theo's head and telling him to drink. It tasted like dark, red wine.

As the boy drank hungrily, Lafou spoke softly. "At Fort Assumption, you drink whatever you need to replenish the life that is sucked from you."

When the bowl was empty, Theo licked it clean, covering his face with blood. And Lafou filled it again, bowlful after bowlful until Theo was drunk.

The sky was getting lighter when he staggered up and reeled his way back toward Fort Assumption. But drunk as he was, he didn't get far, before splashing face down in the swamp. He emerged, screaming, staring wide-eyed into the empty sky. But he didn't wear Theo's face anymore. He wore the face of Theo's father.

Freeze frame. Super: full credits roll.

The lights came up in the theatre. Examining his hands and his clothes, Theo climbed awkwardly to his feet. The back row was empty. He ran up the aisle toward the exit into the street and all the way home.

When he got there, he phoned the Legion Hall and the police, but as he somehow expected, nobody had seen his father. Finding an unopened bottle of navy rum in the liquor cabinet and an inch of warm cola in the bottle beside it, Theo mixed them into his glass, hand shaking so badly he could barely pour. As he stared into the swirling liquid, he realized his father had wandered far too deep into that wilderness to ever emerge. He tilted back the glass and savored its flat, ironic flavor.

MIRROR MONSTER

by
Stephen Meade

Dissatisfied with his work in Halifax as an advertising copywriter and freelance journalist, the peripatetic Stephen Meade has, since 1982, worked at various times as a carnival barker in Quebec, a lumberjack in northern Ontario, a gravestone cutter in Toronto, ski instructor in Banff, a house detective in Winnipeg, and a hotel clerk in Whitehorse, Yukon. He has in that time, as he puts it, "witnessed more than my share of human quirks and follies."

P enfield sat on the oddly uncomfortable chair without fidgeting. He was as excited as he had ever been in his life—and knew that if he handled it right, the excitement was only beginning. But he held himself in rigid control, determined to impress his hero. As he had rather expected, Ordan did not look the part: an avuncular grey-haired man in his vigorous early fifties, with watery green eyes.

"There's nothing wrong with me, Dr. Ordan. That is, I have no physical complaint. I came here to see you in regard to a personal matter."

"This is a busy clinic, Mr. Penfield. You could have come to my home."

"I feel safer here, sir." Watching closely, he saw Ordan's damp eyes narrow slightly. "This office seems secure. Are there any recorders in circuit? Please," he said, as Ordan began to speak, "I'm not concerned with doctor-patient confidentiality. I think I can take it for granted, I simply want to be *certain* no one else can hear us now, for both our sakes."

"My, my, how cryptic," Ordan said, and another might have believed the polite amusement in his voice, but Penfield was still watching the pupils, and exulted inwardly. He could *read* Ordan, see right through his skull! This *was* his hero. "You may speak freely, Mr. Penfield."

He had rehearsed this. "Dr. Ordan, I think of myself as a superior man, and you are my idol. You are an artist, and I am your biggest fan."

"I don't understand, sir. This is an underfunded inner-city clinic; no artistry takes place here, I assure you—"

"Please, Doctor. I am no kind of police; just the opposite. I'm the only one who could have tracked you here because I'm the only one who *knows* you, because I think like you. You are the Mirror Monster, the greatest genius of your age, and I have come halfway across the country to shake your hand and tell you that someone understands."

Ordan's face changed. "That is a serious accusation. The Mirror Monster, as the tabloids call him, is serial murderer, a sexual sadist—"

"A priest of pain, a master of horror. Beside you, de Sade was a half-talented amateur." He stood up slowly. "Doctor, I know that I am in some danger now, because I have startled you , and I want to allay your natural concern, to put you at ease." He began carefully to undress. "I must convince you that I am not wearing a wire or a weapon. Besides, this will look more natural if your nurse should come in."

The doctor watched in expressionless silence until he was done and seated again. The uncomfortable chair seat felt splintery against his bare buttocks, but he ignored it. "What is it that makes you think I am the Mirror Monster, Mr. Penfield?" Ordan asked.

"Study of your work," he replied at once. "I know of at least six certain kills aside from the eighteen attributed to you, and I'm sure there are more. I read all the sex-horror magazines, subscribe to several clipping services, collect videos that can't even be bought in Times Square. I study refinements of cruelty. There's been not one like you since Caligula, and you have technology that didn't exist then.

"Don't worry, Doctor, the police will never find you. Policemen tend to be simple sadists. They fail to perceive wit, subtlety, humor, so they will never understand you well enough to track you as I did. They assume, for instance, that since none of the cuts look surgical, you are not a medical man. But I reasoned that a really ingenious sadist would *learn* and employ medical techniques—unless he had already had a surfeit of them in his work, already exhausted the creative possibilities. So then it was a matter of triangulating on your location by known-body distribution, and looking for the most intelligent doctors. I used grades and IQ scores, and rejected any candidates who were not above reproach, on the assumption that an artist like yourself would cover his tracks superbly. The soundproofed basement in your home was an indicator. And then your background in phsyiochemistry nailed it down. You see..." Penfield smiled proudly, admiringly. "...I know about the anaesthetic."

Ordan did not move a muscle. "Do you really?"

"Brilliant. The first major breakthrough in the field since the discovery of electricity. I *deduced* it, doctor. Had to, of course: it must break down too rapidly and completely for any autopsy to ever find it."

Ordan regarded him for a long moment with those watery eyes. Then he lifted his phone. "Cancel the rest and go home, please, Nurse." He broke the connection. "You are a very clever man, Mr. Penfield."

"I am your student," he said modestly, preening inside. "The utter pellucid horror of using a perfect analgesic for purposes of torture is something I could never have conceived."

"Then how did you deduce it?"

" The sheer amount of the damage. It did not seem reasonable that your victims could survive so many hours of such intense agony before succumbing to heart failure, not even the strong young girls you usually choose. Their hearts should have burst much sooner, if they were going to at all. And of course there were the mirrors themselves. Why would such an artist use mirrors, when videotape would be so much more satisfactory? Why was there always a clock facing the site, even when there was no need for hurry?

"There is a morgue attendant who shares my...interest, a fool who is under my control: I arranged several hours in private with three of your victims. Magnificent work, Doctor; I believe you extracted every possible increment of suffering. The creative use of eye sockets... in any case, after careful study and meditation I found the tiny pinpricks near the top of each spine, obscured by the greater damage. I pondered for days—and then the answer came to me. It's been terribly hard, keeping it to myself."

"Say it."

Penfield grinned uncontrollably. "You string them up and anaesthetize them utterly. Not paralyze them, or they couldn't scream; you merely numb them. You may well use video, for yourself, but you set the mirrors up for *them*, so that they will see everything that is going to happen, every indignity, every splintered bone, every ruined organ.

Then you tell them precisely how long the anaesthetic is going to last. Then you set to work."

Ordan smiled for the first time. "There's a charming quality to the screams once you've taken the tongue. I like to do that first thing. And if you can arrange to be approaching orgasm just as the analgesic is wearing off, the ride is...exhilarating. But perhaps the best moment is somewhat earlier, the one when they first grasp the fact that they have sustained damage too great to survive—and have hours of life left, with the worst to come. Watching that realization dawn is *better* than orgasm."

Penfield felt his penis thicken, and blushed. "So I imagined. I salute you, sir."

Ordan regarded him with interest. "Are you another government recruiter? And if so, which government?"

Penfield blinked. "Oh my, no. I am a private citizen, a connoisseur."

"What is it you want of me, Mr. Penfield?"

He took a deep breath. "I want to hear about the ones that didn't make the papers, for one thing. If there are videos, I would consider it an honor to view them: I would not dare hope for copies. And if you don't mind, I'd like to work with you, once or twice."

"Why should I take that risk?"

"Three reasons. First, once we've done one together, I can no longer be even a hypothetical danger to you. Second, I know your work better than anyone else, probably *including* your victims. Most men— and many women—get a thrill from a newspaper account of your work, and suppress it. A few are willing to admit to themselves that they admire it, that they half-wish they had the courage to emulate you— they collect clippings of Manson and Ng and Bernardo/Homolka and other journeyman practitioners and hide them under the mattress. You have sold a *lot* of copies of the New York *Post*. We all have a monster inside us, men and women. We all see ourselves in your mirrors...

"I confess that I myself have never acted out my fantasies as yet; thanks to you I haven't needed to. But I am a serious student, and I think I know you almost as well as you know yourself. I know, for instance, that you'd never select victims from among your poverty-patients here at the clinic. Not from fear of arousing suspicion, but because there is no great challenge in degrading the kind of women I saw out there in your waiting room." His penis was stirring, beginning to lift. "Your victims are ladies."

"You said three reasons."

Penfield smiled. "I have developed a few little ideas of my own. Nothing as ingenious as yours, to be sure—but I think you may find them interesting amateur work. For instance, there's one I call the Zipper: ten battery-clamps in a row, on a rope..." Naming his invention aloud for the first time in his life was profoundly thrilling.

Ordan took cigarettes from a drawer and lit one. "Mr Penfield, I scarcely know what to say—"

"Doctor, please! Let me work with you—you're the best! You make Spring-Heel Jack look like a common mugger. You've even inspired a competent copycat!"

"The so-called Gay Mirror Monster? You've studied him?" Ordan put the pack away again.

"Briefly. Who cares what faggots do? Or imitators?" His burgeoning erection made him shift position; some part of the chair poked him. "*You* are the real genius."

Ordan smiled warmly and took his hand from the drawer. "Thank you, Mr. Penfield. It is nice to be appreciated. As you will see."

Penfield blinked rapidly. "Beg pardon?" Warm in here...

"Perhaps you felt a little prick in your ass just then? No? No matter; there'll be a bigger one later. How do your feel, Mr. Penfield?'

"—'ll righ'—" Curious. Why was he slurring his works?

"I *do* take an occasional subject from my clinic; I merely have to be a bit more careful. I imagine by now you're feeling very suggestible. Is that right?"

"Yes." He struggled to form additional words, failed.

"Why don't you say, 'Yes, *sir*'?"

"Yes, sir."

"Good boy. You made a basic error. The same one the police and newspapers do. Because you're a monosexual, you assumed that the Gay Mirror Monster was someone else." He smiled beatifically. "A truly great artist, Mr. Penfield, cannot be a monosexual. You're a second-rater, and you don't know me at all."

He sat back, puffed contentedly on his cigarette. "But since you're a connoisseur, perhaps I will tell you about one that didn't make the paper. I *have* been wanting to tell someone, and you'll appreciate it. Besides, it will fill the time while we wait for the hypnotic to take full effect. I took a vacationing family once, from a state campground, young couple and a little boy and girl. They invited me to join their campfire, and were imprudent enough to drink the lemonade I gave them. I did them all, in each others' presence, one at a time, over four days. I saved the mother for last—and then I cheated her. *I let her live.* Blind, deaf, dumb, quadriplegic. With her memories. Isn't that *marvellous?* She's on life support in an institution. I visit her from time to time. She knows it's me: I can tell. Probably by smell, or taste. She hates it when I use her, even more than when the attendants do. She could last another decade, and she has no way to suicide. Strong woman. Sometimes wish I'd left her hearing. Talk over old times..."

He smiled reminiscently, then raised himself slightly to peer over the far edge of his desk. "Ah, excellent, Mr. Penfield. It *is* nice to work with a canvas of a proper size. Have you ever had bisexual leanings. Mr. Penfield?'

"No, sir."

"Excellent. The best victims *are* monosexual, when they come to one. And imaginative, like yourself." He glanced meditatively at his cigarette, stubbed it out in his ashtray with some reluctance. "Get dressed again—you can leave off the briefs—and come along. We're going for a ride. I'm keen to hear about these 'interesting little amateur ideas' of yours..." He giggled suddenly. "Have you ever heard the expression, 'hoist by his own petard'?" The giggle became a full blown laugh.

Penfield's last rational thought was a flash of dismayed contempt. His hero had feet of clay. A man as ingenious as Ordan should have known, without being told, that Penfield would leave a letter in his safe deposit box to protect himself. And by the time the hypnotic had worn off and Penfield had control of his vocal cords again, his tongue would be gone—a shame he would never get to see Ordan's face when...

Then his mind melted and he did as he was told.

TRANSFER

by
Stephanie Bedwell-Grime

Stephanie Bedwell-Grime has had stories published in the anthologies *Northern Frights 3*
and *365 Scary Stories: A Horror Story A
Day*. Her novelette, "Until Death," was released as a chapbook by Cogswell Publishing.
She is a three-time finalist for the Aurora
Award. When not writing, she teaches Multi-
media and Digital Animation programs at a
nearby college, where she can walk to work
instead of riding the subway.

Metal slaughtered metal, sounding for all the world like a woman screaming.

Cassandra jerked awake, embarrassingly certain that in her sleep her lolling head had been bouncing against the shoulder of the next subway passenger.

Oh no! The screeching faded to a whisper as the wheels ground to a halt. A sickening feeling of dread already churned in her stomach. *Please don't let it be an emergency, not this morning with the Marchand presentation first thing.* Fate refused to listen to her desperate wishes. The train remained stubbornly at a dead stop. Dread became certainty. Damn, she was going to be late.

She sat up, blinking fragments of dreams from her mind. She had to get to a phone, call Ernie and head off this disaster in the making. Instead of the claustrophobic crush of a multitude of densely packed bodies, she found the train in silence, darkness.

And completely empty.

The rasp of her suit jacket against the plastic seat sounded disproportionately loud in the hushed interior. Around her seats sat empty. Diffuse light illuminated the interior with a silver glow.

She couldn't possibly have been the only passenger on the train to Union Station. Usually it was standing room only with passengers making connections to the GO trains and others taking the loop around to University Avenue.

If she wasn't at Union Station, where was she?

None of the amber emergency lights shone from the overhead panels, yet the wan illumination shone like a distant moon. The overhead speakers that usually crackled with distorted, high-volume messages lay silent.

Did they take the train out of service while I slept? She'd meant to close her eyes for only a few minutes, a power nap to erase the fatigue of having worked late and worried all night about the upcoming presentation. The one Ernie was counting on her to ace. She'd spent extra care on her morning routine, the contacts, the makeup, the power suit. She'd boarded the train at Finch, the north end of the line, at eight sharp. Of that much, she was certain. Deciding to take advantage of the 45-minute commute to Union, she'd rested her head against the seat partition and fallen asleep as she had every morning for the past two years. The shriek of the rails as the train rounded the corner between King and Union woke her as surely as an alarm clock.

Except this morning. She'd overslept. Had the train completed its run and gone elsewhere, taking her with it?

Ernie's going to have a fit! The thought of her boss sent her snatching up her briefcase. Smoothing out the wrinkles in her suit, Cassandra stood up.

And stopped short.

Her shoes left a trail of footprints in the layer of oily gray dust that coated the floors. It covered everything, she realized looking around, the seats, the floor, her briefcase, even her navy suit.

How long have I been here? She glanced down at her watch. Five to nine. She sighed with relief. Then she realized the tiny red second hand was frozen at one second after twelve.

The grogginess of sleep was rapidly giving way to waves of panic. Concern for Ernie and Marchand played a distant second to the blinding urge to be gone from this place. A scream lodged in her throat. She choked it down.

Wildly, she looked around her, realizing suddenly that the back window that usually looked into a long line of identical subway cars looked out only into darkness. She rubbed at the grime-encrusted window. Through the streaked dirt, she could make out a platform, illuminated in the same ghostly light as the subway car. She raced the length of the car. Hauling open the engineer's door, she nearly tumbled into the empty booth. No one had been at the controls for a long time, if the layer of dirt was any indication. Slowly, Cassandra backed out of the booth. If there was a station out there, surely it had a staircase that led to the surface, to taxis and phones and normalcy.

Cassandra strode purposely toward the door, coming to a stop a few feet from it, realizing with another pang of growing dread, she had no idea how they operated. And if the power in the train was out, then the doors likely wouldn't operate, either.

But as she approached, the doors slid silently open, admitting her to the platform.

Cassandra stepped tentatively onto the tiled platform. At least it had been tile at one time. The same thick layer of dust covered everything. Her leather pumps left footprints in it as if she walked through an inch of fresh snow. Gray walls were tiled with the same nondescript tile as some of the other stations, Bay, Islington. Yet no black letters proclaimed her destination. She remembered reading an article in the Star that abandoned stations like Bay Lower were sometimes used as movie sets and to store old escalator parts. Could that be where she was?

But if the station had once been used, surely there'd be some identifying marks. Nothing. No station name, no out of date movie posters, no machine parts. Nothing.

With a whisper, the doors slid closed behind her.

"Hey!" She pounded against the metal doors. But they remained seamlessly shut. Nowhere now to go, but up, she thought.

Her heels clicked against the tile, oddly muffled, as she walked toward the other end of the platform. Somewhere there had to be an escalator, a staircase, something leading to ground level.

Cassandra squinted down the line of the dusty tile. At the far end the platform a cylindrical tunnel gaped like a hungry mouth. Silver rails trailed off into the darkness inside and disappeared. No, she wasn't going that way. Not willingly.

She felt her way along the tiled wall, looking for a door, a phone, anything. But beneath the dirt, lay only the same grimy, featureless tile as the floor. No phones proclaimed their presence with little blue signs. No overhead lights marked the Designated Waiting Area with its intercom to the ticket booth and the transit police. Come to think of it, there wasn't a ticket booth. Nor was there another platform on the far side for connecting trains. Whatever came into the station apparently left by the same route.

A chilling thought occurred to her. *What if things that came into the station didn't leave?*

No, that thought was just too stupid. Her eerie surroundings made her paranoid. She'd find the person in charge, get things straightened out with Ernie, and then make a very public complaint to the transit company.

Which was all fine, except she hadn't seen a single soul.

"Hello?" Cassandra put all the volume she was capable of into the inquiry. Sound died around her as if she shouted through a thick blanket.

Cold fingers of terror closed around her heart. Hysteria beckoned. She couldn't give in to its seductive call. Her only salvation lay in keeping a level head. Afraid stopping for even a second would send her reeling over the edge, Cassandra took refuge in action and kept walking.

The opposite end of the platform vanished into shadow. A hallway maybe? Cassandra quickened her pace. As she approached she made out the soft whoop, whoop of an escalator.

The shadow gave way to an alcove. She rounded the corner, high-heels skidding against the tile and came to an abrupt halt.

Sure enough, there was an escalator. An ancient wooden one, steps worn black by years of use. Wooden steps flattened, then unfolded at a rapid-fire rate. Like rotten teeth, parts of stairs were missing. Time had reduced the hand rails to shredded spikes of hardened rubber. But it offered the only way out of...wherever. Clutching her briefcase to her chest, Cassandra leapt for the first solid-looking stair.

Instantly, she was whisked downward into darkness as impenetrable as trying to see through blackout curtain. The upper floor disappeared from view.

And then it hit her. She'd seen no matching "up" escalator.

Adrenaline hit her bloodstream. In the utter darkness beneath her came the pulse of something breathing. Panic absorbed all other thought. Pivoting on the narrow stair, she scrambled for the only light above.

One high heel caught in the wooden stair, dragging her downward. Pain stabbed through her ankle. She wrenched her foot, heedless of the hot needles in her ankle. Her heel came loose with a loud snap. The shoe tumbled down into the shadows.

She didn't hear it land.

Terror shoved her forward. Grasping hands floundered in empty air beneath a missing stair. The teeth of huge gears gleamed in the darkness. She screamed, a lingering scream with no echo.

Her fingers closed on the railing. Heedless of the spikes cutting into her palm, she closed her hand around it and scrambled upward.

With one bare foot, she lunged up over the missing stair. The one above it didn't look any more solid. She barked her shins against the splintered wood. The stair cracked. She scrambled for the next. Shards of wooden knives speared down into the darkness.

Hauling herself along the bannister, she leapt for the solid floor above. Nails scraped along the tile leaving claw marks in the he dust.

Her briefcase slid from her grasp. The lock sprang open. Leaves of white paper littered the air. She watched as they spiraled down into nothingness.

The briefcase didn't hit bottom, either.

Cassandra swung her leg up onto the tile. Her skirt tore, another muffled sound without substance. She scrambled back from the edge until her back met the cool tile of wall behind her.

A soft hiss brought her head up sharply.

"No!"

Casting off her remaining pump, she dashed after the departing train. Dust kicked up a gray cloud before her. Stocking feet slid on the smooth tile. She sprawled face down in the dirt. Through the haze, she watched the ghostly shape disappear into the tunnel.

Ignoring the protest of a myriad strained muscles and a dozen scrapes, Cassandra picked herself up off the platform. If the train went out in that direction, then so could she. Wincing, she lowered herself down onto the rails.

Gravel cut through the feet of her shredded stockings. Cassandra forced herself forward. She couldn't let the train get away. It offered the only route out.

She could still hear the dull rush of its engine ahead in the tunnel. She bolted after it, putting all her strength into keeping her battered feet moving. Shadows closed in around her, impenetrable, absolute. Metal wheels screeched against the rails. Far off in the gloom came a hint of light. Cassandra raced toward it.

Impact hit in a shower of white agony. Ecstasy followed in a wave of soft darkness.

Screams shattered the air. Heavy machinery shrieked to a sudden stop. Commotion fought for her attention.

From far away she heard the murmur of a crowd gathering. Announcements echoed through overhead speakers. Gravel crunched beneath the footsteps hurrying in her direction. Her eyelids flickered, she caught a glimpse of a blue uniform. Another set of boots appeared out of the periphery of her vision. The driver perhaps. She couldn't turn her head from the unnatural angle.

"Why this station?" The conductor's voice rose in hysteria. "Why do so many people jump at this station?"

Voices faded to a distant murmur. She found herself on an escalator.

Moving rapidly downward into darkness.

NOCTURNE

by
Sandra Kasturi

Pain wanders through
My bones like a lost fire.
What burns me now?
Desire, desire, desire.

-Theodore Roethke

I have not witnessed the rise of the sun
nor have I felt its slow burn on my flesh
in uncounted, untold centuries,
but I no longer keep time
in this dark dance of many decades,
for the shadow night
my inamorata
cradles my heart
and I have other pleasures now.

I do not find
that the years weigh on me—
the nights sift into one another
until what my memory retains
is a luminous mosaic
of *scent* and *sound* and *vision*,
a whirling minuet of color
that floats before me,
each facet divided by moonlight,
as the sun used to divide the stained glass
of the church
into color-scattered figures
on the stone floor.

I have heard it said
that I cannot dream
but this is a lie,
yet another
in that endless catalogue
of half-truths and superstition,
as much a myth
as I am legend.

I will tell you
that I do dream
after a fashion
only to awaken, disturbed
sometime after sunset
to find myself remembering
only blurred images of the whole
and then the sudden shock
of isolated fragments

a young girl, her face buried in an armful of flowers
a small animal, bloody, on the highway
and the church
Yes
always the church

Were there emotions
involved in these bright pageants of dream?
If so, I would not know the truth of them,
for what passions I feel on waking
seem ill-fitted to these memories
and I am left again to wonder
if I ever felt anything
for the girl,
the girl with her blood-rich arms full of flowers,
other than the voracity
of appetite.

There are those hushed and velvet nights
when the hunger declines to take me
and I lose myself in ancient tomes
pursuing
I know not what,
or I drift unseen
amongst the powerless others,
those who pretend to hunt the night as I do,
but perhaps they too search
for something
as intangible
and difficult to grasp
as I myself am.

But the other nights,
ah, the other nights are filled with rapture and majesty
there is no need to question
no need
for anything
but the epiphany that takes me
lofts me into the rich darkness
that shrouds me
fills me
devours me
just as I
devour
and am filled
with your life's-blood,
my beloved.

THE PIT-HEADS

by
David Nickle

Among his mounting credits, David Nickle has had work featured in each of our four *Northern Frights* volumes. His story in *Northern Frights 2*, "The Sloan Men," was reprinted in *The Year's Best Fantasy and Horror* (St. Martin's Press, 1995), and has recently been filmed as an episode in a major television anthology series.

Paul Peletier and I drove up to Cobalt one last time, about seven years ago. It was my idea. Should have been Paul's—hell, almost two decades before that it *was* his idea, going to Cobalt to paint the pit-heads—but lately he hadn't been painting, hadn't been out of his house to so much as *look* in so long, he was convinced he didn't have any more ideas.

"Bullshit," I said to him, ignition-keys jangling in my fingers, coaxing him outside. "You're more of an artist than that."

"No," he said. "And you're not either."

But Paul didn't have much will left to fight me, so he grumbled around the house looking for his old paint-kit, the little green strongbox filled with the stuff he euphemistically called his Equipment. Then he climbed into the cab of my pickup, grunted, "Well come *on*, Picasso, let's do it," and we headed north.

Just to see.

There are other things to paint in Cobalt, after all: the black-and-umber tarpaper houses, built high on the rock with materials as likely stolen as they were bought; the roads wending dangerously through the lips of bedrock, like the untended streets of a medieval town; the grocery, built on top of an old mine shaft, a three-hundred-foot deep root cellar where the owners dangle their overstock of meat and cheese against the improbable heat of high summer in northern Ontario.

We'd painted them all before, in every season and under every sky, and when the pit-heads were still up, they never got old.

So we turned off Highway 11, parked by the grocery and set up our easels. Paul dallied a bit in his strongbox—took out the old silver chain and put it around his neck, muttered a little prayer from his Catholic school days. And then, because there was nothing more but to get started, he reached into his kit and took out a blank pallet, squeezed out some acrylic from the little magazine of ancient paint-tubes he kept in a dark recess of the kit.

I even remember what we were painting. I've still got the panel at my studio—it's not very good, a not-very-confident study of one of those houses, rambling up a slope of rock and perched on a foundation of cinderblock. In a fit of whimsy, I included the figure of a man, bending down at the septic tank, tool box at his feet, an expression of grim determination painted on his tiny face. In fact, no one came out of the house the entire time we painted.

Or should I say, the entire time that *I* painted. Paul just sat there, lifting his brush, swirling it on his pallet. Setting it down again.

"Nothing here anymore, Graham," said Paul, fingering the chain at his neck, and squinting over the still rooftops of the town in the too-bright summer sun. "They're gone."

"They're buried, you mean."

Paul shook his head, and he smiled. "The mining companies all say it's because of taxes. Hailiebury taxes dearly for a pit-head, next to nothing for a cement plug over a dark shaft."

Then he looked at me, the tiny pewter Jesus at the end of the chain caught in a vise-grip between his thumb and the hard stem of his brush.

"As long as the price of silver stays low, the pit-heads stay down. Holes stay covered, to keep the weather out of the shafts. That's the story, eh Graham?"

"I guess those miners had the right idea, then," I said. "I guess it's time to go."

"I guess so," said Paul.

And so we packed up our brushes and pallets and paintings, and we followed the miners' example. Paul was inordinately cheerful on the way back, and so was I, I have to admit. There was an ineffable feeling of freedom leaving that town—finally admitting it was over for us there; we were strictly on our own, from that moment on. We made jokes, shared a few carefully-chosen reminiscences, were just like old friends again on that four-hour drive south.

But much later, back at my own place in the cold dark of the early morning, I woke up with the once-familiar scream in my throat—memories of the miner Tevalier's age-yellowed flesh, his cruel and hungry grip, renewed in my blood.

Trembling alone in my bed, I vowed to myself that I would not call Paul Peletier, and I would not go to Cobalt again.

Paul was the first one of our little group to visit Cobalt, and when he reported back on it, he didn't tell us the whole of the story. Not by far.

It was 1974, just a year after Paul's divorce, and he was making ends meet teaching landscape painting classes to art clubs in and around North Bay. In April, he drove up to Cobalt at the invitation of the Women's Art League of Hailiebury, and spent a weekend critiquing the septuagenarian League ladies' blurry watercolors out at the Royal Mine #3. He told us about it in July, when the four regulars in our own little Art League—Paul, Jim Osborne, Harry Fairbank and myself—were camped on the south arm of Opeongo Lake, on what would turn out to be our last annual mid-summer painting trip together.

"I wasn't up there to work, which is why it was such a damned shame. It was all I could do to keep my paints in their tubes," he said, leaning against the hull of his canoe as he spoke.

Jim took a swill from his thermos and grinned. Jim worked as a lawyer back in the city, and at the end of the year I figured he bought almost as many paintings as he produced. Privately, Paul told me that he thought Jim Osborne painted pictures the way that other men went fishing: he didn't want to catch anything, just get out of the rat race for a few days every summer and escape to the bush.

"Keep your paints in the tubes." Jim rolled the words thoughtfully. "Or did you mean keep your tube in your pants? Those art club biddies can be pretty spry, I hear."

Paul laughed, but it was a distracted sound, barely an acknowledgment. He was never easy with vulgarity.

Paul continued: "The geography around this town is spectacular. It's all rock and scrub, a few stands of poplar and cedar here and there, and it's had the life mined out of it. But I don't think it's possible to make a bad painting there."

Jim was about to say something, but I shushed him.

"High recommendation," I said.

Paul grinned. "The pit-heads outside Cobalt are a Mecca for those ladies—they swear by them, and I can't argue based on the results."

"Practice makes perfect," deadpanned Jim.

Paul gave Jim a look, but I cut in before he could comment. "Just what kind of pit-heads are these?" I asked. I was only 25 then, and almost all of the out-of-town painting trips I'd been on had been with Paul and the rest—which pretty much limited me to Algonquin Park and one quick trip up to Lake Superior.

Paul pulled out his sketch pad and began roughing out an illustration: "Here's what they look like."

Harry put down the paint-smeared panel he'd been swearing over all afternoon and studied Paul's drawing in the failing light.

"Do you want to do a trip there?" Harry finally asked.

Paul swatted at a black fly on his neck, and examined the little bloody speck on his hand. "It'll be one hell of a drive—about eight hours from your place in good weather, and I want to go up in November when the snow will have started. It's a long way to go for a painting."

Harry took another look the sketch, then at his own failed oil painting. "This—" he threw his arms up, to include the entire, Group-of-Seven, Tom-Thomson splendor of Algonquin Park on a clear summer evening "—is already a long way to come for a painting. And by the looks of things tonight, I don't even have a decent one to show for it. Give me a call when you've set a schedule; I'm in."

Paul smiled and set down the sketch on the flat of a rock for all of us to see. It was crude, but I think it may have been the most accomplished work we'd ever seen from Paul to that date. His carpenter pencil had roughed out the thick spruce beams that splayed out from the narrow, peaked tower head, which Paul had represented with a carelessly precise rectangle of shadow. The trestle emerged from the far side, a jumble of cross-beams and track that draped like a millipede over the spine of a treacherous spill of rock. The thin curves and jags suggesting hills and a treeline seemed like an afterthought—although Paul would scarcely have had time for one. He had completed the whole, perfect sketch in less than a minute.

"Any other takers?" Paul asked, in a tone that suggested there might have been a real question.

The forecast had called for frozen rain in the Hailiebury area, but by the time we pulled onto the mine road the air was just beginning to fill with fine, January-hard snowflakes. They caught in the crevasses and crannies of the low cliffs that rimmed the mine-road, making thin white lines like capillaries of frozen quartz.

I watched Paul's tail-lights through the scratch of snow. He drove an old Ford panel van, and he had set up a small household in the back of it—a foam-rubber mattress near the back for sleeping, a little chemical toilet tucked in a jury-rigged bracket behind the driver's seat, a big cooler filled with enough groceries to feed him for several weeks if need be. And a 12-gauge shotgun with a box of ammunition, in a case beside the mattress, for painting trips during bear season. Paul made his living from his painting, but it wasn't enough of a living to spring for a week in a motel every time he went off on an overnight painting trip. The rest of us followed his lead.

It was scarcely four o'clock, but darkening towards night already, when we finally reached the pit-heads of the Royal Mine. We pulled up on the edge of a wide gravel turnaround maybe three hundred feet downslope from the nearest of the two pit-heads.

The turnaround was near the top of a great boulder of a hill, gouged by glaciers from the tiny slit of a lake that was barely visible through a stand of poplar to the north. The two ancient pit-heads rode that hill's peak, like signal-towers for some forgotten empire.

"We won't have enough light to get any work done tonight," said Paul as he emerged from his van. "But we should be able to go up and have a look inside before nightfall." He hefted a big, ten-battery flashlight on a shoulder-strap he'd tied together from old boot-laces.

Harry put his hands in the small of his back and stretched, making a noise like an old man. "Are those things safe?" he asked.

Paul tromped past him up the slope towards the nearest pit-head. "Not entirely," he said simply. "No, not entirely."

The pit-head was in disuse that year, so the main room under-neath the tower was black and empty. Before anyone went in, Paul speared the flashlight beam inside and ran down a brief inventory of what would otherwise have filled the darkness: the great cable spool, driven by a diesel motor in the back of the hoist house, connected to a wheel that would perch in the very top of the tower, where the belfry would be if this were a church. The bare rock floor of the hoist-house was empty, though, the tower just a dark column of cold, lined by beams and tarpaper; according to Paul, the Royal company had moved their operation out of here three years ago, and had warehoused any-thing remotely portable in Hailiebury. He ran the flashlight beam across the floor in the middle of the chamber, where the cable would have attached to the lift platform. At first, I couldn't even see the mouth of the pit: Jim had to point it out.

"It's pretty small," said Jim, and he was right: the hole leading into the depths of the Royal Mine wasn't more than eight feet on a side.

"This was one of the first mines in the area," said Paul. "One of the ladies from Hailiebury told me it dates back to 1903, when the whole silver rush got its start. Story goes that a prospector found a vein of silver by accident, getting his boot out from where it stuck in a crack in the rock. This pit wouldn't be legal if it'd been dug today—the minimum width now is something like ten feet."

"You sound like a god-damned tour guide," I said.

Paul chuckled. "Why don't you go in and take a look for yourself, Graham?"

Not taking my eyes off the pit, I stepped inside the structure. The top of the tower was partly open, and the north wind blew a steady beer-bottle C-sharp across it.

"How deep is it?" asked Harry.

"I didn't ask." Paul's flashlight beam followed me like a spotlight as he spoke.

As I got closer to the edge of the pit, it seemed as though the ground were actually sloping inward towards it, growing unsteady beneath my feet. A smell of machine oil and something like must wafted out of the hole. I stepped back.

"That's good, Graham," said Paul, motioning me back to the wall with the flashlight. "Don't get too close to the opening. I'd hate to have to tell your mother we left you at the bottom."

Both Jim and Harry sniggered at that, and I laughed as well, with deliberate good humor. I backed up a few more steps, until my shoulders were pressed against an old wooden ladder. The wood felt soft, ancient; like it would crumble under my weight.

"You find this place inspirational, do you Paul?" I asked, fighting to keep the quaver out of my voice.

"The Art League ladies swear by it."

The ladder shifted minutely behind my back. From up high, a sprinkle of sand fell, catching like a miniature nebula in the flashlight beam. I tried to imagine how far that sand would fall into the earth before it found something to settle on.

"Well, we can't let Graham here soak up all the juice," said Harry. He stepped inside and peered up into the dark, nose wrinkling.

"Smells in here," he said finally. Jim stepped inside, sniffing.

Behind me, the ladder shifted again, and more dirt fell into the mine. The wind shifted up a half-tone in pitch and with it, the timbers high in the tower creaked. I let go of the ladder and inched further along the wall. I felt like a reluctant suicide on a high-rise window ledge.

"Paul, be a good man and swing that flashlight up there," said Harry, pointing to the top of the ladder. His voice was quiet, almost a monotone. Paul obeyed, and slashed the beam up through the cascade of sand, to the place where Harry pointed.

"Jesus H. Christ!"

I don't know which one of us yelled it; it might have been me, for all the attention I was paying. The only thing I know for sure is that it didn't come from the narrow platform at the top of the ladder, where the light-circle finally came to rest.

There was a man at the top of the ladder.

The light reflected back at us three times: dimly in each lens of the round safety goggles that he wore underneath his helmet, much brighter from the Cyclops-lens of his own helmet-mounted light. He wore a snowsuit, bright yellow underneath, but obscured by thick, hardening smears of mud. A shadow from a cross-beam fell on his chest and chin, enshrouding his features utterly. His arms dangled at his side, and in the mitten of his left hand, he clutched a crow-bar.

Harry lifted his hands—as though the crow-bar were a rifle, and the miner were a policeman placing the four of us under arrest.

"Hey fellow," he said. "Just thought we'd take a look around before it got too dark up here. Hope we're not trespassing."

The stranger stood stock still, and didn't answer immediately. He was about fifteen feet above us, on a narrow platform that seemed to extend around the entire second storey of the mine-head. The ends of the narrow-gauge tracks that the mine carts rode on extended out into space from the platform near his feet.

"*Bonjour, Monsieur Peletier.*" The voice was deep and gravelly, and the man up top didn't move as he spoke. It was almost as though the voice had come from somewhere else—the top of the pit-tower, maybe the depths of the mine itself. But Paul answered readily enough, and with an easy familiarity that sent a premonitory chill through me.

"*Bonjour, Monsieur Tevalier. Ils sont ici — oui, mon pere, ils sont toutes ici.*"

Paul's Northern Quebec French has always been a challenge for me, but even without the benefit of my Grade 10 French, the meaning of that simple sentence would have been unmistakable:

They are here—yes, my father, all of them.

No sooner had Paul spoken than the miner's left hand opened and the crowbar clattered to the floorboards over our heads. He stepped back, and for the briefest instant as the shadows passed from his face, we could see him—an absurdly weak chin framed by mutton-chop sideburns the color of dirty snow; hard yellow flesh, drawn tight as a drum skin across high cheekbones; and of course, we could see his teeth. They were like nails, hammered down through the gums so far that they extended a full inch over the lips.

Paul turned the light away as the creature leaned forward. As it raised its arms to fall, I heard the flick of a flashlight switch and that light disappeared. Something moved in front of the door, and the darkness of the pit-head became absolute.

The creature took Harry first. He was the oldest among us, he'd been slowing down for years, and from that sheerly practical stand-point, I guess he made the easiest target. There were no screams; just a high whimper. The sound a beaten dog would make, if that dog were Harry Fairbanks.

"The rest of you, stand where you are," said Paul, his voice preposterously calm. "One wrong move, and you could find yourself dead at the bottom of the shaft."

"Oh, you bastard," said Jim, the words coming out in sobbing breaths, "oh you think you got us trapped in here, oh you God-damned *bastard.*"

"Only for a moment," said Paul. "Only a moment. Stand still, and we'll all walk out of here together."

The whimper had devolved into a low moan, and it was quickly joined by another sound: dry clicks, the sound old men sometimes make with their throats, as they swallow their soup.

It was at that point, I think, that it occurred to me that Paul's warning to Jim didn't really apply to me: my back was still against the wall, and so long as I kept in contact with that wall, I'd be safe from making a wrong step into the pit. And the ladder to the second floor was only a step away.

Harry let loose a horrible, blood-wet cough, and with it, my decision was made: left hand still pressed against the rough tarpaper wall, I reached out and grabbed a rung of the ladder with my right. It was just as soft as I remembered it, but I didn't take the time to worry whether or not it would hold and in a single motion, swung myself around and started to climb.

The bottom rung snapped under my foot, but I was working on momentum at that point and managed to pull myself past it. The climb couldn't have taken more than a second or two, but it seemed like hours. I was torn between two dreads: of the moment the rungs snapped —beneath my feet, or my hands, or both—and I fell back into the mine; and of the instant that the creature below stopped swallowing, and reached up with whatever kind of claws it had hiding under those big miner's mitts, to grab my ankle and pull me back towards the pit.

But the clicking continued, and the ladder held, one rung and the next rung and the next, and finally when I reached for another rung, my hand fell instead on the rim of the second floor. As I scrambled to get up, my hand closed around the cold metal of the crow-bar the creature had dropped, and when I got to my feet, I hefted it in front of me like a club. There was marginally more light up here, and I took a moment to get my bearings. What remained of the day filtered in through cracks in the far wall, and reflected dull steel gleam off the mine-cart tracks even as they converged toward that wall. I couldn't see clearly, but I knew there would have to be a door there—those tracks would lead out to the trestle, and the jagged heap of rocks that it traversed.

"Graham! For Christ's sake!" It was Paul, but I didn't take time to answer him. Something more important had suddenly occupied my attention:

The clicking had finally stopped.

And the ladder creaked under new weight.

I turned and ran towards the light. The floor was clear, but the boards had heaved over the years and I almost tripped twice before I finally fell, against the huge door at the end of the tracks. It rattled on its runners as I righted myself. Behind me, I heard the sound of wood snapping, and something grunted—a sound a pig would make.

I found a metal handle about half-way up and lifted, but the door wouldn't budge. So I wedged the tip of the crowbar between the floor and the bottom of the door, and stepped on it. There were more splintering sounds; this time coming both from the door in front of me and the ladder behind me.

"Graham! Get back here!"

"Forget it, Paul!" I was surprised at how giddy my voice sounded, echoing back at me through the darkness.

"I'm doing you a God-damned favor!"

Whatever was holding the door shut gave way then, and I nearly lost the crowbar as it shot up with the force of the released tension. In a fast motion, I scooped up the crowbar under one arm, and lifted the door up with the other. The pit-head was briefly filled with gray November daylight and I let the door rest on my shoulder.

The creature was at the top of the ladder. It had cast off its helmet and goggles, revealing patchy whips of hair on a mottled yellow scalp, eyes that seemed all pupil—they glittered blankly in the new light. Its chin and beard were slick with Harry's blood and its hands *were* claws. The gloves had been discarded on the way up, and they poked out of the snowsuit's sleeves, dead branches blackened by flame.

The thing held its arm up against the light for only an instant before it launched itself at me.

I swung my head under the door and, checking my footing on the trestle outside first, let go. The door clattered down, even as the creature fell against it.

I backed up a few steps and raised the crowbar again, this time holding it over my shoulder, like a baseball bat.

I don't know how long I stood there before it dawned on me that I could climb down any time I wanted; that it wasn't coming out.

Before it dawned on me just what kind of creature the thing inside the pit-head was.

I threw the crowbar ahead of me, and in careful fits and starts, made it to the ground.

Paul raised his hands and stepped away from the van. I held his 12-gauge cocked and ready at my shoulder, an open box of ammunition on the floor of the van beside the chemical toilet, which I was using as a stool. If the gun were to go off, it would do so with both barrels, and take Paul's head away in the process.

"Stay where I can see you," I told him, and he made no move to disobey. He was framed perfectly in the open panel. "But don't come any closer. No more tricks, all right?"

"I'm glad you weren't hurt," he said, and at that I swear I almost did shoot him.

"No thanks to you."

"No, Graham," said Paul, his voice very cool and reasonable considering his circumstances, "if you'd done what I told you to, stood still and waited for it, believe me—you'd thank me."

"Yeah, Paul. Just like Jim and Harry are thanking you now. I want you to hand over the keys to the van."

"So you can just drive away? Leave all this, leave your work behind?" Paul stood still, kept his eyes on mine as he spoke. "I'm disappointed."

I'd been in the back of Paul's van for about an hour before he'd shown up, and once I'd pried open his gun case and found where he'd kept the ammunition, I'd had little to do but think. Paul had set us up—

set us up for something awful—that much was clear. Other things were clear too, but it was the wrong kind of clarity; I needed confirmation.

"That miner—that thing in the mine—it drinks blood, doesn't it?" I demanded. "We're talking about a vampire, aren't we?"

"It's not the only one," replied Paul. "There are maybe twenty or thirty of them, living down in the tunnels. When the mine's active, they feed on the miners."

"And when it's not active, they kill the tourists."

Paul actually smiled at that. "Don't be stupid. They don't kill anyone; how long do you think they'd be able to survive here in these mines if they did? They just—" he searched for the word "—just feed, they milk us if you like. And they always give something back. It's a transaction."

"So that thing in the pit-head—the vampire—didn't kill Harry?"

"He's sleeping in his car."

"Or Jim?"

"They're both fine."

I sat back and let that sink in for a moment. If Paul were telling the truth, my original plans—stealing Paul's van at gun point, hightailing it to the OPP station in Haileybury and reporting a brutal triple-killing-by-exsanguination at the Royal mine-head north of Cobalt—would all bear some serious rethinking.

"What's the deal, Paul?" I finally asked. "Why'd you do this to us?"

"I didn't do it *to* you," he said, sounding a little exasperated. "I did it *for* you—particularly for *you*, Graham."

"So you keep saying."

"Look, when you joined our little group three years ago, you were just out of art college. And even though you're pointing my own shotgun at my head and it's probably not the wisest thing for me to do, I'll tell you: your work wasn't much to look at then, and three years later, it's still not much to look at. You might as well be doing paint-by-numbers. You've got technical skills that Jim and Harry would both probably kill for—hell, you went to art school for two years, you'd better have learned something—but artistically? You're all cast from the same mold."

When Paul was done, I lowered the shotgun. If I'd left it trained on his forehead, the temptation to pull the trigger would have been too great to resist.

"It may hurt to hear that," continued Paul, "But I think it's the case. It's the case for all of you, and more days than not, it's the case for me too. Which is why when this opportunity arose, I couldn't pass it up. And I couldn't have let any of you pass it up either."

"What opportunity?" My voice sounded like metal in my head.

Paul shook his head. "How do you think," he said slowly, "the Women's Art League of Hailiebury managed to produce such consistently good work here? You think they were born with talent? Or maybe that it was God-given? They made an arrangement, Graham—just like I did."

There was a rustling in the darkness behind Paul, and I raised the shotgun again. I could barely see Paul in the vanishing light; the shadows that emerged from the stand of spruce behind him seemed insubstantial.

"Let them inside," said Paul. "They'll change the way you see."

"Go to hell," I said.

The cold was fierce through the night, but I was glad for it; I managed to stay awake for all but a brief hour before dawn. Paul came by every so often, to check on me—he was waiting, I guess, for me to slip, for the miners to take me the way they'd taken the rest of them, so he could get inside and use his cot for the night. He would pound on the side of the van, shout— "Still corporeal, Graham?" —and tromp off laughing every time I told him to go screw himself.

For their parts, the miners weren't half as annoying. Their claws made a noise like branches as they caressed the side of the van, but they stayed clear of the windows after I made it clear that I was quite willing to shoot the next one that tried to smash its way through the glass of the front windscreen, or tried to jimmy the door locks with its long talons. They kept clear of me to the extent that when I finally did nod off, at about 6:30 in the morning, it was Paul and not the miners that woke me up.

"Rise and shine, young Graham!" he hollered. "The sun's almost up, and it's time to get to work!"

I snapped alert, hefting the shotgun from where it had slid down between my legs. I looked out the front window and confirmed it was safe. Dawn was a thin wash of rose watercolor on the flat gray sheet of November cloud.

"You're not still mad at me, are you?" Paul stepped into view outside the windscreen. "Come on, Graham, at least give me the Coleman and the cooler—the guys want some coffee."

I let go of the shotgun with my right hand, flexed my fingers; I could barely feel them. My feet were similarly numb. And the prospect of hot coffee was impossible to resist.

"I'm still mad at you," I said, and set the shotgun down on the floor. "Yes, you could say that."

I made the fingers of one hand into a claw around the handle of the side door; the thumb of the other hand pushed up the lock. The door slid open, and the fresh morning cold pushed the stale chill of my first night alone in the van into the vaults of memory.

I don't know why I stayed on the week. Harry, neck swathed in gauze and looking perversely healthy, better than he had in years, apologized for the troubles. He offered me a lift into town, even to pay for my bus ticket home if I wanted.

"The painter's life isn't for everybody," said Jim, still relishing his new artist's eye as he peered at the trees and hills through the "L" of his thumb and forefinger. "No shame in admitting that now rather than later."

Paul crouched against the wheel of Jim's Buick and stared at the pit-heads. They were black as coal in the scant morning light.

"No." I rubbed my hands together—feeling was beginning to return to my fingertips, and I figured that by my second cup of coffee I'd be able to hold a brush again. "I came up here to paint some pictures."

"Suit yourself," said Harry.

And so I fell into the ritual of genial artistry that the three of them had established a decade ago and I had joined three years past. After an early breakfast, we all readied our paint kits, slung them on our shoulders and set out in different directions, to find our spots for the morning. Then it was work, about five hours straight, and back to the camp to compare notes and share some lunch.

In the afternoon, we'd go back to work—sometimes in the same spot as the morning, sometimes we'd swap. We tried to avoid one another while painting—there was no point in two of us working the same view—but we'd occasionally wander by between panels, just to see how the other fellow was doing.

As the week wore on, I found that I was doing most of the wandering. After finishing a half-dozen so-so studies of the pit heads, the lake below them, the remains of a fallen spruce tree that lay smashed across the back of a boulder bigger than Paul's van, it seemed as though I'd exhausted the possibilities of the place.

So I wandered. And I watched, as Jim and Harry, even Paul, found their art in the skies and the soil of the Royal mine-head, and turned out some of the most accomplished work of their lives.

Harry painted the pit-heads almost exclusively. At first, he chose the highest vantage-point, and worked intight series' of sketches that took my breath away. He used primarily shadow in preference to line to define form, spotting nuances in the light that I, with my art-school trained eye, could only see in the land after studying one of Harry's panels.

Jim did a couple of studies of the pit-heads, then moved off downslope to the lake, where he watched the ice as it spread its crystals, submerging and cracking here and there as winter struggled to solidify its hold on the mine lands. His paintings were abstracts, eggshell whites and stipples of gray and blue—November ice was personified there. It was a complete departure for Jim that was no less shocking to him than it was to the rest of us.

Paul stayed with the pit-heads too. But unlike Harry, who circled them almost daily, Paul remained in a single position, and worked a single canvas, three feet on a side. In the past, Paul's work had always been characterized by a broad brush-stroke, form suggested rather than stated. Color had always been his medium.

With this canvas, Paul had discovered detail. And with his nightly visits to the pit-head with the other three, he had found the art with which to convey it. As I watched the intricate tapestry of his painting take form, the realization came to me:

Paul Peletier wouldn't need to teach art lessons in Cobalt any more. With work like this, he'd be able to write his own ticket.

None of the three were very good company when I visited them. Part of that no doubt was my fault; I'd been staying in Paul's van—alone, awake most of the night and with a shotgun on my lap. It was clear that I made them uncomfortable. And they, frankly, had better things to do than pass the time with me—they moved brush between pallet and panel with the hungry compulsion of newfound genius.

In my sleep-starved state, I compared badly against them. My outlines were tentative, frequently poorly-drafted; my colors became muddy and indistinct as I tried again and again to correct them, make them match the land there, the sky.

On the fifth morning at the pit-heads, I knew I couldn't put it off any longer. When we finished breakfast and split up for the morning's work, instead of getting my paint-kit, I went back to Paul's van and picked up the shotgun, a box of shells, his flashlight, and a coil of yellow safety rope. As stealthily as I could, I made my way back up to the pit-head.

The cloud had broken that day, and the mine-heads were bathed in clean sunlight for the first time since we'd arrived. But as I stepped inside, it was as ever, as dark as midnight.

I tied the rope off against one of the larger beams supporting the tower. The shotgun had a strap, and I hung it over my shoulder while I wrapped the flashlight string around my forearm. It dangled aiming downward as I lowered myself into the pit.

By this time, I'd stopped being angry with Paul. I still wasn't about to come around to his way of thinking, but I realized that he hadn't been lying to me—he was only thinking of my best interests as an artist when he brought me here. He was doing me a favor, opening a door.

And he was, in large part at least, right. The destination beyond was a place that I very much wanted to be. It was just that Paul's door was not the route I wanted to take to get there.

I wrapped the rope twice around my waist, looped and tied the end, and, kicking the last vestiges of snow off my boots, lowered myself into the shaft.

I only lost my footing twice, both times near the end of my descent. The walls had become slippery with ice, and the first time I managed to recover my footing perfectly. The second time came just before the opening of the topmost tunnels, where rock had given way and crumbled around thetunnel's edge. I clutched the rope as it burned against my mittens, swinging free in the narrow shaft. Eventually I propelled myself inside.

The smell I'd first noticed at the top of the pit was stronger here: Heated metal and smoldering engine oil, an underlying *badness* that pervades old industrial sites—or, I guess, mineshafts that've gone dry.

I slung the flashlight in front of me, lowered the shotgun to my side, and peered ahead.

At the time, I don't think I knew precisely what it was that I was looking for. I certainly wasn't there to let the miners—the creatures, the *vampires*—feed on me; I didn't want to cement any transaction in that way. I still like to think that, had they been given a choice, Jim and Harry would have come to the same conclusion.

These miners had something, all right. But they weren't only doling out art lessons—those miners took something different away in return for their blood. And simply because they had so far only bestowed in exchange for blood was no reason to assume that blood was the only coin they understood—or that trade was the only way to draw the genius out of them. I hefted the shotgun to remind myself of that possibility.

The tunnel was wider than it was high at first, and I had to stoop under lips of shale and thick, tarred cross-beams as I moved along. After a time, the tunnel widened out to a space that must have been used as a lunch room when the mine was active. I played the light over the few artifacts that the miners had left: a metal-topped table, surrounded by four folding metal chairs; a stack of more chairs, leaning against an oblong wooden box—an oblong box! —which I pried open with shaking hands only to find it empty but for three badly-corroded car batteries.

Sitting on the table was a fabulous anachronism—an ancient oil lamp, with a single crack snaking up from its base. Layers of soot made the glass nearly opaque. It would make a good still-life, I thought, and laughed quietly.

I should have brought my paint-kit down.

Beyond the lunch room, the tracks ended and the tunnel took a steep downward slope. There were no steps, but long stems of cedar had been bolted to the rock wall on either side, making banisters. I descended the staircase, such as it was, and at the bottom found a room filled with buckets, made of wood slats and iron hoops and filled with a black liquid that was, after all, only water. The tunnel continued beyond that, and as I followed it I noticed that the long wires and wire-mesh lighting fixtures that had been stapled to the ceiling had been replaced by ornate lamp-shelves,such as one might have found in a home around here, before the advent of electricity.

I had stopped for a moment, resting against the wall between two of these low sconces, when the miners found me.

Three of them stepped into the light, and stood frozen there as I hefted my shotgun. Unlike the first creature I'd seen in the pit-head, these wore nothing but a few rags over limbs that were taut with sinew. Their eyes were round and reflected back the flashlight beam like new pennies. The hair on their scalps and their chins was thin, and shockingly white.

"Don't come any closer," I said.

In response, the tunnel filled with a low chattering. I caught fragments of thick Quebecois French, mixed with other sounds: whistles, clicking; a pig-grunt; a wet, bronchial wheeze.

I don't think they understood me any better than I understood them. But they understood the shotgun all right. The trio watched me for a moment longer, then one of them turned and vanished into the dark. When the other two followed, I was after them.

We ran deeper into the mine. If the floor had been rough as the upper tunnels, I don't think I would have been able to keep up. But the rock down here was so smooth it seemed to have been carved, not dug.

The creatures finally escaped me in a wide room—so wide that its walls were beyond the reach of my flashlight. It had a low slate ceiling, supported with thick wooden posts at regular intervals. I stopped, scanned my flashlight across the shadows around me.

"Bonjour, mon petit."

It was the same voice we'd heard in the pit-head. The one that had spoken to Paul, with such familiarity.

Paul had called it, what? *Monsieur Tevalier. Mon Pere.*

Father.

"Show yourself," I said.

Monsieur Tevalier's breath made a frosting on the hairs of the back of my neck.

I whirled, barely in time to face him. But I couldn't get the shotgun up as well. The flashlight fell to the ground and I felt his talons dig into my coat. I only caught the barest glimpse of his face as he lifted me into the dark. The mutton-chops had darkened, and the flesh on his cheeks had reddened, plumped out with the new blood.

"Vous étudiez avec le maître," said the vampire—then, in thickly-accented English: *"I show you the way."*

How was it for Paul, the rest of them? How was it for the miners, for that matter—who made their own dark bargains here in the earth beneath Cobalt?

I can't say for sure, but it must have been different than the darkness was for me. The twin punctures of the vampire's teeth would have been an utter shock to them—until the moment it occurred, they would have had no reason to expect such a complete invasion as the vampire would have perpetrated.

I was prepared for the attack, though. Where five days earlier I might have looked away—forgotten the assault—as Monsieur Tevalier pierced the flesh of my throat in the rooms beneath Cobalt, I did not lose myself.

Tevalier spoke through my blood, and I was attentive.

He and his kind had been in the land here for as long as the mines had been in Cobalt, moving between the great rocks that remained when the world last thawed. As my blood pulsed down his throat in clicking gulps, he showed me: the earth pulsed too, and the essence that moved through it also flowed through Tevalier, through me. If Tevalier drained me, swallowed all my blood, then the earth's pulse would be all there was. The clarity would be absolute, because I and his land would be as one. In the early days of Cobalt, before the pit-heads, I wondered at what the miners, the prospectors, would have made of that clarity.

Because there was the secret of Tevalier's gift. It dwelt in the razor-line between my heartbeat, absolute insularity—my life—and the earth's simpler rhythm, a final subsumation to the external—my death.

Should I ever stray too far, one way or the other, there would be Tevalier, waiting in the pit-head to nudge me back onto the artist's one true path. *Did I understand the depth of my dependency?* he asked me through my blood. I felt his tongue on my neck, rough like a cat's. Then, with the care of a physician removing a long hypodermic, he withdrew.

I thought again about the prospectors—thought about the strange town they had built on the earth above, the mining companies that had prospered in it, and the terrible bargain that had founded it.

Did I understand the depth of my dependency?

Before he could withdraw completely, I swung the barrels of the shotgun up, pressed them against the brittle flesh and bone that covered the vampire's heart.

"*Je comprends,*" I whispered, and pulled both triggers.

The hardest part of getting out of the mine-head was the climb up the rope, something I hadn't expected. But the run up along the tunnel had proven exhausting, and I was light-headed already with the loss of my blood. When I fired off the last two shells back into the tunnel, the recoil nearly knocked me into the shaft. The buckshot did its job though, sending the two vampires that followed me screaming back into the depths. I wanted to rest then, wanted the escape to be finished, but of course I could not, and it was not. I had to ascend the rope.

I lost the shotgun, and nearly lost the flashlight on the way up. Finally I did have to rest, so I tied myself off and dangled there in the shaft, the timber creaking above me and my limbs feeling like meat below; I had the feet of a hanged man.

From the depths, the vampires whispered a cacophony. I had removed their head with Tevalier, taken the one who had made them, shown them their own line—evidently, they had much to discuss. When I resumed my ascent, the whispers had grown quieter, and nearer.

It was near noon when I reached the top of the shaft, and that may have been what saved me. Cobalt is too far north for the sun to have shone straight down the open tower in November, but it made a bright yellow square among the upper rafters, and the light filtered down through the dust to make the pit-head brighter than I'd ever seen it. Clutching at the numbness in my throat, I stumbled to the door and out into the afternoon.

Only as the sun set, five hours later, was I able to calm Paul down and convince him that we had to leave Cobalt before dark. And then, I think it was only the screaming, hungry and subterranean as it echoed from the dark of the pit-heads, that convinced him:

Tevalier was gone; and with him went the razor-line that protected us, and gave us our art.

That summer, the Women's Art League of Hailiebury disbanded, after an early-June tragedy that made the national news reports and forced a six-week coroner's inquest. But throughout that inquest, not one witness stepped forward to charge that the deaths of Elsie LaFontaine and Betty-Ann Sale were the result of anything other than stepping too close to the edge of the mine-shaft.

In 1978, the shanty-town houses of North Cobalt were destroyed by a fire so huge it lit the sky for a hundred miles and kept them warm in Quebec. The Ontario Fire Marshall's office raised the possibility of arson a number of times in the course of its inquiries. But never was it remarked—at least not in public—how close some of the old mine tunnels came to the surface in that section of town. The news reports never dwelt upon the prevailing view in southern Cobalt—that North Cobalt wasn't so much burned, as it was cauterized.

Painting was good in that time. We took precautions, of course; when he got back to his studio, Paul went down to the library in town and came up with a whole list of them. Chains of garlic; Catholic-blessed Holy Water; crucifixes, one for each neck; and silver coins, to cover the eyes. He put them together in a green strongbox, and never came within a hundred miles of Cobalt without his Equipment. I preferred the simpler approach, and as my painting career allowed me to afford it, I expanded my arsenal to the very limits of the prevailing Canadian gun laws.

When the vampires came to our camp outside the pit-heads, we knew how to deal with them. We only allowed them enough blood to complete the transaction: attempts to get any more were met with garlic and holy water and buckshot. The razor's edge remained, even in Tevalier's absence.

It paid off for us all over the years. Jim went professional in the early 1980s and moved to New York in '86. Paul abandoned oils and embraced watercolor, and for five years made a fortune off royalties from art books and calendars featuring reproductions of his hyper-realistic landscapes and naturalist paintings.

We nearly lost Harry in 1981, when he got too close to the edge one night; after that he got spooked and stopped coming out. But he'd produced some damned fine panels in the meantime, and I know they'd pleased him.

And for myself, I did fine, I think; a lot of good work over those years. The rise of my career was far from meteoric—I have yet to see my work on postage stamps, the biggest interview I ever gave was to the North Bay Nugget, and I've still never been able to afford a new car. But groceries are never a question and I keep the furnace going all winter long.

The mining companies finally surrendered in 1985, and tore down every one of the pit-heads, capped the holes. In a way, I'm surprised it took them as long as it did; for Paul and Jim and Harry and me, adaptation was relatively easy—we were only up there two or three weeks out of the year, and when we were there, we knew how to behave. But the men who ran the companies in Cobalt didn't adapt so well; they didn't even have enough sense to put a guard-rail around the edges of their shafts—let alone recast the bargains that had made them wealthy in the early years.

It was a scary time for us, in the years after the pit-heads came down. Paul stopped painting altogether, and has sat in an artistic paralysis ever since. Jim traded on his reputation and actually made the cover of Esquire after he hired a loyal coven of apprentices to do the actual painting, while he busied himself with what his publicist calls conceptualization, articulation. He's done quite well for himself, but I don't think he'll ever work again.

I, on the other hand, kept on painting. My work's gotten repetitive over the years, but I keep a couple of dealers in Toronto happy—if nothing else, my pictures are a good match for the style of sofa-beds and arm-chairs that well-heeled doctors and their wives favor as they furnish their cottages in Muskoka.

Art is in the narrow line between life and death—Tevalier was right on that score. I walked that line with Jim and Harry and Paul for more than a decade, against all my better judgment; and I'll admit, it does offer its intoxication.

Now, the pit-heads are down, the pictures there are done. Cobalt has been bled dry—of silver; of art; and of blood. The bargain, whatever coin it was that sealed it, is finished.

But here's the thing: in that bargain's wake, the town of Cobalt persists—a little quieter, maybe, hunched a bit around the scarred land and flesh that the Tevalier and the prospectors and the mining companies that came after left behind. But the town accepts its strange shape, acknowledges its new limitations. Within them all, it persists.

I've been warped by Tevalier's knowledge, too, and bent again by its absence. But when I wake up in the morning, after I've driven away the nightmares with my coffee and an egg and seen to the other mundane chores, I still pick up my brush and set to work.

Because even if the art is gone now, the land remains. And whatever crimes Tevalier's grave-cold shade accuses me of, in the small, quiet hours of the night...

I don't need anyone's permisson to paint it.

ICE BRIDGE

by
Edo van Belkom

A frequent contributor to *Northern Frights*, Edo van Belkom is a three-time Aurora Award nominee and the author of over 100 short stories of horror, fantasy and science fiction appearing in a wide variety of magazines and anthologies. He is the author of four dark fantasy novels: *Wyrm Wolf,* (a finalist for the First Novel Bram Stoker Award), *Lord Soth, Army of the Dead* and *Mr. Magick.*

T he continuous diesel-driven thrum of the loader was only occasionally drowned out by the crash of logs being dumped into place. The
loud noise was followed by the faint groan of metal and the slight
rumbling of frozen earth as the truck dutifully bowed to accept its load.

Rick Hartwick mixed his coffee with a plastic stir-stick and
walked casually toward the far end of the office trailer. At the window,
he blew across the top of his steaming cup and watched his breath
freeze against the pane. Then he took a sip, wiped away the patch of ice
that had formed on the glass, and watched his truck being loaded one
last time. As always, the loader, a Quebecois named Pierre Langlois,
was making sure Rick's rig was piled heavy with spruce and pine logs,
some of them more than three feet in diameter. Langlois liked Rick, and
with good reason. Every other week throughout the season, Rick had
provided Langlois with a bottle of Canadian Club. He'd been doing it
for years now, ever since he'd called a loader an asshole during a card
game and wound up driving trucks loaded with soft wood and air the
rest of the winter.

He'd been lucky to hang on to his rig.

The next winter he began greasing Langlois' gears with the best
eighty proof he could find and since then he'd never had a load under
thirty tonnes and only a handful under thirty-five.

He owned his rig now, as well a house in Prince George.

As he continued to watch the loading operation, Jerry Chetwynd,
the oldtimer who manned the trailer for the company came up behind

Rick and looked out the window. "That's a good load you got going there."

"Not bad," said Rick, taking a sip.

"Are you gonna take it over the road, or take a chance on the bridge?"

Rick took another sip, then turned to look at the old man. They said Chetwynd had been a logger in the B.C. interior when they'd still used ripsaws and axes to clear the land. Rick believed it, although you wouldn't know it to look at him now, all thin and bony, and hunched over like he was still carrying post wood on his back. "Is the ice bridge open?"

Chetwynd smiled, showing Rick all four of the teeth he'd been able to keep from rotting out. "They cleared the road to MacKenzie last night and this morning," he said. "But the company decided to keep the bridge open one more day seeing as how cold it was overnight."

Rick nodded. Although the winter season usually ended the last two weeks of March, a cold snap late in the month had lingered long enough for them to keep the bridge operating a whole week into April. And while they'd been opening and closing the ice bridge across Williston Lake like a saloon door the past couple days, the few extra trips he'd been able to make had made a big difference to Rick's finances—the kind of difference that translated into a two-week stay at an all-inclusive singles resort on Maui.

"Anyone use the bridge today?"

Chetwynd scratched the side of his head with two gnarled fingers. "Not that I know of. Maybe an empty coming back from the mill. Harry Heskith left here about an hour ago... But he said he wasn't going to risk the ice. Said the road would get him there just the same..."

"Yeah, eventually," Rick muttered under his breath.

The ice bridge across Williston Lake was three kilometres long and took about four minutes to cross. If you took the road around the lake you added an extra fifty kilometres and about an hour's drive to the trip. That might have been all right for Harry Heskith, with a wife, mortgage, two-point-three kids, and a dog, but Rick had a plane to catch.

Maui was waiting.

"Up to you," Chetwynd said, shrugging his shoulders as he handed Rick the yellow shipping form.

The loader's throaty roar suddenly died down and the inside of the trailer became very quiet.

Uncomfortably so.

Rick crushed his coffee cup in his hand and tossed it into the garbage. "See you 'round," he said, zipping up his parka and stepping outside.

"If you're smart you will," said Chetwynd to an empty trailer. "Smart or lucky."

The air outside was cold, but nothing like the -35 Celsius they got through January and February. Between -15 and -35 was best for winter logging -- anything colder and the machinery froze up, anything warmer and the ground started getting soft. The weather report had said -15 today, but with the sun out and shining down on the back of his coat, it felt a lot warmer than that.

Rick slipped on his gloves and headed for his rig, the morning's light dusting of snow crunching noisily underfoot.

"You got her loaded pretty tight," he called out to Langlois, who had climbed up onto the trailer to secure the load.

"Filled the hempty spaces wit kindling," Langlois said with obvious pride in his voice.

"Gee, I don't know," chided Rick. "I still see some daylight in there."

"All dat fits in dare, my friend, is match sticks hand toot picks," Langlois' said, his French-Canadian accent still lingering after a dozen years in the B.C. interior.

Rick laughed.

"You know, I uh, I 'aven't seen you in a while and I been getting a little tirsty... You know what I mean?"

Rick nodded. Of course he knew what Langlois meant. He was trying to scam him for an extra bottle before he went on holidays, even though he'd given the man a bottle less than a week ago.

"I'll take care of you when I get back next week," Rick said, knowing full well he wouldn't be back for another two.

Langlois smiled. "Going somewhere?"

"Maui, man," said Rick, giving Langlois the Hawaiian 'hang loose' sign with the thumb and little finger of his right hand.

"Lucky man... Make sure you get a lei when you land dare."

"When I land," Rick smiled. "And all week long."

The two men laughed heartily as they began walking around the truck doing a circle check on the rig and making sure the chains holding the logs in place were tight and secure.

"You load Heskith this morning?" Rick asked when they were almost done.

"Yeah."

"What do you figure you gave him?"

"Plenty of air," Langlois smiled. He had struggled to pronounce the word *air* so it didn't sound too much like *hair*.

"How much?"

"Twenty tonnes. Maybe twenty-two."

"He complain about it?"

"Not a word. In fact, he ask me to load him light. Said he was taking the road into MacKenzie."

Rick shook his head. "Dumb sonuvabitch is going to be driving a logging truck into his sixties with loads like that."

"Well, he's been doing it twenty years already."

"Yeah, and maybe he's just managed to pay off his truck by now, huh?"

"He seem to do okay," Langlois shrugged. "But it's none of my business anyway, eh?"

"Right," said Rick, shaking his head. The way he saw it, truck logging was a young man's game. Get in, make as much as you can carrying as much as you can, and get out. So he pushed it to the limit every once in a while. So what? If he worked it right he could retire early or finish out his years driving part-time, picking and choosing his loads on a sort of busman's holiday.

They finished checking the rig.

Everything was secure. "How much you figure I got there?" asked Rick, knowing Langlois could usually estimate a load to within a tonne.

"Tirty-six. Tirty-seven."

"You're beautiful, man."

Langlois nodded. "Just get it to the mill."

"Have I failed you yet?"

"No, but dare will always be a first time."

"Funny. Very funny."

There was a moment of silence between them. Finally Langlois said, "So, you taking it over the ice?"

"The bridge is open isn't it."

"Yeah, it's *open*."

Rick looked at him. Something about the way he'd said the word *open* didn't sit right with him. It sounded too much like *hope* for his liking. "Did Heskith say why he wasn't taking the bridge?"

"Uh-huh," Langlois nodded. "He said he had no intention of floating his logs to the mill."

Rick laughed at that. "And I got no intention of missing my flight."

Langlois nodded. "Aloha."

For a moment, Rick didn't understand, then he smiled and said, "Oh, yeah right. Aloha."

The interior of the Peterbilt had been warmed by the sunlight beaming through the windshield. As Rick settled in he took off his hat and gloves and undid his coat, then he shifted it into neutral and started up the truck. The big engine rattled, the truck shivered, and a belch of black smoke escaped the rig's twin chrome pipes. And then the cab was filled with the strong and steady metallic rumble of 525 diesel-powered horses.

He let the engine warm-up, making himself more comfortable for the long drive to the mill. He slipped in a Charlie Major tape, and waited for the opening chords of "For the Money" to begin playing. When the song started blaring, he shifted it into gear and slowly released the clutch.

His first thought was how long it took the rig to get moving, as the cab rocked and the engine roared against dead weight of the heavy load. It usually didn't take so long to get underway, Rick thought. Must be a bit heavier than Langlois had figured.

Inch by inch, the truck rolled forward. At last he was out of first and into second, gaining small amounts of momentum and speed as he worked his way up through the gears.

A light amount of snow had begun to fall, but it wasn't enough to worry about, certainly nothing that would slow him down.

The logging road into MacKenzie was wide and flat, following the southern bank of the Nation River for more than a hundred kilometres before coming upon the southern tip of Williston Lake. There the road split in two, one fork continuing east over the ice bridge to MacKenzie, the other turning south and rounding the southern finger of Williston Lake before turning back north toward the mills.

Rick drove along the logging road at about sixty kilometres an hour, slowing only once when he came upon an empty rig headed in the opposite direction. Out of courtesy, he gave the driver a pull on the gas horn and a friendly wave, then it was back to the unbroken white strip of road cut neatly through the trees.

The snow continued to fall.

When he turned over the Major tape for the second time he knew he was nearing the bridge. He hated to admit it, but a slight tingle coursed through his body at the thought of taking his load over the ice.

When Rick first began driving logging trucks the idea of driving across lakes didn't sit all that well with him. To him, it was sort of like skydivers jumping out of perfectly good airplanes—it just wasn't right. Six-axle semi-trailers loaded with thirty-five tonnes of logs weren't meant to be driven over water—frozen or otherwise.

It was unnatural...

Dangerous.

But after his first few rides over the ice, he realized that it was the only way to go. Sure, sometimes you heard a crack or pop under your wheels, but that just made it all the more exciting. The only real danger about driving over the ice was losing your way. Once your were off the bridge there were no guarantees that the ice beneath your rig would be thick enough to support you. And if you did fall through, or simply got stuck, there was a good chance you'd freeze to death while searching for help.

Even so, those instances were rare, and as far as Rick knew, no one had ever fallen through the ice while driving over an open bridge.

And he sure as hell didn't intend to be the first.

Up ahead the roadway opened up slightly as the snow-trimmed trees parted to reveal the lake and the ice bridge across it. In the distance, he could see the smoke rising up from the stacks of the three saw mills and two pulp mills of MacKenzie, a town of about 5,000 hardy souls.

He turned down the music, then shut it off completely as he slowed his rig to a stop at the fork in the road.

He took a deep breath and considered his options one last time.

Across the lake at less than three kilometres away, MacKenzie seemed close enough to touch. But between here and there, there was nothing more than frozen water to hold up over thirty-five tonnes of wood and steel.

He turned to look down the road as it curved to the south and pictured Harry Heskith's rig turning that way about an hour before, his tracks now obscured by the continuing snowfall.

The road.

It was Heskith's route all right...

The long way.

The safe way.

But even if Rick decided to go that route, there were no guarantees that the drive would be easy. First of all he was really too heavy to chance it. With its sharp inclines and steep downgrades there was a real risk of sliding off the snow-covered road while rounding a curve. Also, although it hadn't happened to him yet, he'd heard of truckers coming across tourists out for Sunday drives, rubbernecking along their merry way at ten or fifteen kilometres an hour. When that happened, you had the choice of driving over top of them, or slamming on the brakes. And on these logging roads, hard braking usually meant ending up on your side or in the ditch, or both. And that might mean a month's worth of profits just to get back on the road.

But even if he *wanted* to take the road, it would mean spending another hour behind the wheel and that would make him late for his flight out of Prince George. Then he'd miss his connecting flight out of Vancouver which meant...

No Maui.

And he wasn't about to let that happen, especially when he'd been told that the resort he'd be staying at discreetly stocked rooms with complimentary condoms.

Man, he couldn't wait to get there.

He looked out across the lake again. The snow was still falling, but a light crosswind was keeping it from building up on the ice. He could still clearly see the thick black lines painted onto the ice surface on either side of the bridge. With those lines so visible, there was really no way he could lose his way.

He took one last look down the road, thought of Heskith heading down that way an hour ago and wondered if he'd catch up with good ole Harry on the other side.

If he did, maybe he could race him into Mackenzie.

The thought put a dark and devilish grin on Rick's face.

He slid the Charlie Major tape back into the deck, turned up the volume and shifted the truck into gear.

"Here goes nothing," he said.

The rig inched forward.

It took him a while to get up to speed, but by the time he got onto the bridge he was doing fifty, more than enough to see him safely to the other side.

The trick to driving over the ice was to keep moving. There was incredible amounts of pressure under the wheels of the rig, but as long as you kept moving, that pressure was constantly being relieved. If you slowed, or heaven forbid, stalled out on the ice, then you were really shit-out-of-luck.

He shifted into sixth gear, missed the shift and had to try again. Finally, he got it into gear, but in the meantime he had slowed considerably and the engine had to struggle to recover the lost speed.

Slowly the speedometer's red needle clawed its way back up to sixty, sixty-one, sixty-two...

And then he heard something over the music.

It was a loud sound, like the splintering of wood or the cracking of bone. He immediately turned down the music and listened.

All he could hear was the steady thrum of his diesel engine.

For a moment he breathed easier.

But then he heard it again.

The unmistakable sound of cracking ice.

It was a difficult sound to describe. Some said it was like snow crunching underfoot, while others compared it to fresh celery stalks being snapped in two. Rick, however, had always described it as sounding like an ice cube dropped into a warm glass of Coke—only a hundred times louder.

He looked down at the ice on the bridge in front of him, realized he was straddling one of the black lines painted on the ice and gently eased the wheel to the left, bringing him back squarely between the lines.

That done, he breathed a sigh of relief, and felt the sweat begin to cool on his face and down his back.

"Eyes on the road," he said aloud. "You big dummy—"

Crack!

This one was louder than the others, so loud he could feel the shock waves in his chest.

Again he looked out in front of his truck and for the first time saw the pressure cracks shooting out in front of him, matching the progress of his truck metre for metre.

Finally Rick admitted what he'd known all along.

He was way too heavy.

And the ice was far too thin.

But 20/20 hindsight was useless to him now. All he could do was keep moving, keep relieving the pressure under his wheels and hope that both he and the pressure crack reached the other side.

He stepped hard on the gas pedal and the engine responded with a louder, throatier growl. He considered shifting gears again but decided it might be better not to risk it.

He firmed up his foot on the gas pedal and stood on it with all his weight.

The engine began to strain as the speedometer inched past seventy... He remained on the pedal, knowing he'd be across in less than a minute.

The sound grew louder, changing from a crunching, cracking sound to something resembling a gunshot.

He looked down.

The crack in front of the truck had grown bigger, firing out in front of him in all directions like the scraggly branches of a December birch.

"C'mon, c'mon," he said pressing his foot harder on the gas even though it was a wasted effort. The pedal was already down as far as it would go.

Then suddenly the cracking sound grew faint, as if it had been dampened by a splash of water.

A moment later, crunching again.

Cracking.

He looked up. The shoreline was a few hundred metres away. In a few seconds there would be solid ice under his wheels and then nothing but wonderful, glorious, hard-packed frozen ground.

But then the trailer suddenly lurched to the right, pulling the left-front corner of the tractor into the air.

"C'mon, c'mon," Rick screamed, jerking back and forth in his seat in a vain attempt to add some forward momentum to the rig.

Then the front end of the Peterbilt dipped as if it had come across a huge rent in the ice.

"Oh, shit!"

The tractor bounced over the rent, then the trailer followed, each axle dipping down, seemingly hesitant about coming back up the other side, and then reluctantly doing so.

And then, as if by some miracle...

He was through it.

Rolling smoothly over the ice.

Solid ice.

And the only sound he could hear was the throaty roar of his Peterbilt as he kept his foot hard on the gas.

He raced up the incline toward the road without slowing.

When he reached the road, he got off the gas, but still had plenty of momentum, not to mention weight, behind him.

Too much of both, it seemed.

He pulled gently on the rear brake lever, but found that his tires had little grip on the snow-covered road. His rear wheels locked up and began sliding out from behind.

He turned the wheel, but it was no use.

He closed his eyes and braced himself for the rig to topple onto its side.

He waited and waited for the crash...

But it never came.

Suddenly all was quiet except for the calming rattle of the Peterbilt's diesel engine at idle.

Rick opened his eyes.

He breathed hard as he looked around to get his bearings.

He was horizontal across the highway, pointed in the direction he'd come.

He looked north out the passenger side window and saw the puffing smokestacks of MacKenzie, and smiled.

He'd made it.

Made it across the bridge.

The moment of celebration was sweet, but short-lived...

Cut off by the loud cry of a gas horn, splitting the air like a scream.

He turned to look south down the highway.

Harry Heskith's rig had just crested the hill and was heading straight for him.

Rick threw the Peterbilt into gear, stomped on the gas and popped the clutch.

The rig lurched forward, but he was too slow and too late.

All of Heskith's rear wheels were locked and sliding over the snow like skis. Heskith was turning his front wheels frantically left and right even though it was doing nothing to change the direction he was headed.

And then as he got closer, Rick could clearly see Heskith's face. What surprised Rick most was the realization that the old man was shaking his fist at him.

Shaking his fist, as if to say he was a crazy fool for taking the bridge.

But as the two trucks came together, all Rick could think of was how *he'd* been right all along.

The dangers of the ice bridge had all been a cakewalk compared to—

THE DEEP
by
Carolyn Clink

It prowls the tip of the Bruce Peninsula.
Gnarled pines clinging to barren cliffs watch
as wind-tossed waves smash the narrow shoreline.
Shoals and reefs pluck the unlucky
down into its lair of cold serenity.
Glass-bottom tour boats peer into the beast's
frigid heart. Voyeurs view the bones of its prey,
scattered across the crystal blue depths of Georgian Bay.
Ill-fated ships caught like flies in amber,
suddenly transformed from life to afterlife.
Skeletons preserved in glacial eternity.

THE FISHER'S DAUGHTER

by
Thomas S. Roche

San Francisco-based Thomas S. Roche has had stories featured in the anthologies *Razor Kiss, Gothic Ghosts*, and *The Mammoth Book of Pulp Fiction*, among others. He is editor of the anthologies *Noirotica* (Rhinoceros Books), *Sons of Darkness* (Cleis Press) and *Gargoyles* (Ace/Berkley). His short fiction is collected in *Dark Matter* (Rhinoceros Books, 1997).

Across the steel-gray sea on certain damned nights still comes the keening of Cathleen, the Fisher's Daughter. The people of the town know her well, though there are few fishers left and the piers crumble worm-eaten in the water. What fishers there are now do not fear her, for her banshee wail tastes merely of agonies, and to see her is only to breathe the stink of death. Times have changed everywhere, and the people of the Nova Scotia coast are a hardy folk; death carries no currency there. Only life is at a premium, and hard to come by.

Despite this, in days past Cathleen's ghost was greatly feared, perhaps because in her death-song she pronounced the words that would kill the past, and damn the future.

All would shut their eyes, plug their ears, close their hearts. Except for the one whose name the Fisher's Daughter called out—and that girl had her own subtle agonies to torment her. She would meet with her lover on the seacoast at midnights, their screams mingling in furtive trysts in the dank fog of the rocky coast. Fate, though, had played its cruel joke upon the lovers, and the ghosts could not touch. And so they would weep, and the night itself would tremble.

In those days the Fisher gave up his boat and took to whiskey. His boat languished, decaying. McCoppin the boathand had long ago left the Fisher's employment. The Fisher grew more emaciated, his color worse, every day. The other fishers went away, cursing, and found other places to search for their cod, lobster, and haddock. Some of them had long tied their boats at the Orphan's Harbor, as it was called, but the day came when Cathleen's father was the only fisher with a boat left in the harbor, which is why we may call him the Fisher.

The Fisher locked himself inside his house to drink, fearing the waves. For the Fisher's Daughter haunted only the water: land was forbidden her, given the manner of her death.

When the Fisher did make his way down to the pier, perhaps to visit his shrinking and shriveled boat, to grope after a forgotten memory of this time on the water, he would hear his daughter's voice wailing and would lose his sea-legs in an instant. He would then scramble back to his house, there to hide with his morose and bitter wife, drinking cheap whiskey.

But his daughter's wails still haunted his nightmares, and there in the dark of the Fisher's bedroom she would wail the single word over and over again: her lover's name.

Cathleen's lover lived, gone as mad as Cathleen's ghost. She haunted the Fisher's house, walking slow circles around it and calling out Cathleen's name. She was called Adrienne, and she was haunted by her love of the dead girl. Such a string of hauntings can only end in tragedy, then as now.

The Fisher cursed at his wife when he saw the girl circling the house, a living ghost condemned to land.

"If it wasn't for her—Cathleen would—" the Fisher would snarl, and his wife would shatter a glass or a plate, stopping him before he could once again bemoan his ill luck.

"If it wasn't for you—" howled the woman, old before her time, stooped almost down on her haunches, snarling like a she-wolf — "she would be alive and happy! What you did was unthinkable! Unmentionable! Unforgivable!"

"Love is not meant to be—"

"Enough!" spat the Fisher's wife, her lips pulled back in a snarl.

And the Fisher would turn to his drink, his wife hissing at him and scampering away while the young woman's mourning grew louder outside.

Adrienne wandered the spaces around the Fisher's house, weeping salty tears, perhaps imagining the texture of the many afternoons she had spent in the house. She wept and wailed Cathleen's name. While on the waves, Cathleen called for her.

Inside, the Fisher would once again curse the name of Adrienne, for it was she who had brought such despair upon their daughter. Without her love, their daughter would be alive. And yet the Fisher knew his wife was right. He was ultimately to blame.

Adrienne's own mother, the Widow, tried everything she could do to bring the poor girl solace. But she could not stop her daughter's mourning; she could not console the girl.

Sometimes, on the pier, Adrienne would kneel and reach out over the waves, calling her lover's name. And Cathleen would reach for Adrienne as well, but their fingers would pass through each other, the two girls forever separated, the land and water keeping them apart.

"If only Cathleen had stabbed herself," wept Adrienne, sprawled on the pier as icy rain pelted her. "If only she had thrown herself from the church steeple; why couldn't she have hung herself? If only my lover hadn't done what she did, I could cast myself upon her grave and perhaps we could touch."

The Widow took Adrienne to the beauty parlor, for expensive procedures that were supposed to make her ever-more-beautiful. In the beauty parlor, the beauticians would clean the sand from under Adrienne's nails and ask her if there were any boys she liked. Adrienne would mumble incoherently with her bluish lips and the beauticians would giggle grotesquely and prattle on, buffing her nails. They would listen to the radio and hear the latest song from Frank Sinatra. Adrienne's mother would sing along loudly and out-of-key as she sat under the dryers, but Adrienne would merely stare, the curlers and toxic chemicals bleaching her raven hair into a haggard parody of sunlight. After, Adrienne's immaculate blackberry nails would break against the wood of the pier and the rocky sands of the beach; her bleached hair would grow out ratted and filthy, the black roots showing; her radiant lipstick would take a cockeyed half-turn across her mouth; her eyes would grow sallow and decayed again. Soon she would look worse than before, misfortune making her into a wraith. She would wrap herself in the tattered wool coat Cathleen had left behind, and weep under the battering of the freezing rain. It could only end in tears.

The girl had always liked the boat. When Cathleen was young, her father would take her out on the waves when she would sink into one of her sorrowful and unconsolable fits of depression. McCoppin was with him even then, and McCoppin liked the girl. The boathand would teach Cathleen how to tie the ropes, how to run the motor, how to cast the nets. No matter how iconsolable the girl had seemed on land, she would cheer up at sea. The Fisher knew such things were not necessary for girls to know, but she seemed to love it. And anything that would cheer her up was a Godsend as far as the Fisher was concerned.

McCoppin was lame and nearly deaf, having been injured badly in an accident long ago, the accident that scrapped his own fishing boat. But he had a strong back and did not talk much when they were at sea. And his sea legs were as intact as ever; you would swear he was only lame when walking on land. The girl Cathleen loved the things he taught her about charts, maps, winds, currents.

And so a few days after it happened, the Fisher took Cathleen out in the boat. He felt sure that his daughter hated him for what he did, but equally sure that her disappointment would pass.

"It's not right," the Fisher would tell his daughter endlessly, over and over again. "It's not proper. It wasn't meant to be. You shan't see her again. It's for your own good. It's the way it must be. I'm your father, you'll do as I say."

Cathleen, the Fisher's Daughter, would respond with a helpless look of agony.

And so the Fisher did what he had always done; he took her with him, to wander the waves with McCoppin and him as they cast their nets across the ocean for fish.

A mile out to sea it became clear that Cathleen did not plan on cheering up.

"Fine, then," spat the Fisher. "Stay back here, don't get in our way—we've work to do!"

The Fisher turned and left her to her miseries in the stern, having gazed for the last time on his daughter's living face.

And Cathleen came wailing across the waves, screaming her lover's name, haunted by the unfortunate living as the living were haunted by the unlucky dead. When Adrienne's mother saw the policeman coming in to the beauty parlor, she knew the truth before the man opened his mouth—but something caused her to shriek desperately "No!" —her scream mingling with the radio.

It was fitting, perhaps, that Adrienne should die by drowning. The Baker's Wife had seen it. The waters had frozen and the land-dweller, Adrienne, had wandered desperately out to meet the ghost of ocean-dweller, Cathleen. The sun was blocked by swirling clouds, and perhaps the ghost of Cathleen sensed her lover's presence, for she appeared at the edge of the ice, reaching her arms out for the girl. They had shared one brief kiss as the clouds broke; the sun shone down in a single molten shaft. Like gunshots there were the sounds of fracturing ice. Cathleen, walking the frozen waters, scrambled to take her lover's hand, but the girl was already gone, swallowed through the crack in the ice.

She was blue when they dragged her body out of the freezing water. Her lips had gone an even more unnatural shade and her white-black hair was tangled with stiff seaweed. But she was not yet dead. They struggled to save her, but she had lost the will to live.

The priest said Last Rites over the shivering girl, and she passed on soon after.

She had loved a ghost of the waves, and so it was fitting that she die at sea.

But what was to be done? A sea burial wouldn't be proper. It was simply not permitted. She was dressed in her best gown, the black mourning gown Cathleen had left her. And buried on the hill overlooking the water.

The girl came wailing across the beach, shrieking her lover's name, moaning the agonies of the damned. Their shimmering fingers reach out for each other; their blackened lips nearly touch.

The fishing hasn't been good in recent years. Last season, some enterprising huckster set up a souvenir stand, selling Cathleen dolls, fragments of Adrienne's coat, doctored photographs of the two ghosts touching on the waves. He did a good business for a while, but tourists soon forgot about the girls and chose to return to their warmer climes. The beaches grew deserted and the pier fell into disrepair. The Fisher's boat was sold off for scrap and the Fisher died of drink. McCoppin was found frozen beneath a sycamore tree and buried in an unmarked grave. The Fisher's wife entered an asylum. Adrienne's mother, the Widow, married a Banker and moved to Ontario. The hairdressers all became grotesque with their own unholy ministrations, and eventually moved *en masse* to Las Vegas. A new crop of fishing people took up residence, unafraid of the dead, untouched by fear, unamused by spectres.

Over the years the girls seemed to grow resolved to the fact that they could never touch, could never kiss. Their wailings grew less frequent and they came to merely watch each other, Cathleen on her waves, Adrienne on the hill overlooking the beach. They did not weep or mourn, and they might be said to be at peace.

But occasionally the harbor freezes. On those rare nights, sometimes, there is the flash of translucent skin, the wail of a beloved's name. A kiss in the foggy midnight.

THE INNER INNER CITY

by
Robert Charles Wilson

Toronto's Robert Charles Wilson, whose award-winning novella "The Perseids" was a highlight of *Northern Frights 3*, is the author of such outstanding novels as *Mysterium, The Harvest,* and the forthcoming *Darwinia*. His latest story is one that *The Science Fiction Encyclopedia* might have anticipated when they wrote of the author, "He expresses with vigor and imagination the great Canadian theme (for the sense of being on the lonely side of a binary has sparked much of the best Canadian SF) of geographical alienation."

"**I**nvent a religion," John Carver said, and for the first time I really took notice of him.

It wasn't the invitation. All of us in the group had been asked to do stranger things. It was the way he said it. I had pegged Carver as one of those affluent post-grads perfectly content to while away a decade in a focusless quest for a Ph.d, one of the krill of the academic ocean. He would float until he was swallowed...by the final onus of a degree, or by an ambitious woman, or by his own aimlessness. In the meantime he was charming-enough company.

But he posed his challenge with an insouciance and an air of mischief that took me by surprise. He perched on the arm of the leather recliner and looked straight at me, though there were fifteen of us crowded into the living room. He wore casually expensive clothes, perfectly-cut jeans and a pastel sweatshirt, the sort whose brand names I felt I was expected to recognize, though I never did. His face was lean and handsome. Not blandly handsome—*aggressively* handsome. He looked, not like a rapist, but like the sort of actor who would be cast as one.

Deirdre Frank peered at him through the watery lenses of her enormous eyeglasses. "What kind of religion? *Any* kind of religion?"

"A new religious doctrine," Carver said, "or dogma, article of faith, heresy, occultism, cosmology. Original in its elements. Submissions marked on a ten-point sliding scale, we all mark each other, and in the event of a tie I cast the deciding vote." All this was as usual. "Are we game?"

Someone had to go first. In this case it was Michelle, my wife. She opened the carved-basswood jewellery box we kept for the occasion and slipped a hundred dollar bill inside. "I'm in," she said. "But it's a toughie, John."

In the end we all anted up, even Chuck Byrnie, a tweedy atheist from the U. of T. chemistry department, though he grumbled before committing himself. "Somewhat unfair. More in Deirdre's line than mine."

Most of us were faculty. Deirdre was our chief exception. She had no credentials but an arts degree, class of '68, and a long perambulation through Toronto's evolving fringe cultures: Yorkville, Rochdale, Harbord Street, Queen Street. She owned the Golden Bough Gem and Crystal Shoppe, where Michelle worked part-time. She was perhaps the paradigm of the aging hippie, grey-tressed and overweight, usually draped in a batiqued kaftan or some other wildly inappropriate ethnic garb. But she wasn't stupid and she wasn't afraid to match egos with the rest of us. "Stop whining, Chuck. Even the physicists are mystics nowadays."

"You've read Mary Baker Eddy. You have an advantage."

"Oh? And where would you guys be without Roger Bacon? Admit it—all you science types are closet alchemists."

Fifteen hundred dollars in the kitty. Michelle locked the box in our safe, where it waited for a winner. Gatherings were held weekly, but the contest was quarterly. We had three months to play Christ, Buddha, Zoroaster. Winner take all.

The challenge sparked an evening's conversation, which was the purpose of it. What *was* religion, exactly, and where did you start? A new paganism or a new Christian heresy? Did UFOs count? ESP?

From these seeds would spring our ideas, and after tonight we wouldn't mention the subject again until the results were presented in November. It was our fifth year. The contest had started with a friendly wager between Michelle and a self-styled performance artist, something about whether Whitman was a better poet than Emerson. I had ended up refereeing the debate. Our Friday night social circle rendered final judgment, and we all enjoyed it so much (excepting the loser, who vanished soon thereafter) that we made it an institution, with rules. A Challenge, a Challenger, a hundred-dollar ante, judgment by tribunal.

Challenges had ranged from the whimsical (re-write your favorite fairy tale in the style of William Faulkner) to the devilish (explain the theory of relativity using words of one syllable, points for clarity and brevity). Our best pots had topped two thousand dollars.

John's challenge was...*interesting*, and I wondered what had prompted it. To my knowledge, he had never shown much interest in religion or the occult. I remembered him from my course on the Romantics, blithely amused but hardly fascinated. Something Byronesque about him, but without the doomed intensity; say, Byron on Zoloft. Tonight he was animated and engaging, and I wondered what else I had missed about him.

Sometime past midnight I stepped out onto the balcony for a breath of air. We had lived in this apartment for ten years, Michelle and I. Central but a little north, seventeen stories up, southern exposure. The city scrolled away from it like a vast and intricate diagram, as indecipherable as the language of the Hittites. Lights dim as stars cut into the black vastness of Lake Ontario, all quivering in the rising remains of the heat of the day. Here was a religion, I thought. Here was *my* religion. My secret book, my Talmud.

I had known this about myself for a long time, my addiction to the obscure beauties of the city. For most of my life I had consoled myself in its contradictions, its austerities and its baroque recomplications. Here was the answer to Carver's challenge. I would make a city religion. An urban occultism. Divination by cartography. Call it *paracartography*.

Carver came through the sliding door as if I had summoned him. His presence broke the mood, but I was excited enough to describe my notion to him. He smiled one of his odd and distant smiles. "Sounds promising. A sort of map..."

"A *sacred* map," I said.

"Sacred. Exactly. Very clever, Jeremy. In fact, I—"

He would have said more, but Michelle barged onto the balcony to regale him with some idea of her own. She had been reading too many of Deirdre's New Age tracts, or simply drinking too much; she was flushed and semi-coherent, tugging Carver's sleeve as she talked, something about post-temporal deities, model worlds, gods from the end of time.

The party wound down around two. We gently hastened hence our last guest an hour later and went to bed without washing the dishes. Michelle was less feverish but still feeling the alcohol; she was impatient about making love. Drinking makes her eager, but I don't drink and have always found her occasional drunkenness an anti-aphrodisiac; her breath smelled like a chem lab and she looked at me as if she wasn't quite sure who had tumbled into bed with her.

But she was still fundamentally beautiful, still the brash and intelligent woman I had married a dozen years ago, and if our climaxes that night drew us deeper into ourselves and farther from each other...well, here's a mystery I have never understood: ecstasy hates company.

One more thing I remember from that time. (And memory is the point of writing this.) We woke to breakfast among the ruins. Actually we took breakfast about eleven, on the balcony, because the weather had turned lovely and cool, and the sun came slantwise between the bars of the railing and warmed our feet. Michelle mimed a hangover but said she actually felt okay, just a little rueful. Wide sheepish grin. We turned our faces to the breeze and sipped orange juice. We didn't talk about the contest, except this:

"Carver's interesting," she said. "Funny, I never really noticed him before."

"You noticed him last night."

"Well, that's the point. He used to be so quiet."

Did he? He struck me as evasive, mercurial—the whole *idea* of Carver had become suddenly slippery. I wondered aloud who had brought him to the group.

Michelle looked at me curiously. "You did, genius—last year sometime."

Was that possible? Carver had audited one of my classes—that was the first I saw of him—but afterward?

"A couple of meetings at Hart House," Michelle supplied. "He read your Coleridge book. Then you brought him to a Friday night and introduced him around. You said he was bright but a little withdrawn, sort of a lost puppy."

Funny thing to forget.

I let the challenge slide for a month or so. By daylight, it lost some of its charm. Labour Day passed, classes resumed, and I was obliged to untangle the annual knotted shoestring of schedules and lectures, the endless autumn minutiae. In what began as a half-gesture toward the contest, I took up walking again.

Not that I had ever completely abandoned it. By "walking" I mean long, late walks—walks without destination, often after midnight, sometimes until dawn. Compulsive as much as therapeutic. I lived in one of the few cities in North America where such urban walking was less than mortally dangerous, and I had learned which places to avoid—the after-hours clubs, the hustlers' alleys, the needle parks.

Of course, this kind of wandering constitutes suspicious behaviour. Cops are apt to stop you and read your I.D. into their dashboard databanks. Young male steroid abusers from the suburbs on a gay-bashing *soiree* might turn their attention your way. Some years ago a belligerent drunk had broken my jaw, for reasons known only to himself.

I think even Michelle wondered about these expeditions at first. I wouldn't have been the first dutiful husband with a secret career in the midnight toilet stalls. But that wasn't it. The only solace I wanted or needed was the solace of an empty street. It clears the mind and comforts the soul.

At least, it used to.

Walking took my mind off my work and turned it back toward Carver's challenge. I was neither religious nor dogmatically atheistic— I had shelved all those issues in a category marked "Unanswerable Questions," after which what more was there to say? I had been raised in a benign Anglicanism and had shed it without trauma. But I wasn't empty of the religious impulse. It's no secret that my fascination with the Romantic poets was equally a fascination with their opiated gnosticism, their sense of an *aeternitas* haunting every crag and glen.

What is perhaps strange is that the city gave me the same sensation. We contrast the urban and the natural, but that's a contemporary myth; we're animals, after all; our cities are organic products, fully as natural as a termite hill or a rabbit warren. But how much more interesting: how much more complex, dressed in the intricacies and strange exfoliations of human culture, simple patterns iterated into infinite variation. And full of secrets, secrets beyond counting.

I think I had always known this. When I was seven years old and allowed to stay up to see *The Naked City* (intrigued even then by the title), it wasn't the melodrama that drew me but the opportunity to hear the opening credits, the ABC announcer's lugubrious "There are a million stories in the Naked City," which I understood as a great and terrible truth.

Obviously my religion of the city would have to unite the two, the gnostic impulse and the urban mandala. Paracartography implied the making of maps, city maps, a map of *this* city, but not an ordinary map; it must be a map of the city's secret terrains, the city as perceived by a divine madman, streets rendered as ecstasies or purgatories; a map legible only at night, in the dark.

Too complex and senseless a piece of work, even with fifteen hundred dollars at stake, but I couldn't dismiss it, and wondered if some hint of the idea might be enough to take the pot.

I thought about it as I walked—one night a week, sometimes two, rarely three. I carried a notebook in case of inspiration. Paracartography became one of those ideas so paradoxical and odd as to inspire a strange fascination. I found it was always in the back of my mind, waiting for a free hour or a tedious subway ride or, best of all, an evening's walk.

And yet the walks were still their own reward. Even after almost a quarter century of restless exploration there were still neighborhoods and terrains that took me absolutely by surprise, and surprise was the purpose and reward of the exercise: to come around a corner and find some black and shadowed warehouse, some abandoned railway siding, a hidden angle of moonlight on a crumbling silo that catches the heart with an inexplicable poignancy.

What I rediscovered that autumn was my ability to get lost. Toronto is a forgiving city, essentially a gridwork of streets as formal and uninspiring as its banks. Walk in any direction long enough, you'll find a landmark or a familiar bus route. As a rule. But the invention of paracartography exercised such trancelike power that I was liable to walk without any sense of time or direction and find myself, hours later, in a wholly new neighborhood, as if my unattended feet had followed a map of their own.

Which was precisely what I wanted. Automatic pathfinding, like automatic writing. How better to begin a paracartographic survey?

The only trouble was that I began to look a little ragged at work. Friends inquired about my health. I didn't feel the sleep deprivation, but I began to use drops to disguise the inevitable red-eye. My best friends worried more than I thought appropriate.

One afternoon early in October I phoned Michelle to tell her I'd be late, took transit to the Dundas subway station, transferred to a streetcar and rode it east until I felt like getting off. Heady, that first moment of freedom. The air was crisp, the sun was about to set on the other side of the Don River Valley. I remember a cheap meal, curry and chapatis at a Pakistani diner while I watched the traffic through a cracked and steam-fogged window. Then out again into the fresh night. I walked west, where the wind-scrubbed sky was still faintly blue.

I remember the first evening star over the Armory, I remember amber streetlights reflected in the barred and dusty windows of Church Street pawnshops, I remember the sound of my own footsteps ticking on empty sidewalks....

But memory falters (more often now), and apart from a general sensation of cold and uncertainty, the next thing I remember is finding myself in full daylight about a half-block from Deirdre's gem shop.

According to my watch it was after ten, a sunny Saturday morning. There was no place I had to be. But Michelle might be worried. I stopped by the shop to use the phone.

Deirdre was at the back, hanging dream-catchers from the peg-board ceiling. Kathy, her other part-timer, lounged behind the counter looking impatient. "Morning, Dr. Singer," she trilled.

Deirdre looked down from her stepladder. "Hey, Jeremy. Geeze, look at you. Been eroding the shoe leather again?"

"It shows?"

"Sort of a Bataan Death-March look...."

"Tactful as ever. Mind if I call Michelle?"

"My guest."

Michelle was relieved to hear from me, said she hadn't been worried but would I be home for lunch? I told her I would and put the phone back under the counter.

"Don't sneak off," Deirdre said. "Kathy can mind the store a while. Buy me coffee."

I said I could spare half an hour.

She stopped at a hardware store across the street and bought a box of houseplant fertilizer. "For the ladies?" I asked.

"The ladies."

Deirdre's "ladies" were the female marijuana plants she grew in her basement. If Deirdre trusted you, she'd tell you about her garden. I had seen it once, a fragrant emerald oasis tucked into a closet and illuminated with a football-sized halide bulb. She grew cannabis for her own use and to my knowledge never sold any, though Deirdre was so customarily level-headed and so seldom publicly stoned that I wondered what exactly she used it *for*. She was a pothead but not a social pothead; she kept her intoxications to herself.

We bought coffee at the Second Cup and found a window table. Deirdre gulped half her latte and frowned critically at me. "You really do look like shit, Jeremy. And you don't smell much better."

Half-moons of sweat under my arms. I was aware of my own stink, the low-tide smell of too much exercise on a cold night. My thighs ached and my feet were throbbing. I admitted I might have overdone it a little.

"So where'd you go?"

"Started out across the Don, ended up here."

"That's not an all night walk."

"I took the scenic route."

"And saw—?"

I realized I didn't have an answer. An image flitted past my mind's eye, of a grey street, grey flagstone storefronts, shuttered second-story windows, but the memory was sepia-toned, faded, fading. "Shadows on a cavern wall."

"What?"

"Plato."

"You're so fucked up sometimes." She paused. "Listen, Jeremy, is everything okay between you and Michelle?"

"Me and Michelle? Why do you ask?"

"That's an evasion. Why do I ask? I ask because I'm a nosy old lady who can't mind her own business. Also because I'm your friend."

"Has she said something?"

"No. Nothing at all. It's just—"

"Just *what*?"

She drummed her fingers on the table. "If I say it's a hunch, that doesn't cut much ice, huh?"

"If it's a hunch, Deirdre, I'd say thanks for thinking of us, but your hunch is wrong. We're fine."

"There's something that happens to married people. They lose track of each other. Everything's routine, you know, dinner and TV and bed, but meanwhile they're sailing separate boats, spiritually I mean. Until one of 'em wakes up in an empty bed going, 'What the fuck?'"

"Thank you, Dr. Ruth."

"Well, okay." The last half of her coffee chased the first. "Are you writing another book?"

"What?"

"That little notepad sticking out of your pocket. And your pen's starting to leak, there, Jeremy."

I grabbed the ballpoint out of my pocket, but the shirt was going to be a casualty. As for the notebook, I began to tell Deirdre how I kept it around for inspiration regarding the Challenge, but it was empty so far...except it *wasn't* empty.

"Good part of a book right there," Deirdre said, watching me flip through the pages.

Every page was filled. The handwriting was tiny and cramped, but it looked like my own.

Only one problem. I couldn't read a word.

Here the question becomes: Why didn't I see a doctor?

It wouldn't have helped, of course, but I didn't know that then. And I had read enough Oliver Sacks to realize that the combination of periodic fugues and graphomania spelled big trouble, at least potentially.

Nor was I afraid of doctors. In my forty-one years I had made it through an appendectomy, a kidney stone, and two impacted wisdom teeth. No big deal.

Of course a brain tumor *would* have been a big deal, but the idea of talking to a doctor didn't even occur to me; it was beyond the pale, unnecessary, absurd. What had happened was not a medical but a *metaphysical* mystery. I think it half-delighted me.

And half-terrified me, but the terror was metaphysical too: if this new discontinuity was not imaginary then it must be external, which implied that I had crossed a real boundary, that I had stepped at least a little distance into the land beyond the mirror.

In short, I didn't think about it rationally.

But I did think about it. Come November, I thought about it almost constantly.

The details of a descent into obsession are familiar enough. I came to believe in my own psychological invulnerability even as friends began to ask delicately whether I might not want to "see someone." I let my work slide. Missed a few lectures. I told myself I was achieving a valuable insight into the Romantic sensibility, and I suppose that was true, in a twisted sense; Novalis's sad hero forever seeking his blue flower could hardly have been more single-minded. Single-mindedly, I began to assemble my map.

I won't tell you how I did it. In any case there was no single method, only materials and intuition. I will say that I obtained the largest and most comprehensive survey map of the city I could find and then began to distort and overlay it according to my own perceptions, certain that each new palimpsest of ink and color, each new mylar transparency, was not obscuring but actually revealing the city—the occult, the *hidden* city.

I kept the work private, but we all did, in a Challenge; even Michelle and I were competing for that fifteen hundred dollars (though the money was the least of my considerations). She didn't mention temporal deities to me. And although she knew something had gone awry—for one thing, our sex life suffered—she said very little. Humoring me, I thought. The good and faithful wife. But she didn't have to speak; I read a volume of recrimination in her frowns and silences, and there were moments when I hated her for it.

"You realize," Deirdre said, "he's fucking us over."

November had come in on the last breath of autumn, sunny and warm. Deirdre had shown up early for our Friday night, the night we judged the Challenge. Michelle was busy in the kitchen. I sat with Deirdre on the balcony, the fragile heat of the day evaporating fast.

Deirdre wore XL denim bib overalls and a baseball cap turned sideways. She took a joint from the grimy deeps of her purse and held it up. "Mind?"

"Not at all."

She hunted for a lighter. "We don't even know who he is—where he comes from."

She was talking about John Carver. "He's been shy about his past, true."

"He's not shy about anything, Jeremy. Haven't you figured that out? If there's something he hasn't told us, it's 'cause he doesn't want us to know."

"That's a little harsh."

"Watch him tonight. He's the center of attention. We huddle at his feet like he's Socrates or something, and people forget it wasn't always like that. Better yet, keep your eyes off Carver and look at the crowd. It's like hypnotism, what he does. He radiates this power, this very deliberate sexual thing, and it *pins* people. I mean, they don't blink!"

"He's charismatic."

"I guess so. Up to a point. I don't get it, myself. And he does not welcome criticism, our Mr. Carver."

"He doesn't?"

She lit the joint and exhaled a wisp of piney smoke. "Try it and see."

If I had been less concerned with my map I might have paid Deirdre closer attention. But I was nervous. Now that the map was about to become public it began to seem doomed, chimerical, stupid. I considered forfeiting the prize money and keeping my obsession to myself.

More guests arrived. The group was slightly diminished lately. A few regulars had stopped showing up. There were seven of us present when we took up the Challenge.

Each participant was allotted ten minutes in which to convince the others he or she deserved the prize. Showmanship counted. The contest was graded pointwise and we were scrupulously fair; it benefited no one to deliberately mark down the competition—and we were honorable people, even with fifteen hundred dollars at stake.

I forget who went first. Some ideas were novel, some half-hearted. Ellie Cochrane, one of Chuck Byrnie's students, proposed a sort of techno-divination, reading the future in blank-channel TV noise. Ted Fishbeinder, an Arts Department teaching assistant, did a funny riff on "esthetic precognition," in which, for instance, the Surrealist movement represented a "psychic plagiarism" of contemporary rock videos.

Then it was Michelle's turn.

She used more than her allotted time, but nobody said a word. We were astonished. Myself most of all. Michelle wasn't much of a public speaker, and her part in previous Challenges had always been low-key—but this Challenge was different.

She spoke with a steady, articulate passion, and her eyes were fixed on Carver throughout.

Suppose, she said—and this is the best recollection I can muster—suppose that sentient creatures become their own God. That is, suppose God is human intellect at the end of time, a kind of teleological white hole in which consciousness engulfs the universe that created it. And suppose, furthermore, that the flow of time is not unidirectional. Information may be extracted from the past, or the past recreated in the body of God. Might not our freshly-created supreme being (or beings) reach back into human history and commit miracles?

But take it another step, Michelle said: suppose the teleological gods want to recreate history in miniature, to re-run each consecutive moment of universal history as a sort of goldfish bowl at the end of the universe.

Would we know, if *we* were such a simulation? Probably not...but there might be clues, Michelle said, and she enumerated a few. (Physics, she said, asks us to believe in a discontinuous quantum-level universe that actually makes more sense if interpreted as information—a "digital" universe, hence infinitely simulatable...or already a simulation!)

And there was much more, speculation on teleological entities, the multiple nature of God, wars in heaven—but memory fails.

I do remember John Carver returning her stare, and the silent communication that seemed to pass between them. Mentor and student, I thought. Maybe he'd helped her with this.

When she finished, we all took a deep breath. Chuck Byrnie murmured, "We seem to have a winner." There was scattered applause.

It was a tough act to follow. I let Michelle dash to the kitchen before I screwed up my courage and brought out the map—poor feeble thing it now seemed. A round of drinks, then the crowd gathered. I stumbled through an explanation of paracartography that sounded incoherent even to me, and then I displayed the map—by this time a thickly layered palimpsest of acetate and rainbow-colored acrylic paints and cryptic keys legible only to myself. Nobody reacted visibly to it, but for me the map was a silent reassurance, pleasant to stand next to, like a fire on a cold night. Maybe no one else sensed its power, but I did —I felt the promise of its unfollowed and hidden avenues, the scrolls of spiritual code concealed in its deeps.

The map, I thought, would speak for itself.

Eventually Chuck Byrnie averted his eyes from it. "Enterprising," he said. "More art than map. Still, it's quite wonderful, Jeremy. You should be proud. But why is it empty at the center?"

"Eh?" The question took me by surprise.

"I mean to say, why is it blank in the middle? I can see how it bears a certain relationship to the city, and those arteries or veins, there, might be streets....but it seems odd, to have left such a hole in the middle."

No one objected. Everybody seemed to think this was a reasonable question.

I stared at the map. Squinted at the map. But try as I might, I couldn't see "a hole in the middle." The map was continuous, a single seamless thing.

I felt suddenly queasy. Byrnie waited for an answer, frowning.

"*Terra incognita,*" I said breathlessly. "Here there be tygers, Chuck."

"I see."

I didn't.

Deirdre was the last contestant, and we were all a little tired. Midnight passed. Michelle had brought out the basswood box, and it rested on the coffee table waiting for a winner—but it had ceased to be the centerpiece of the evening.

Chuck Byrnie yawned.

Deirdre wouldn't win the prize, and I think we all knew it. But this wasn't only *pro forma*. *Watch Carver*, she had said. And I did: I watched Carver watch Deirdre. He watched her fiercely. No one else seemed to notice (and I know the obvious is often invisible), but the expression on his face looked like hatred, hatred pure as distilled vitriol. For a moment I had the terrifying feeling that an animal was loose in the room, something subtle and vicious and quick.

Deirdre said, "I think we should reconsider the history of divine intervention."

She looked frail, I thought, for all her twenty or thirty excess pounds, her apparent solidity. Her eyes were bright, nervous. She looked like prey.

Every culture, she said, has a folk tradition of alien visitations. Think of Pan, the *sidhe*, Conan Doyle's fairies, Terence McKenna's "machine elves," or any of the thousands of North American men and women who fervently and passionately believe they've been abducted by almond-eyed space creatures.

It isn't a pretty history, Deirdre said. Look at it dispassionately. Much as we might want to believe in benign or enlightened spirits, what do these creatures do? Kidnap people, rape women, mutilate cattle, substitute changelings for human infants, cast lives into disarray. They mislead; they torture.

If these creatures are not wholly imaginary, Deirdre said, then we should regard them as dangerous. Also sadistic, petty, lascivious, and very powerful. However seductive they might sometimes seem, they're clearly hostile and ought to be resisted in any way possible.

Carver said, "That seems a little glib. What do you suppose these creatures want from us? What's in it for them, Deirdre?"

"I can't imagine. Maybe they're Michelle's 'temporal deities'—half-gods, with the kind of mentality that delights in picking wings off flies. There's a sexual component in most of these stories. Sex and cruelty."

"They sound more human than divine."

"I think we're a playground for them. They inhabit a much larger world—we're an anthill, as far as they're concerned."

"But why the hatred?"

"Even an ant can bite."

"Time's up," Chuck Byrnie said.

"Thank you, Deirdre," John Carver said. "Very insightful. Let's tally the votes."

There's a city inside the city—the city at the center of the map.

I couldn't see the hole in the map because for me there *was* no hole: the gap closed when I looked at it, or else the most important part of the map was invisible to anyone but myself.

And that made sense. What I had failed to understand was that paracartography must necessarily be a private matter. My map isn't your map. The ideal paracartographical map charts not a territory but a mind, or at least it merges the two: the inner inner city.

Michelle took the prize. She seemed less pleased with the money than with John Carver's obvious approval.

Deirdre took me aside as the evening ended. "Jeremy."

"Mm?"

"Are you blind or just stupid?"

"Do I get another choice?"

"I'm serious." She sighed. "There's something in you, Jeremy, something a little lost and obsessive, and he found that—he dug it out of you like digging a stone out of the ground. He used it, and he's still using it. It amuses him to watch us screw around with these scary ideas like little kids playing with blasting caps."

"Deirdre, I don't need a lecture."

"What you need is a wake-up call. Ah, hell, Jeremy.... This is not the kind of news I love to deliver, but it's obvious she's sleeping with him. Please think about it."

I stared at her. Then I said, "Time to leave, Deirdre."

"It matters to me what happens to you guys."

"Just go."

Michelle went wordlessly to bed.

I couldn't sleep.

I sat on the balcony under a duvet, watching the city. At half-past three, the peak (or valley) of the night, I thought I saw the city itself in all its luminous grids begin subtly to shift—to move, somehow, without moving; to part and make a passage where none had been.

I closed my aching eyes and went inside. The map was waiting.

My department head suggested a sabbatical. She also suggested I consult a mental-health specialist. I took the time off, gratefully. It was convenient to be able to sleep during the day.

There is a city inside the city, but the road there is tortuous and strange.

I glimpsed that city for the first time in December, late on a cold night.

I was tired. I'd come a long way. The lost city was not, at first sight, distinctly different. It possessed, if anything, a haunting familiarity, and only gradually did I wake to its strangeness and charm.

I found myself on an empty street of two or three-story brick buildings. The buildings looked as if they might have been built at the turn of the last century, though the cap stones had no dates. The brick was gray and ancient, the upper-story windows shuttered and dark. Remnants of Depression-era advertising clung to the walls like scabs.

The storefronts weren't barred, though cracks laced the window glass. The goods dimly visible behind the panes were generic, neglected, carelessly heaped together: pyramids of patent leather shoes or racks of paperback books in various languages. The businesses were marginal—tobacco shops, junk shops, shops that sold back-issue magazines or canned food without labels. Their tattered awnings rattled in the wind.

It sounds dreary, but it wasn't, at least not in my eyes; it was a small magic, this inexplicable neighborhood glazed with December moonlight, chill and perfect as a black pearl. It should not have existed. *Didn't* exist. I couldn't place it in any customary part of the city nor could I discern any obvious landmarks (the CN Tower, the bank buildings). Streets here parted and met again like the meanders of a slow river, and the horizon was perpetually hidden.

The only light brighter than the winter moon came from an all-hours coffee shop at a corner bereft of street signs. The air inside was moist but still cold. Two men in dowdy overcoats sat huddled over a faded formica tabletop. Behind the cash counter, a middle-aged woman in a hairnet looked at me blankly.

"Coffee," I said, and she poured a cup, and I took it. It didn't occur to me to pay, and she didn't ask.

Things work differently at the heart of the heart of the city.

And yet it was familiar. It ached with memory. I'd been here before, I knew, at some time outside the discourse of history.

I took my notebook from my jacket pocket. Maybe this was where I had invented my ideoglyphs, or where the invisible city had generated them, somehow, itself. I flipped open the notepad and was only mildly surprised to find the words suddenly, crisply legible. This did not astonish me—I was past that—but I read the contents with close attention.

Every page was a love letter. Concise, nostalgic, sad, sincere, my own. And every page was addressed to Michelle.

Finding my way home was difficult. The hidden city encloses itself. There are no parallel lines in the hidden city. Streets cross themselves at false intersections. There are, I think, many identical streets, the peeling Edwardian townhouses and bare maples deceptively iterated, unnavigable. I don't know how long it took to find my way back, nor could I say just where the border lay or when I passed it, but by dawn I found myself on a pedestrian bridge where the railway tracks run south from Dundas, among the wind-haunted warehouses and empty coal-dust factories of the city as it should be.

I checked my pocket, but the notebook was gone.

Most of the universe is invisible—invisible in the sense of unseen, unexperienced. The deserts of Mars, the barrens of Mercury, the surfaces of a million unnamed planets, places where time passes, where a rock might tumble from a cliffside or a glacier calve into a lifeless sea, invisibly. Did you walk to work today, or take a walk after dinner?

Every day things become or remain invisible: the mailbox you passed (where is it exactly?), the crack in the sidewalk, the sign in the window, this morning's breakfast.

I think I didn't see Michelle. I think I hadn't seen her for a long time.

Have I described her? I would, but I can't. What memory loses is rendered invisible; it merges into the seas and deserts of the unseen universe.

I'm writing this for her. For you.

Michelle wasn't home when I looked for her. That might have been normal or it might not. I had lost track of the days of the week. I went to look for her at Deirdre's store.

Winter now, skies like blue lead, a brisk and painful wind. The wind ran in fitful rivers down Bay Street and lifted scrap newspapers high above gold-mirrored windows.

The store was closed, but I saw Deirdre moving in the dim space inside. She unlocked the door when I tapped.

"You look—" she said.

"Like shit. I know. You don't look too good yourself, Deirdre."

She looked, in fact, frightened and sleepless.

"I think he's after me, Jeremy."

"Who, Carver?"

"Of course Carver."

She pulled me inside and closed the door. Wind rattled the glass. The herbal reek of the store was overpowering.

Deirdre unfolded a director's chair for me, and we sat in the prism light of her window crystals. "I followed him," she said.

"You did what?"

"Does that surprise you? Of course I followed him. I thought it was about time we knew something about John Carver, since he seems to know more than enough about us. Did he ever tell *you* where he lives?"

"He must have."

"You remember what he said?"

"No..."

"No one remembers. Or else it didn't occur to them ask. Don't you find that a little odd?"

"Maybe a little."

"Turns out he lives in the Beaches, out near the water-treatment plant. Here, I'll write down the address for you."

"That's not necessary."

"The fuck it's not necessary. Information about John Carver has this interesting way of disappearing."

"I came here to ask you about Michelle."

"I know."

She scrawled the address on the back of a register receipt. "And Jeremy, one more thing."

"What?"

"Be careful of him. He's not human."

Don't be ridiculous, I began to say, but the words stuck. In the realm of what was possible and what was not, I seemed to have lost all compass. "Do you really believe that?"

"I've spent a lot of time reading the strange books, Jeremy, and talking to the strange people. It's hard to believe in hidden information in the information age, but there are still some mysteries that haven't made the Internet. Trust me on this."

"What should I do?"

She looked away, ashamed of her impotence. "I don't know."

Long story short: I went home, Michelle hadn't shown up, nor did she come home that night.

I didn't sleep. I watched TV, and when that was finished I watched the minute hand sweep around the face of Michelle's bedroom clock. Michelle didn't believe in digital clocks—hated them. The only digital clock in the apartment was the one on my wrist. She believed in the tick and sweep of old-fashioned time.

I fell asleep at dawn and woke to find the daylight already fading, snow on the windowsill, snow falling in sheets and ribbons over the city. No Michelle.

I tried phoning Deirdre. There was no answer at the store or at her home number.

Then I remembered the address she had scrawled for me—John Carver's address.

I was in my jacket and headed for the door when the phone rang.

"Jeremy?"

Deirdre, and she sounded breathless. "Where are you?"

"Doesn't matter. Jeremy, don't try to get hold of me after this."

"Why not?"

"They busted my garden! Raided the store, too—on principle, I guess."

"The police?"

"It wasn't the fucking Girl Guides!"

"You're in custody?"

"Hell no. I was having lunch with Chuck Byrnie when it happened. Kathy managed to warn me off." She paused. "I guess I'm a wanted criminal. I don't know what they do to you for growing grass anymore. Jail or a fine or what. But they trashed my house, Jeremy, and my place of business, and I can't afford legal fees." She sounded near tears.

"You can stay here," I said.

"No, I can't. The thing is, only half a dozen people knew about the garden. Somebody must have tipped the police."

"I swear I never—"

"Not you, asshole!"

"Carver?"

"I never told him about the plants. Somebody else must have."

The wind scoured grains of snow against the balcony door, a sandpaper sound.

"You're saying Michelle—"

"I'm not pissed at Michelle. It comes down to John Carver, and that's why I called. He means business, and he isn't pleased with me— or you."

"You can't be sure of that."

"I can't be sure of anything. I think he's been manipulating us from the word go."

"Deirdre—"

"My advice? Throw that fucking map away. And good luck, Jeremy."

"How can I reach you?"
"You can't. But thanks."

Time passes differently in the secret city. Day follows night, sunlight sweeps the sundial streets, seasons pass, but the past eats itself and the future is the present, only less so. We pace the sidewalks, we few citizens of this underpopulated city, empty of appetite, wordless, but how many others are keeping secret diaries? Or keeping the same diary endlessly reiterated, all stories worn smooth with the telling.

I took a last look at the map. The map was mounted on a pressboard frame leaning against the wall of my study.

The map was sleek, seductive, inexpressibly beautiful, but I didn't need it anymore. It had never been more than a tool. I didn't need the map because I contained it—I *was* the map, in some sense; and it would be dangerous, I thought, to leave so potent a self-portrait where strangers might find it.

So I destroyed it. I carved it into pieces, like a penitent debtor destroying a credit card, and then I pushed the pieces down the garbage chute.

Then I went to look for Michelle.

What Michelle hadn't said, what Michelle hadn't guessed and Deirdre hadn't figured out, was that a temporal deity, even a minor and malevolent one, must have *all* the maps, all the ordinary and the hidden maps, all the blueprints and bibles and Baedekers of all the places there are or might be or have ever been.

I took the Queen car east. The scrap of paper on which Deirdre had written Carver's address was in my pocket—more out than in, really, since I felt compelled to check it and check it again as the streetcar stuttered past the race track, the waterworks. The numbers were elusive.

The address was well off the transit routes. What I found when I approached on foot was an ordinary Beaches neighborhood, snow-silent and still. The houses were fashionable restored freeholds above the frozen lakeshore, a few lights still burning in second and third story bedroom windows. Carver's was no different. I wondered whether he owned it or rented, whether money had ever been a problem for him. I doubted it.

And now what: should I knock on the door and demand to see Michelle? What if she wasn't there—what if Deirdre and I had drawn all the wrong conclusions? I stood in the snow and felt useless and foolish.

Then—I presume not coincidentally—Carver's door opened, and I stepped behind a snowbound hedge as he came smiling into the night.

Michelle was on his arm.

She wore her navy winter coat with the collar turned up. She looked cold and bewildered, both very young and very old. Carver wore jeans and a flannel shirt, and the snow seemed not to touch him.

I blinked—and they were at the end of the block. I called Michelle's name. She didn't look back—only inclined her head, as if an errant thought had troubled her.

There was nothing to do but follow them.

He turned corners I had never seen before. Narrow alleys, a corridor of trees in an empty park, a wood-paved ravine walk dense with swirling snow.

I ran, they strolled, but the gap between us widened until Michelle was a distant figure, vague among the snow-spirals, and Carver—

Carver, I believe, began to grow translucent, not-quite-invisible, became a gap in the falling snow that might have been a human shape or something taller, more agile, sleek, potent, pleased.

At last he turned and looked directly at me. I felt but couldn't see his smile. His eyes, even at this distance, remained distinct: yellow, vulpine.

He smiled, folded his arm around Michelle as if claiming a trophy, and turned a corner I have never been able to find. I suppose it had been a sort of contest all along—the ultimate Challenge.

That was the last I saw of her.

The invisible city seals its exits. Enter once and walk away. Enter twice and the way back to the world is more elusive.

Enter a third time—

I walked for hours—it might have been days—but every road turned back to the elliptical streets and jigsaw alleys of the hidden city.

Only a few of us live in the secret city, and we seldom speak. Things work differently here. It is, I think, a sort of mirror world, an empty and imperfect shell of a city, sparsely colonized.

Its shabbily furnished upper rooms are mainly empty. I live in one now. I sleep on its crude spring mattress and I gaze through its grime-crusted windows and I breathe its dry and dust-heavy air. I eat what I find in unattended stores—canned food without labels. The stock is periodically replenished. I don't know how.

Something in the hidden city inhibits curiosity, and memory...memory fades into the air like morning fog.

I write to remember. I write in these lined tablets of cheap pulp paper manufactured in Taiwan or Indonesia, places incomprehensibly far away.

I think I'm not the only one. I think there are others scribing their thin and thinning memoirs, diary entries that grow more stark with each passing day, letters to lovers whose names we have forgotten.

Spring now. The wind is cold, wet, cutting.

I do not despair of finding a way home. Just yesterday I thought I saw Deirdre wandering the precincts—looking for me, perhaps; but if she's found the hidden city, she needs to be warned.

I called her name, but she vanished.

If you find this, will you warn her?

And if you know Michelle, if you see Michelle, please give her these pages.

I mail the pages from my window. I mail them on the wind. As yesterday. As the day before. On a good day the wind carries the yellow leaves of paper up above the stone capitals and pebbled roofs, above the tarpaper and the wind vanes and the chimneys of the hidden city, and I hope and believe that for the wind there are no borders; the wind, I think, is utterly invisible and utterly free.

RED MISCHIEF

by
Michael Rowe

Michael Rowe's first published horror story ("Wild Things Live There," *Northern Frights 3*) was optioned for the movies and selected for Honorable Mention in *The Year's Best Fantasy and Horror*. He has since made his debut as an editor with *Sons of Darkness*, an anthology of vampire stories co-edited with Thomas S. Roche, as well as a sequel, *Brothers of the Night*. His first novel, *Darkling I Listen*, a ghost story, is slated for publication from Richard Kasak Books.

"**Y**ou got the canteen?" Tyler called over his shoulder to Mitch, whose pack felt twice as heavy as when he'd slipped it on this morning. His t-shirt was soaked. A wave of heat rolled out at them as they left the green patch of woods and stepped into the shattering sunlight refracted on the rockface. Mitch squinted behind his Revo sunglasses. Behind them, the cliffs and chasms of Glen Eden rose up to meet the cerulean sky like great shoulders of granite. Below them, shimmering in the August heat, lay the town of Milton. The surrounding Halton Region farmland spread out like a patchwork quilt of green and brown. A hawk circled lazily in the air above them, so close that Mitch felt that he could reach out and touch it.

"I got the canteen," he puffed. "But I think it's empty. You drank it all. I think there's some Tab, though. You want it?"

"No, I don't goddamn-well want warm *Tab*!" spat Tyler. "And I *didn't* drink all the water. It was half full last time I checked. You musta drank it all. You're a hog, Mitch."

Tyler wiped his face with a grimy red bandanna and sat down heavily. He removed his pack. Mitch, who outweighed him by thirty pounds, followed suit. Mitch was seventeen, Tyler would be nineteen on Christmas Day. *Little Baby Jesus*, his sister Elsa called him, and never nicely.

Mitch and Tyler were best friends, and had been best friends since the first day of classes at E.C. Drury highschool, going on five years now. They were graduating in September, and they dearly wished they knew what the hell they were going to do with the rest of their lives.

One thing was certain, though—they would be doing it together. Mitch wanted to go travelling in Europe for a year together. Tyler wasn't sure about Europe—he thought maybe Australia instead. Together they argued the merits of each destination, but these discussions left them with the warm feeling of being in the adventure together. Tyler's father had left when Tyler was six, and Mitch's parents had all but adopted him. In return, Tyler, two years older than Mitch, had become something of a big brother figure. At school, anything that any bully had to say to Mitch they could say to Tyler first. Where Mitch was slow on his feet, Tyler was fast with his fists. They had navigated the treacherous waters of adolescence as an inseperable team of two. Both spent summers working at Don Cherry's in the kitchen—Mitch as a prep-cook, Tyler as a waiter. One hot summer night two years ago they had named themselves brothers, and swore it would be forever.

The hikes to Glen Eden were a celebration, an affirmation of their bond. They occurred once every season: spring, summer, fall, winter. No girlfriends were allowed. It was strictly Mitch-and-Tyler, and both of them knew it would never be any other way.

"Christ, it's hot," Mitch whined. "Why did we go climbing today of all days? We coulda stayed inside, or gone swimming at my house. This was your idea, not mine."

Tyler grunted. He'd learned long ago that Mitch was a bit of a puss, and when he got to whining like he was right now, ignoring him was best. And besides, Tyler had already said he would die of thirst unless he got some water right away. They had hiked from the townhouse development on Childs Drive where Mitch lived, past the Milton Mall, into the centre of town, down Martin Street, past the boarded-up red house where old lady Winfield had lived until she disappeared in 1971, straight up Steeles, then followed the country roads until they reached Glen Eden. Mitch and Tyler had been making this hike for years, and in every season, but Tyler would be goddamned if he could remember a day as hot as this one had turned out to be. Though already late afternoon, the heat was fierce. He felt light-headed, not the greatest thing to be while navigating the treacherous ledges of the escarpment.

"Let's go," Tyler said. "I don't feel so good." He rose unsteadily to his feet and shouldered his backpack.

"You'll feel better when we're in the pool," Mitch said, relieved that they were heading back. He scrambled after Tyler. They trudged down the path together in the direction of town. The trees offered them little shade, but Mitch was grateful for what there was.

Turning a bend in the trail, he saw the stream. It coursed along the opposite rockface like a river of liquid silver, throwing rainbows and spray where it crashed against the pebbles.

"Water!" screamed Tyler jubilantly. "Water! I'm not going to die of the heat after all!" He shrugged off his pack and skirted the edge of the rockface until he was at the edge of the water. He flung himself on his belly and plunged both hands into the water. He brought them to his face and began to rinse the dirt and sweat from his face. "Mitch, c'merc! This is totally great! The water is freezing!"

"I dunno." Mitch looked doubtfully at the stream. "You don't know what it is."

"It's *water*, doofus! The whole *town* is fed by streams like this. Maybe the rain made it happen this summer or something. Oh, God," he moaned, scooping up a handful of the water. He drank deeply. "This tastes so good! Mitch, come here and taste this water. It's so cold!" Mitch shivered. "I've never seen that stream before, and we've come up here a coupla hundred times. Plus, it smells funny around here. Don't you smell it, Ty?"

"No, I do not smell 'it' Mitch. Whatever you mean by 'it'." He giggled. "There're flowers over there on the path. Those yellow ones. It's probably wild garlic or something. What's your damage, anyway? Aren't you burning up?" Tyler stripped off his shirt and rolled in the stream, splashing his arms and neck. He closed his eyes, shrieking in ecstasy.

"Quit screaming," Mitch said sourly. "Those Brownies we passed will think there's been an accident. Come on, let's go. I don't like this place!"

"It's an artesian stream or something, Mitchell," Tyler said patiently. "We've read about them in school. It tastes amazing, just like water ought to taste on the *day* from *hell*, and I now feel like I'm going to survive the walk home." Tyler stood up and blotted himself dry with his t-shirt. He looked sideways at his friend. "You ought to live a little, Mitch. You sound like an old woman sometimes."

"Well, you say 'old woman' now," Mitch said grimly, "but you just wait till you die of poisoning or something, then we'll see who's laughing."

"If I die of poisoning you'll be *laughing*?" Tyler shot Mitch a look of mock-heartbreak. Mitch was bent over the yellow flowers. "*Now* what're you doin'?" Tyler snapped. "First you bitch about hangin' around, and now you're pickin' flowers. You makin' a *bouquet* or somethin'?"

"Hah, hah, very funny," Mitch grunted. "Everything's a laugh-riot with you, Tyler. No, I am *not* making a bouquet, I am picking one of these stinkweed plants in case you die after drinking that water, so we know what killed you." He shoved the yellow flower into his pocket.

"Thanks ever so much, Mitchell," Tyler said gravely. "Jeez, I knew that there was a reason I've been putting up with you all of these years. Maybe I should just *marry* you this fall."

"*Fag alert!*" Mitch howled, and they both burst out laughing at the same time. Perspiring furiously in the torpid summer heat, Tyler chased Mitch down the hill and past the gates of Glen Eden, where a bored and sweaty Parks and Recreation Authority officer barely glanced up to see them race past his booth.

The two boys trudged down the path till they hit Steeles Avenue. Mercifully the air cooled as they approached the town. They walked slowly down Martin Street through the cathedral of green light filtering down from the tall trees which flanked the street like ancient sentries, savouring the summer-warm scent of roses and freshly cut grass. Although Mitch had lived in Milton all of his life, the beauty of the town in moments like this always, somehow, stunned him with the clarity of it's perfection. Mitch's thoughts drifted as he and Tyler walked in companionable silence. He didn't hear the taxi pull up slowly behind them until Tyler elbowed him in the side.

"Uh-oh," Tyler said. "Something wicked this way comes."

"What?" Mitch looked up from the pavement and turned to Tyler.

"The taxi," Tyler replied tensely. "Behind us. Don't look now, but it's Wild Angus. He's been following us for awhile, I think."

"How do you know it's him?"

"Shut *up* Mitch," Tyler said in a fierce whisper. "Keep walking, and don't look at him."

The navy-blue Borealis Cab Company taxi had been following behind them at a discreet distance. It gradually increased it's speed until it was keeping pace with Tyler and Mitch. The driver was hunched over the steering wheel. Mitch saw thick black hair, tied back in a ponytail, and large, powerful hands. Slowly the driver raised his head and turned towards the two boys. Wild Angus was rumoured to have been an outlaw biker before he moved to Milton. If Mitch, who never placed much faith in small-town gossip, ever once doubted the veracity of that particular rumour, he didn't doubt it at that moment.

Wild Angus stared at Tyler for a full minute. Then slowly, he began to grin.

There was nothing pleasant there, or warm. It was a vulpine smile, hungry and curiously inquisitive, as though Wild Angus was scenting the air like an animal marking territory. Through the heavy beard and moustache, Mitch glimpsed strong white teeth set in an oddly-fixed cruel-looking mouth. In the gold-flecked dark brown eyes that looked past him, boring into Tyler, Mitch sensed savagery. And he knew, with a momentary terror so perfectly exquisite that it felt like joy, that the only thing separating him and Wild Angus at that moment was the steel and glass of the taxicab.

The car inched closer to the sidewalk. Mitch shuddered and looked back down at the pavement. He heard Tyler make a sound like air being let out of a balloon, and then the taxicab swept past them and turned right on Main Street, disappearing from view.

"Sweet Jesus," Tyler whispered.

"What the hell was that all about? Why did he stare at you that way?"

"How should I know?" Tyler said weakly. "I don't even know the guy. Christ, I want to go home. I think I just about pissed my pants there. Jesus Christ, what a freak."

"Look," Mitch said tightly, "let's just get up to the mall, OK? It'll be all right when we're around people. He just spooked us there. It didn't mean nothing."

They crossed Main Street and hiked back up towards the Milton Mall on Ontario Street. They entered the mall through the Shopper's Drug Mart doors. They stopped at Pam's coffee shop for a Coke. The cool air of the mall made Mitch feel a little sick, coming at him so soon after being outside. He looked up to tell Tyler how he felt, but stopped. Tyler's face was ashen, and beads of sweat dotted his forehead and upper lip. For once, Mitch felt less inclined to complain about his own well being.

"Hey, man," Mitch said. "You OK?" He reached towards his friend Tyler, who flinched slightly, and backed away. "Hello?"

"I'm OK, I'm OK," Tyler gasped. "It's just the heat. Man, I feel like shit all of a sudden. Everything got all woozy there for a second."

"It's that water you drank," Mitch said darkly. "What an afternoon this is turning out to be. Freaks in the street, poisoned water in the forest."

"Let's leave the fuckin' water alone, OK?" Tyler snapped. Some color had returned to his cheeks, though he still looked pale to Mitch. "I just want to go home and lie down for awhile. I'll call you later." Tyler rose unsteadily to his feet and shouldered his pack. He turned and headed towards the glass doors of the mall. Mitch stared after him, open-mouthed.

"How're you going to get home? You want a lift?"

"Nah, I'll be OK."

"Hey!" Mitch called out, but Tyler had already stumbled through the mall's swinging doors into the late afternoon sunlight.

And then Mitch caught a whiff of something bitter in Tyler's wake. The air had moved, and Mitch had smelled something that momentarily disoriented him, something wild, like berries gone bad, like moss on the inside of caves that never saw sunlight.

"Dad," Mitch began, "do you know anything about that guy who just started to drive for Borealis?"

"Who?" Mitch's father, Frank, dabbed the corner of his mouth with a paper napkin. "What are you going on about, Mitchell?"

"They call him Wild Angus," Mitch explained. "Looks like a biker? They say he used to be some kind of Hell's Angel or something. Somebody said he lives in a rundown farmhouse in Campbelville. They say he sells drugs."

"Well," said Mitch's father. "*They* certainly have this poor man all figured out, don't *they*?" He appraised Mitch coolly over the top of his horn-rimmed glasses. "If *they* had half the sense that God gave a jackass, *they'd* read a book every once in awhile instead of spreading all of these rumors, and maybe the library in this town would be open on Mondays and the hairdressers would be closed." Frank paused for a moment, then pursed his lips disapprovingly. "Of course, if he were all of those things, he couldn't be working for a more appropriate firm. The Borealis taxicab company has been rumored to employ persons of dubious-enough backgrounds. I remember when there was only one cab company in this town, and we all knew who the drivers were. These Borealis people just showed up, bold as brass, and helped themselves to half the town's taxi business." Frank shook his head slightly, then remembered himself. He cleared his throat. "What have your mother and I told you about coming in here with gossip?"

"I'm not gossiping," Mitch protested, "I'm asking." He turned to his mother who was washing the dishes. "Mom? Do you know anything about him?"

"My, it's pretty out there tonight," sighed Flora-Jean, Mitch's mother. She stood at the kitchen sink staring out the window into the back yard. "I do dearly love a full moon in the summer. Look at it, like a big ball of orange fire in the sky. And the sky looks almost purple tonight, doesn't it?" She sighed again, and smoothed her hair. "It's a lover's moon, and that's the plain truth of it." She absentmindedly half-turned to Mitch and said, "Who were you asking about, sweetie?"

Mitch looked up from the table, where he had been removing the carrot and celery shavings from the quivering blob of green Jello on his plate with a surgeon's precision. Beneath the Jello were the faces of Charles and Diana. His mother had won a commemorative set of dessert plates at the Bingo, the year the star-crossed Prince and Princess of Wales announced their engagement. Mitch, who hated Jello, blindfolded Diana with a strip of carrot.

"Never mind, Mom. It isn't important."

Frank, reached up and switched off the overhead fluorescent. The full moon flooded the kitchen with blood-orange light.

"I'll say it isn't," said Frank as he walked up behind Flora-Jean and put his hands on her ample hips. He leaned into her and nuzzled her beige perm. "Grrrr. It's a wolf moon. How'd you like to go for a walk in the forest, Little Red Riding Hood?"

Flora-Jean giggled and swatted him away. Frank growled louder.

"Go away now, shoo!" Flora-Jean said creamily. "The *mischief* men get up to when the moon is full! You're such a *monster* sometimes." Frank whispered something in her ear, and she shrieked with laughter. Frank made loud smacking noises. "A girl is hardly safe," Flora-Jean whispered coyly, batting her eyelashes.

"Gross," Mitch muttered. Then louder, he announced, "I'm still a *kid*, you know. You guys are gonna warp me or something with that stuff. You two are, like, forty years old. That's too old to be carrying on like that."

"Don't you have homework, son?" Frank asked, without turning around. His face was still buried in Flora-Jean's hair.

"It's July, Dad. Of course I don't have homework."

His parents continued to nuzzle each other, and giggle.

"May I please be excused? I'm gonna drive over and see how Tyler's doing."

"Sure you may be excused, sweetie. Your father and I are going to go upstairs and watch a little telly. We'll be down later."

"Much later," Frank growled.

"Oh, *la lune*!" sighed Flora-Jean. "It's like that movie, with Cher." She giggled again. "Now Frank, *stop it!*"

"Don't wait up, son" Frank panted, grinding his hips into his wife's behind. Flora-Jean screamed with laughter. His parents must be going through some sicko mid-life thing, Mitch thought disgustedly as he walked through the darkened living room.

Mitch opened the door and stepped outside. The August heat enfolded him. The full moon overhead was dull orange, shrouded in dense black clouds. The familiar front yards and townhouses of Childs Drive were etched tonight in a weird twilight of amber phosphorous. In the streetlamps, bats wheeled and flirted. To his right, in the distance, Mitch saw the neon glow of the all-night lights from the Milton Mall. It would be empty now, except for the security people. *Graveyard shift*, Mitch thought for no good reason at all, and he shivered. He walked quickly down the street to where his Mustang convertible was parked. Mitch unlocked the car and climbed behind the wheel. He turned the key in the ignition, and started the motor. He backed out of the cul-de-sac where he'd parked, and began to drive. The fields were an ocean of dark earth on either side of the car as Mitch sped past houses and barns, the night wind keening through the open window.

After driving for fifteen minutes, Mitch turned left on the dirt road, then left again into Tyler's driveway. Mist from the fields bordering the house danced in the Mustang's headlights, making tunnels of light and fog. Mitch swung the car round, and pulled in front of the garage.

A sudden flurry of motion just outside his peripheral line of sight caused Mitch to swivel around. For a moment, he could have sworn he'd something—a bear? A man?—stumbling past the headlights of the Mustang, into the darkness of the woods behind the house. He stared harder, willing himself to see in the dark. And there had been something else, too. His subconscious had registered it immediately.

Something red in the headlights, Mitch thought, *like...eyes*? Maybe a deer, or a racoon. *Standing upright? You're still spooked, Mitch old boy.*

"Anybody home?" Mitch shouted. The wind rustled through the trees above his head. The kitchen light was on in the house, but there was no answering bellow from Tyler. He knocked on the door. He waited. And then he tried the door handle.

"Hello?" It came out as a whisper. "Ty? Is anybody here?"

The door swung inward. Mitch stepped into the darkness of the hallway. He took a step forward. The darkness surged forward greedily to meet him. The lamp in the kitchen down the hallway provided a little light, enough to make out the dining room table propped up against the wall. No, not propped. It looked as though it had been tossed against the wall.

Tossed? You can't toss a table, doofus.

Mitch stared stupidly through the dining room doors. He groped for the light fixture behind him, and flicked the switch.

The dining room suite had been smashed to pieces, as though someone had taken an axe to it for firewood. The white-flocked walls of the dining were spattered with blood. The curtains had been shredded like tissue paper. What looked like holiday garlands, but upon closer inspection proved to be entrails, were looped festively along the window sills. The doors and walls had been clawed apart.

Mitch numbly surveyed the dining room, aware that any second now, the horror of what he was seeing would probably drive him mad, and then the monsters would get him.

A bundle of bloody rags in the kitchen doorway. No, not rags. A roast? No, a roast would be cooked brown. *Raw meat on the dining room floor?* He walked slowly across the room. The audible grinding of the smashed dinner plates beneath his feet carved the sound of his tentative progress into the gloom. Mitch looked down.

It was Tyler's mother's head. He recognized the gold and enamel earrings Tyler had bought her at Christmas. Her face had been savaged. Flaps of skin hung in tatters along her jaw as though she had been peeled. There were teeth marks on her forehead. Her remaining eye, torn from it's socket, lay against her cheek.

Mitch backed away, stumbling over furniture, and then he tripped over something else. Flailing to keep himself from falling, his hands found something warm and wet.

It was the rest of Mrs. Ross, and part of Tyler's sister Elsa. The bodies had been gutted from abdomen to throat.

When the smell hit him, Mitch began to heave. He emptied his stomach in the hallway, and as he wiped his mouth, he heard a scratching at the back door. Something whined, like a large friendly dog looking for a way inside. And then the whining became a deep growl, far deeper than any dog Mitch had ever heard, and no longer at all friendly. The door shivered in it's frame as a series of impossibly powerful blows came from the other side. Mitch heard a crack as the door began to splinter. The growls became excited squeals as the blows redoubled in force.

Blindly, Mitch turned and ran down the hallway. He slipped in a pool of congealed blood and crashed to the floor. A bolt of pain shot up his leg. Mitch scrambled to his feet and limped towards the front door, gritting his teeth to keep from crying out in pain. He reached for the handle of the front door, and twisted it. The night wind blew a flurry of leaves into the hallway from the yard.

The dark shape stood motionless on the front steps, framed by the yellow moonlight. When it reached for him, Mitch screamed to wake the dead.

"Mitch," Tyler said. "What are you doing here?"

"Get out! Get out! Come on! Your family's dead, and some-thing's trying to get in the back door! Run, Tyler! Run!"

Mitch stumbled toward the Mustang, fishing in his pocket for the keys. He turned and looked over his shoulder. Tyler was still standing on the front steps.

"Come on, Tyler!" he screamed. "We've got to get help! Don't just fucking stand there, run!"

"Mitch," Tyler said calmly. "Come back here. It's all right. Nothing's wrong. Just come back here."

Mitch stared. As Tyler loped towards him, Mitch saw that he was naked. His chest and arms were clotted with dried blood. Mitch began to shiver uncontrollably. Tyler smiled and stretched out his arms.

"*You?*" Mitch whispered with dawning horror. "You did this? You killed your mother and your sister?"

"No," Tyler said definitely. "I didn't do this. At least I don't think I did. I was just sitting at the table having supper, minding my own business. I don't remember anything after that. Except," Tyler smiled dreamily, "that it was night. I just woke up walking around outside." Tyler shook himself happily. "I feel great! In fact, I feel better than I ever have."

"Oh Tyler," Mitch sobbed. "Oh man, Tyler. What have you done here?"

"Look at your car, Mitch," Tyler giggled. He pointed at the Mustang.

Mitch turned to look. An enormous black wolf was lying on the roof of the car, it's paws crossed contentedly. The wolf seemed to be grinning. It's red eyes sparkled in the moonlight. A second massive wolf, shaggy and grey-furred, sat on it's haunches as though guarding the driver's side door. Mitch flinched, and took a step backwards. The wolf growled low in it's throat. Mitch looked back at Tyler. Two more wolves padded silently around the back of the house. Several more crept out of the woods bordering the driveway.

As Mitch watched fascinated, the first two wolves raised themselves smoothly to a standing position and shambled towards Tyler, walking on two legs. Tyler squatted on his haunches, studying Mitch. He reached out his hand and caressed the two wolves reverently.

"Does any of this make sense to you, Mitchell?" Tyler asked curiously. "It's all sort of come to me all at once, but then I'm *in it*, you know what I mean? I'm there. It's *about* me."

"Let me go," Mitch begged. "Please..."

"You still don't understand, Mitch, do you? You're my best friend, and I want you to understand everything. Look at this," he said, glancing up at the black-furred wolf lying on the roof of the car. "Watch, now."

The wolf stood up in one smooth fluid motion, leapt to the ground and began to change. The dark fur appeared to pull inward, vanishing below the skin. The wolf's limbs twisted and elongated, becoming powerful arms and legs. The man's white skin glowed eldritch blue in the moonlight, and he stood up. It was Wild Angus. His black eyes glittered like chips of ice. The wind ruffled his wild black hair and beard.

"He tells me I can do that too," Tyler said with a trace of awe. "He tells me I already *have* done it. He says that's what happened tonight at the dinner table. My first change. My first full moon. He tells me that's why my family is dead." Tears streamed from Tyler's eyes. "He says the first thing to go is the guilt."

"Tyler..."

"He says it's a miracle, me finding the stream and drinking from it," Tyler babbled, ignoring Mitch. "He says those yellow flowers we found are called wolfsbane. He says that's how you know that the stream is special. Especially for me, because he says that people who are born on Christmas Day sometimes have what it takes to change."

"Little Baby Jesus," Mitch breathed.

"Yeah. Poor Elsa," Tyler said, wiping away the tears with his bloody fingers. "But yeah, that's pretty much it."

"You realize," Wild Angus growled, "that he can't be allowed to live. I'll have to kill him, or you can. It's all the same to me, and to the others. We're your family now, and you have a duty to us."

"He's my best friend," Tyler said defiantly. "He won't do anything." He turned to Mitch. "Will you?" Mitch shook his head furiously. "I didn't think so. You know, it's so weird...I can smell stuff now. Not *smell* like in smelling perfume or nothing. I mean *smell* as in,

I know things now just by knowing them. I know you're not going to tell. Right?"

"He's going to die!" Wild Angus rasped, taking a step towards Mitch "He's seen to much here tonight. You have a duty to *us* now."

"Give me a break!" Tyler laughed in Wild Angus' face. "Who's going to believe in a pack of werewolves in Milton even if he *did* tell, which he wouldn't? Especially a pack of werewolves running a *cab* company?" He turned to Mitch and winked conspiratorially. "That's why they named it 'Borealis.' You know, like 'Aurora Borealis'? Lights in the northern sky? It's their little joke. Funny, huh? The stories are all true, too. They all used to be bikers."

Wild Angus leapt at Tyler and slapped him brutally across the face. The force of the blow knocked Tyler across the yard. Wild Angus stalked across the driveway and seized Tyler roughly by the arm. "You'll learn to take this seriously boy, or I'll kill you. Then I'll kill this fatboy friend of yours."

Tyler rose slowly and brushed himself off. Then he began to change.

Soft silver fur flowed across his body. His face shifted and melted, becoming long and bestial. His eyes glittered, and he pulled back blackened lips exposing strong white teeth grown long and sharp. He sank to his knees and stretched his arms out in front of him. As Mitch watched, the arms became forelegs, claws like human fingers scraping the soft ground.

Fully transformed, the werewolf turned it's flaming eyes to Mitch. All around him, the wolves began to howl. He looked at Wild Angus, who stood with his arms folded. His face was impassive, but a small, cold smile turned the edges of his mouth upward.

Mitch looked back at the creature that had been his best friend. For a second, Mitch could have sworn he saw a flicker of Tyler in the werewolf's eyes. It made a soft growling sound in the back of it's throat that sounded to Mitch like the word *run*, and then Mitch was looking into the eyes of an animal, from which all traces of humanity had vanished. The growl became a vicious snarl. Mitch closed his eyes, praying for a quick death. And then the werewolf sprang.

The scream of pain and rage caused Mitch to open his eyes, and he stared in disbelief at what he saw. Wild Angus had clearly been taken by surprise, but only just. Older and stronger, Wild Angus recovered his advantage. As Mitch watched, a shadow passed across Wild Angus' body as he effortlessly effected his own change. The black wolf with the blazing red eyes leapt at the smaller yellow-eyed one, clamping his jaws firmly about the silver wolf's throat.

Mitch ran for the door of the Mustang. The howling of the wolves had become deafening. He managed to climb in and slam the door shut just as the first of the werewolf pack charged the small car, jaws snapping on empty air. Mitch jammed the key in the ignition and turned it. The engine stuttered but refused to turn over.

"Come on, come on!" Mitch screamed, banging the dashboard. He heard the thudding of heavy paws on the roof of the Mustang as the werewolves attacked the car. His view through the windshield was obscured as the creatures clambered across the hood and began to hurl themselves at the doors and windows, trying to batter their way inside. He heard a ripping sound and looked up in time to see the razor sharp claws slice through the soft roof. He screamed as one of the werewolves pulled aside the torn flap of the roof an leaned in, green eyes glittering. The jaws opened wide, and Mitch smelled fresh meat and blood on the creature's breath. The howling had become screams of rage and frustration, and he was sure he heard human words in among the bestial snarls of fury. He turned the key in the ignition again.

The engine roared to life. Tyler put the car in reverse and backed up, turning the Mustang around. The abrupt motion of the car knocked the werewolf off the roof. He heard a thud as it sprawled on the driveway. Mitch backed up again, more sharply. He heard a scream of animal pain and felt a crunch as the car ran over the beast's legs.

"*Fuck you!*" Mitch screamed. He was laughing hysterically. He put the car in drive and pressed the pedal to the floor. The wheels spun a rain of gravel and peeled off down Tyler's driveway. Behind him, the baying of the wolves soared to the moon like a demonic symphony. In front of him, Mitch saw the night fog flee as though in terror from his headlights as he careened down the road towards Milton.

By the time Frank and Flora-Jean had calmed Mitch down long enough to make something approaching sense of his story of wolves and blood and murder, they had called the Milton detachment of the Halton

Regional Police Force and explained that something—they weren't quite sure what—had upset their boy terribly, and it wouldn't hurt to check out the Ross house up the escarpment. Things move slowly in a small town, and neither the police nor Mitch's parents were prepared to accept a worst-case scenario. This was Milton—not, after all, Toronto.

Frank was indignant when they asked her about Mitch's use of drugs. Their boy had never used drugs in his life. He didn't even *smoke*, for pity's sake.

"What's that on your pants, son?" Frank asked after he'd hung up with the officer.

"It's blood, Dad. I already told you. This is where I slipped in Elsa's blood."

Frank and Flora-Jean exchanged a worried glance. The story was crazy, but Mitchell wasn't prone to stories, and the blood was something quite apart from normal.

"Mitchell..." Frank began.

"I can't talk about it anymore Dad," Mitch said, then burst into tears. Flora-Jean hurried over to him and put a plump arm around his shoulders.

"Oh sweetie," she murmured. "It's all right. We'll figure it all out. Come and lie down till the police get back to us." She ushered her sobbing son out of the living room, and helped him upstairs to his own room. Mitch took off his jeans and climbed into bed. Flora-Jean, who knew about evidence from watching *Night Heat* re-runs, gingerly picked up the pants by the belt loop, and carried them into the kitchen. She put them in a plastic bag—just in case—and went out to the living room to wait with her husband for a call from the police.

Mitch lay down on his bed. The clock beside his bed ticked rhythmically. Downstairs, he heard his mother making coffee. His mother and father were talking quietly to each other, but Mitch couldn't make out the words. He drifted into a catatonic twilight of sleep and wakefulness.

A sound woke him. He raised himself to his elbows and said, "Mom?" Mitch looked out his window and saw that the moon was going down. A second stone hit the window.

"Tyler?"

Mitch kicked aside the covers and walked to the window. There, in the shadows of the elm tree nearest the house, he saw something white cowering in the dark. Even from the upstairs window, Mitch could see that the naked, huddled figure was Tyler. He had been savagely mauled. The grass upon which he was crouched was stained red. Wordlessly, Mitch crossed his bedroom and opened the door. He listened for his parents. They were still talking in the living room. He'd crept out of the house many times before when he and Tyler had gone adventuring, so he knew which stair creaked, and how to avoid it. Mitch slipped out the back door and hurried around the back of the house to the front yard. The night wind had grown cooler now, and his bare legs were chilled.

"Tyler," Mitch sobbed. "Oh Tyler."

Tyler tried to raise his mangled body slightly. He stared at Mitch, his eyes trying to focus on his friend. He fell back, exhausted by the effort. Mitch cradled him in his arms, his tears mixing with Tyler's blood.

"In the movies...the werewolves...heal quickly," Tyler croaked. His laugh was more like a gurgle. Fresh blood bubbled from his wounded throat. "Not...true."

"Oh, God" Mitch whispered. "Why? Why did all this happen to us, Ty? "

"Just...shitty luck. The water..." Tyler said weakly. "Wild Angus...is dead." He grasped Mitch's arm tightly. "But..the others...know who you are. Be careful...your family too."

"It'll be OK, Tyler," Mitch wept. "It'll be OK. The police are coming. We'll get you to a doctor. Everything's gonna be fine. Fall's coming, and we have to do that Glen Eden climb in September like we always do. You and me together...like always. We can go to Australia if you want. Fuck Europe. Europe's not goin' anywhere. You'll be fine, Tyler. Oh God, please don't die."

"They lied..."

"What? Tyler, what did you say?" Mitch leaned close to Tyler's mouth, straining to hear.

"They lied...about...the guilt. It...doesn't go away." Tyler rested his head in the crook of Mitch's arm and closed his eyes.

In the distance, Mitch heard the scream of many police sirens as they swept along the country roads towards his house. To Mitch, the sirens sounded like screams of rage and frustration, the keening howl of something alive, something cheated. He saw lights being switched on in living rooms along Childs Drive as the wailing sirens came closer. Loudest of all to Mitch was the sound of his own weeping as he cradled Tyler's dead body in his arms, rocking him gently as though he were a baby. He raised his face to the moonless night, looking for the first lightening of the eastern sky.

SKINNY DIPPING
by
Mici Gold

Giggling
On the shore
Stripping off clothes
Bone white skin
In the moonlight

Trees rustling in warning
Unheard

A dare, a chase, a splash
Then another splash
Ripples spreading
In the darkness

Sudden silence on the lake
A small ring of bubbles breaking
The deathly still surface

Over the water
A hungry owl flying
Seeing in the depths
Skin white bones
In the moonlight

Sign in the shadows:
Acid Lake

REASONS UNKNOWN

by
Scott Mackay

Toronto author Scott Mackay's first novel, *A Friend in Barcelona* (Harper Collins) appeared in hardcover in 1991. He has published short stories in numerous magazines, including *Science Fiction Age* and *The Magazine of Fantasy and Science Fiction*, and has been a regular contributor to *Ellery Queen Mystery Magazine* since 1989. His most recent novel, *Outpost*, is due from Tor Books this year.

T om Stanton's horse was dead.

I was seventeen, a shy retiring boy who, living alone with my father in the backwoods of Lambton County, had only two friends, Tom Stanton and his horse, Ace. They both died within days of each other, both of heart attacks. I didn't know horses could have heart attacks until Ace died.

I am now thirty-four. I live in the city and have a wife and two children. I wouldn't have remembered the day Ace died if it weren't for all these old boxes. My father passed away last month. These old boxes are all I have left of him.

I led Ace by the halter down Route 33 the day after Tom Stanton's funeral. Someone had to look after the old horse, and I was the obvious choice. Route 33, an alternate route favored by truckers, climbed a sandy wooded rise and curved out of sight to the left. I crossed with Ace just the other side of the rise, with the hill behind me and the curve still ahead, a bad place to cross, with visibility in either direction less than fifty metres. But at this time of day, just after six in the evening, with the truckers stopped for supper, the road was silent, and I didn't have to worry about traffic.

Ace snorted. That was the first of it. Then he wheezed. He stopped in the middle of that dangerous spot in the road, his grey and white coat moistening, his legs stiffening. Then his front legs buckled and he toppled onto his side. I knelt beside him, and he looked up at me with his right eye.

"Ace?" I said. "Ace, are you all right?"

He scuffed the pavement with his hoof and whinnied. He lifted his head, but he couldn't get it more than a few inches off the ground, wheezed again, then died. I stared at him. I couldn't believe I could lose two such dear friends in the same week.

I hadn't felt such emptiness since the day my mother left my father. With the horse on the road like that, I must have cried. Shy retiring boys of seventeen usually do. But I stopped crying when I finally understood the true nature of my predicament. I had a dead horse in the middle of the highway, with blind spots both north and south, a horse I couldn't possibly hope to move by myself, and no one around to help. I looked at my watch. With truckers finishing supper and pulling out onto Route 33 by the dozens, I had to get Ace off the road as soon as I could, but I didn't know how.

Tom Stanton died that June at the age of seventy-two. I didn't know how I was going to fill the long summer days. Raised alone by my father, my mother having deserted us for reasons unknown, I gained, through Tom, a wider view of myself and of the world around me. Tom was interested in everything. In and around that part of Lambton County they called Tom a man for all seasons. A bee-keeper by trade, his hands were often swollen and puffy from bee stings. He once developed a hybrid strain of sweet blossom clover now used by most of the bee-keepers in the country. His clover isn't much, but it's more than this, these musty smelling boxes crowding around me in the rec-room of my split level home in the city. I have found an old photograph album full of black and white photographs in the mustiest of the boxes and I now hold it open on my knee.

The dead have power over the living. Even now as I sit in the rec-room of my split-level home flipping through this photograph album, I sense my dead father's power, not the same power Ace had, or Tom had, but a deeper power, the power of pity. I pity my father because he couldn't hang onto the woman he loved. My mother's name was Mabel. She was small, bird-like, had silken hair she brushed a hundred times each night, was pretty, at least by Lambton County standards. I have never been able to forgive my mother for leaving us. My father didn't deserve it. My father was a minister of the Methodist Church, a staunch abstainer, a devoted and loving family man, and a vigorous patriot. How he fell in love with an excitable woman like my mother I'll never know. Yet the fact remains, he loved her, and when we lost her, for reasons unknown, he had only this to say.

"Your mother had bad nerves."

I turn to the third page of my father's photograph album and stare at the photograph in the top right-hand corner. It shows a young man wearing stream-wading gaiters with a fishing rod over his shoulder, his hat full of hooks and lures. Underneath, in my father's block capitals, reads the following: TOM STANTON, HURON FALLS, OCTOBER, 1947. Behind Tom I see rapids, trees, and an outcropping of rock. This is the first picture I've ever seen of Tom as a young man, but even as a young man he has the same kind benevolent face, high forehead, and puckish eyes I remember so well.

We buried my father in the small cemetery next to the wood-frame Methodist Church in Holdsworth. You probably don't know Holdsworth. Besides Tom Stanton's outhouse made entirely out of clothes-pins, it hasn't got much to offer. Every dowager in town showed up for my father's funeral. Half the old girls loved him. He could have married any one of them. I don't know why he didn't. I guess he never found anyone he loved as much as Mabel. I have always admired my father for building a useful and moral life out of his heartache and disappointment, and will remain forever grateful to him for raising me single-handedly. As for my mother, well, only tonight, as I stare down at this old photograph of Tom Stanton can I find it in myself to forgive her. I will miss my father. All my life I tried to give him the family life my mother took away from us. I will miss Christmas out at the old place on Route 33; I will miss the way he made hot porridge for me every morning when I was a kid; I will miss the way he took such good care of his garden and how the ladies of the voluntary auxiliary always kept the Methodist Church in Holdsworth bedecked with the gladioli, roses, and 'mums my father grew with such love and care in that half-acre behind the house he called his own personal Eden. I will miss him as much as I miss my mother. As much as I miss Acc. As much as I miss Tom Stanton. But looking at this picture of the young Tom Stanton, I understand that I should celebrate my father's life, not grieve for his loss. This is no ordinary photograph. This photograph is magical. This photograph tells me there is more to life—and to death—than perhaps meets the eye.

On the night Ace died, I gazed up the road, listening. A crescent moon floated overhead, its cusps dagger sharp against the sky. Far in the distance, I heard a car climb the other side of the rise. I ran to the top of the hill, ripped off my white shirt, and waved it like a flag.

The driver saw me and pulled over to the gravel shoulder. It was Ross Patrick, a cigar smoking mountain of a man who owned a bee farm just down the hill, one of Tom's fiercest competitors, a man who had never been able to live down Tom's special hybrid strain of a sweet blossom clover.

"Well, now," he said, once I explained the situation. "Why don't you get in the car and we'll go have a look?"

So I got in the car and we had a look.

At three hundred pounds, Ross Patrick had the strength to drag Ace to the side of the road easily. He got out of the car, hiked up his pants, adjusted his suspenders, and pulled out a fresh cigar. I came around the other side. He looked up and down the road. A grin came to his face. I didn't like the look of that grin. Then he stared at me. I thought he had an idea. About how we could move the horse. But he bit off the end of his cigar and spit the brown little nubby against Ace's rump.

"I never did like that horse," he said. He lit the cigar and exhaled a great cloud of smoke into the air. "Come to think of it, I never liked Tom." He put his hands in his pockets. His grin faded. "No, to tell you the truth, I never liked either of them."

He shook his head, as if he didn't understand how I could get mixed up with someone like Tom Stanton, or ever feel any affection for a horse like Ace, then got back in his car, and, without saying a word, drove away.

I watched his red tail-lights disappear around the curve. How could Ross Patrick drive away? How could he hold a grudge against a dead man, let alone a dead horse? As a shy retiring boy of seventeen I couldn't possibly comprehend the scope of the world's bitterness, or its unwillingness to forgive.

I tried to drag Ace by the head. I tried to drag him by the tail. I walked into the woods, found an old fence post, and tried to pry Ace off the pavement, but my fence post broke. I knelt beside the horse. I didn't know what to do. That's when I saw a bee land on Ace's neck.

I heard someone walking through the woods toward me. Three more bees landed on Ace's face. I looked into the woods, but the shadows still hid whoever was coming. Another six bees landed on Ace's rump. A man emerged. He couldn't have been more than thirty-five. He wore stream-wading gaiters, a hat full of hooks and lures, and carried a fishing rod over his shoulder. He had a kind benevolent face, a high forehead, and puckish eyes.

"What happened?" he asked. He had an easy voice, the voice of a lucky man.

I explained the situation. I told him about Ross Patrick and Tom Stanton. I asked him whether he knew Ross Patrick.

"He's an unforgiving son-of-a-bitch," said the man, as mild as could be. "If he's got something against you, he'll never let it go. It's twisted him right around."

I don't believe in ghosts. But I know the man who helped me drag Ace off the highway that night is the man in this photograph. Or at least I think I do. The young Tom Stanton. Who can say for sure. We looked up the highway. We heard the distant rumble of an eighteen-wheeler coming up the other side of the hill. The man put his fishing rod down.

"Well," he said, "we'd better get him off the road."

He could have pulled Ace over to the gravel shoulder by himself, but, being who he was, he understood that I had to help, that by helping, by giving Tom Stanton's horse this one last dignity, I would better be able to bear the death of the old man, and get through the long lonely days of summer all by myself. So he grabbed one leg and I grabbed the other, and we pulled Ace to the side of Route 33 just as the truck crested the rise. We watched the truck drive past. The driver looked down at us with mystified eyes.

When the truck disappeared, the man picked up his fishing rod. "I'm on my way to Huron Falls," he said. "I hear the fish are biting. I'll see you around some time."

He walked across the highway, a swarm of bees buzzing above his head, and disappeared into the trees.

As I stare down at his photograph in the rec-room of my split-level home in the city, with my father freshly buried in the small cemetery outside the Methodist Church in Holdsworth, I now remember that they dammed up Huron Falls in 1951. The man who helped me move Ace off the road so long ago was years and years too late for Huron Falls. I don't know. This is difficult, especially because of the way I feel about my mother. I'm uncomfortable. I don't believe in ghosts, yet tonight I know they are all around me. I'm glad they're here. Especially the ghost of Tom Stanton. Huron Falls, 1947. I'm glad he's here with me tonight, as he was the night he helped me move Ace off Route 33, because he has made me understand the scope of the world's bitterness and its unwillingness to forgive, taught me to come to terms with it. I glance up from his photograph and look at all the old boxes. How easy to be a Ross Patrick, and how hard to be a Tom Stanton. I have both good and bad memories of my mother, my father, Tom Stanton, Ace, and all the other ghosts who still find the fishing good up at Huron Falls. How easy to hold a grudge, especially against people you love. When my mother left my father, for reasons unknown, it twisted me right around, turned me into an unforgiving son-of-a-bitch. But now after all these years, with both my parents dead, with my kids in bed, and my wife upstairs putting curlers in her hair, and the detritus of my father's life spread out in musty old boxes on the rec-room floor, my mother no longer haunts me so much, the pain isn't so bad, and I know she is gone, that Tom Stanton has risen from the spectral sepia tones of this old photograph and taken her back to Huron Falls for good.

DEAD OF WINTER

by
Carol Weekes

This story came from the author's study of the effects of Alzheimer's disease, as well as hearing stories from elderly relatives about friends who have suffered from the affliction. "In all of the sadness, loss, and terror of this kind of situation," she writes, "I also wanted to weave a small thread of peace regarding the inevitability of our own mortality, and that a lifetime of anticipation about death may be worse than the moment when we leave this life for whatever lays beyond."

John Donovan stood in the bedroom doorway, watching his father doze. The old man's face didn't look peaceful, the way a sleeping face should. The eyelids flickered with the rapid movement of REM. Perhaps his father was dreaming, and John hoped the fantasy would dissipate when he woke his father up. He would be thinking of her again. The room smelled spicy with the after-aroma of flowers. Carpet freshener, perhaps.

Mark Donovan's mouth gave a sudden twist."You promised me, Doreen! DOREEN!"

John winced and felt his gut tighten at the name. He went to turn away...it would be so much easier to walk out now and just keep walking; then, he caught himself and turned back to face the gaunt form in the bed.

"Dad, wake up."

The old eyes flew open and stared, disoriented, around the room. The eyes looked hopeful until they fell on the younger man still standing in the doorway, then they clouded with a misty disappointment. Even worse, no recognition flickered there at all.

"I thought you might be my wife, Doreen," Mark replied wearily. "She's supposed to come back and see me tonight. We've planned for a trip. Who are you?"

John felt his heart sink. "Christ, Dad..." He almost burst out *Do you have to make it so hard? Don't you realize she's dead...* He caught that, too, and bit his tongue. The dementia was a final kick in the ass along with the almost total loss of a lifetime's worth of memories.

"It's me, Dad. John. Would you like a tea and a biscuit?"

Heavily veined hands dug into the comforter, clutching it protectively against the chest. Watchful. "I'm expecting my wife...she might not come if you're here. Please...look for her for me."

"I'll make the tea." John backed painfully into the bedside table, knocking the lampshade askew with his elbow. The lamp wavered back and forth, threatening to spill over the table's edge. John caught it, along with the yeasty stench of stale urine wafting up from beneath the bed covers. He wanted to weep. He steadied the lamp and took a moment to compose himself. Play the game—ease the poor, broken mind. There was no point in trying to argue with the unreasonable any more. Have a tea just like old (forgotten) times, and then go. He wanted to shriek into the room that none of this was fair; that he still wanted to be able to sit with the old man at the backgammon board, a beer in hand and the comforting scent of his father's pipe in the room.

He shut his eyes for a moment before turning towards the closet where the nursing staff kept the towels, facecloths, and the diapers his father now wore. Over the last two months Mark Donovan had stopped remembering to use the facilities. It had been another blow to John, to watch his father retrograde back to an infantile state devoid of its childhood wonder and innocence.

He chose a facecloth and went through the mechanical motions of wetting it with warm water and soap, then carried the cloth and a clean diaper back tothe bed. Outside the January winter howled, shaking the building with hurricane force. The frozen landscape might have been beautiful, were it not for the pulsation of human emotional pain caught like a southern bird within the room providing the view. The thought made him start uneasily. *So, this is aging,* he thought miserably. *The bird wants release.*

"Take it easy, Dad. Let me help you out."

"I don't need your help. I have a wife..."

He used gentle strokes to wash the urine away from the thin, blue-veined limbs before redressing his father. Father and son's hands shook simultaneously, the father with a chill and the son's with the act of holding everything inside. He almost wished he could open the window and let that bird go free, then immediately regretted the thought. John held his father to his chest and bit into his lower lip to stop the tears from coming. He hadn't cried since...

...since his mother's funeral just over a year ago.

Mark Donovan struck out. "Leave me alone! You've done your job, now go!"

"Don't fight me, Dad. God, I love you and I...I'm having a hard time with this." He let the tears run. Screw it. Who was here to see anything except an old man who didn't know his son from a line of strangers, and the bleak staccato tick of ice pellets hitting the window?

The old man's left fist wormed its way out of the embrace and connected with the cheekbone beneath John's left eye.

"Dad!"

"Go away. I don't want you here."

John released the man and strode purposefully into the small kitchen where he'd left a paper bag of groceries and his car keys on the table. He took his jacket off (you could walk out right now) and placed it on the back of a chair, then plugged the tea kettle in to boil. The staff still trusted him with this gadget, although the fuses for the stove had been recently removed after a burner had been left on during the night.

The bird needs to escape...

His father thrashed in the bed behind him, fighting the tight covers holding him in.

"You can't keep me here forever. When Doreen finds out who's responsible you'll be sued!"

John stood with his back to the bedroom door, rubbing at the eye which now watered from the impact. Twenty minutes. It would be about all he could stand. At moments, and they were occurring more frequently lately, he wanted to turn and scream that Doreen Donovan was dead. Buried, frozen, and decomposing like the funeral flowers that had been sealed inside her coffin. The thought sickened him. He focused on the water reaching a near-boil in the tea kettle, grateful for a sound he'd always associated with pleasure and comfort, before death had arrived and left its mark on their doorstep.

He poured the tea and added enough milk to his father's mug to turn the liquid into a lukewarm, tasteless mess—in case he spilled. His mind might be broken, but his nerve endings were still painfully alive. He clicked the heater on as he carried the tea back to the bedroom.

"That'll keep the winter out," he said as cheerfully as he could muster. A fistful of wind slammed into the patio doors of the livingroom, as if in defiance of the words. John jumped and stared through the glass into the night. Hot tea rolled over a rim and scalded his wrist. Only the snow and the dead branches of the frozen season moved out there. He trod into the bedroom and placed the carrying tray down on the night table. The saucers shook as he made himself face the old man again. What did you say to a mind lost in the past? *So, have you met a nice girl, yet?*

He sat down on the edge of the bed and began the mental count-down towards departure, hating himself for it. *Happy fucking new year*, he thought morosely. "Would you like the television on?"

The lips trembled. "No. I might not hear her when she comes in."

He handed his father the tea, noting how the old eyes stared into the night, reflecting the cold wash of light from the arc sodium lamps over the building's parking lot.

"She'll be here at seven-thirty. She's never late, you know. That's why I married Doreen...because I always admired a punctual woman."

John swallowed the tea and thought that he'd never tasted a cup so bitter and repugnant. He patted the hand resting on top of the covers and stood up.

"Do you think the roads are difficult in this storm?" his father queried suddenly. The free hand shot out and gripped John's own, pinching the flesh.

Ignore him and say goodbye.

"She'll show if she can, I'm sure." The words spilling out of his mouth shocked and amazed him simultaneously. Oh, that was bad, that was really bad. It was time to go. He retrieved his jacket, struggled to zip it up, then glanced back into the bedroom. A smile had broken over his father's face, like the first faint ray of sun peeking out beyond the storm's rim. The apartment had warmed up, filling the air with the stink of urine and the annoying floral scent. He had to get out of there.

John walked back into the bedroom. He bent and kissed the thinning hair. He'd told a lie, bolstering an old man's hope of seeing his dead wife, and he supposed that was wrong. At the same time, if it gave his father pleasure - at this point, what did any of it matter any more?

He didn't think it did.

He zipped the jacket up to the neck and turned the television set on for his father to watch before leaving the apartment.

It was when he went to the pocket which always held his keys that he realized where the damn things still were. John slammed a palm against the car roof, knocking a thin veil of ice to the ground. He stared at the building, snow crystals stinging his eyes. He would have to go back inside. Perhaps he could duck past the bedroom door quickly and retrieve the things without his father noticing the movement.

The night blew a long mournful note at his back as he pulled open the doors to the foyer and moved into the entrance. He reached the apartment and let himself in quietly, grateful for the warmth of the building. He glanced at his watch. It read seven twenty-nine. If he hurried he could still make it home for eight o'clock and some kind of an evening with his wife.

The muted tones of the television floated down the hallway to him...followed by an icy wind faintly aromatic with the scent of flowers and age.

John stiffened, confused at the change of air pressure and temperature. Then it hit him—the apartment felt similar to what he'd just left behind in the parking lot.

Winter.

The hallway of his father's apartment felt like a January landscape poking a tentative finger at the newcomer.

He broke into a run towards the living quarters which felt strangely distant. He reached the livingroom and dinette area where his keys lay beside the gloves on the table.

The patio doors of the livingroom sat wide open, allowing swirling strands of snow eddies to circulate into the room.

Mark Donovan moved across the rigid patio stones, his cotton pyjamas billowing about his body in the winds. He held both arms forward, as if about to embrace the night....and suddenly John spotted what his father was moving towards.

Doreen....mother. She seemed to linger in the pause of wind, a halo of a woman highlighted in the apartment's glow. Snow pooled in her shallow eye sockets. It settled along the surfaces of the exposed ribcage poking through the silk dress she'd been buried in.

His father reached for the skeletal hands wavering in the wind, and John screamed. "Dad, she's dead!" His father didn't look back. The hands connected, and John watched time meld....the past, present, and future solidifying into one. They began to move out into the storm together, floating inches above the winter ground. The wind shrieked and the snow dispersed like dust, taking man and wife into the darkness.

The bird has escaped, John thought hysterically, and passed out on the living room carpet.

Dale brought him a hot tea from the hospital dispenser machine down the hallway. No milk to turn it into a soppy mess, he thought depressively.

"The police are still looking for him, John." Dale pressed his arm, lightly. Suddenly she began to cry and reached out for him, drawing his head against her chest.

He felt himself flop forward like a rag doll and couldn't bring himself to return the gesture.

They won't find him, he wanted to tell her. The bird is free.

"I'll be back after supper," she kissed his forehead. "I'll let you know....if they find him."

"Yeah," he said. He avoided looking at her eyes, red-rimmed from crying all night long. She'd been close to Mom and Dad, almost as much as he'd been himself. He didn't want to tell her how close they still really were.

She gripped his hand while he turned terrified eyes towards the window of the hospital room. One corner sat thick with newly accumulated snow, the fine filament fingers of frost gradually inching towards him.

"The police never found his footprints in the snow," she said from a distance. "You were in hysterics when you came to last night. They drugged you...God dammit, this feels all too familiar!" She fumbled for the cigarettes in her purse, then remembered hospital policy and shoved them back inside. She wept silently, holding the emotions back while her shoulders shook. He wanted to tell her he knew exactly how she was feeling, but he couldn't stop watching winter move along the glass.

This bird is afraid. He had years before he could hope for senility to wash most of his memories away.

In the meantime he could scream.

CONSUMING FEAR

by
Colleen Anderson

The author writes: "I went to Orycon in Port-land a few years ago, right after having a laparoscopy. This minor exploratory surgery puts a tiny incision in the navel and one at the edge of the pubic hair region. My stomach was sore and bruised, and at the time I was extremely hungry. I commented to a friend that it felt like I had a black hole in my stom-ach. Consuming Fear was born from that one suggestion."

J enny has a black hole in her stomach. At least, she knows that's what it's called now. It is something dark, that swallows all the bad things she's tasted. But like a black hole it also swallows the good foods she's eaten. She has had the black hole for a while now but Ms. Norton, in science class, just told them about black holes.

Ms. Norton said that even the men—and hopefully some women, Jenny thinks, who spend their lives studying black holes don't know exactly what they are. Jenny knows now that they swallow everything that's within a certain distance and that they exist in space. But, Jenny knows, it's a black hole that's inside her. In the space where her stomach is. Momma's always saying that she doesn't know where all the food goes that Jenny eats and Jenny isn't fat at all.

She frowns and pulls up on her shoulder bag full of books, and notices that she's only a house away from old Mrs. Kreiger's. Amongst the innocently yellow tulips the roses bite with thorns for purchase. Ivy wraps around strangely stunted and pruned cedar bushes. Jenny spots Mrs. Kreiger walking around the side of the house, hose in hand, watering her prizes. Scowling, Jenny loops her hands through the shoulder straps of her pack and runs past, not listening to Mrs. Kreiger's calls of, "Hello, Jen."

Instead, Jenny hums to herself and feels the bounce of her hair on her neck.

Home in a matter of minutes, Jenny bursts into the kitchen. "Hi, Momma!"

"Well, hi there." Momma smiles at her. "Dinner's almost ready. You want to go and wash your hands and set the table for me, please?" Momma's chopping vegetables for a salad.

The warm aroma of something yummy cooking, and the satisfying click click of the knife makes Jenny feel content enough to forget what's in her stomach for a few minutes. "Where's Dean? How come he isn't helping?"

Momma turns and smiles at Jenny, shaking her head. "You two, I swear. He's taking out the garbage and will clear the table after dinner. All right?"

Jenny nods, then runs up the stairs. She dumps her books on her bed then lathers rose-scented soap up to her elbows. Back downstairs she pulls sky blue plates from the cupboard and talks to Momma. "We had art and math and science today. Math was okay, but science was really cool." She puts three plates on the table knowing that Daddy's still out of town. Jenny runs her fingers around the rim of one plate and wonders if her black hole is large and shiny.

"Jen, I asked you what you did?"

"Jenny," she corrects. "Ms. Norton told us about black holes." Dean bangs in the back door but Jenny ignores her older brother and continues. "She said that they swallow everything in sight and nothing can escape them once they get too close."

Dean grabs a celery stick, deftly dodging Momma's swat, and lounges in one of the chairs as Jenny puts glasses and apple juice on the table. "That's what I have, you know."

"What?" Momma asks.

"A black hole. That's why I eat so much."

Dean snorts. "Geez, what a turnip head. Black holes only exist in space and it would have swallowed you up by now."

Jenny glares at Dean and states, "Well my teacher said no one knows everything about them and I have one in me. I know it!"

Momma sets the salad on the table and looks over at them. "That's enough, you two. Jenny just has a vivid imagination; it will help her remember the details. Now, let's eat."

Jenny sits and stares at her plate. Momma dishes up a helping of potatoes, beef and Brussels sprouts. She eats, thinking of her black hole, trying to enjoy the food while she can. The black hole will get it all too soon.

Dean grumbles but Jenny barely hears him. "Aw, Mom, I hate Brussels sprouts. Do I have to eat them?"

"Your sister's eating them."

"Yeah, but she eats everything."

After dinner, Jenny runs upstairs and leaves the dishwashing to Dean. She'll do them tomorrow. She lies on her bed and works out her homework on the solar system and the universe.

Dean stops on the way to his room and leans on the doorframe scowling. "Well, miss goody two-shoes-eats- everything. What a traitor. You used to hate Brussels sprouts as much as I did. Thanks a lot." He saunters off before she can say anything.

Jenny puts her book down and stares at the wall. Did they have Brussels sprouts for dinner? She knows she ate but as always, Jenny can never remember what she's eaten. Nothing. Not breakfast, not lunch, not dinner.... No smell, no taste, nothing.

She doesn't understand why the black hole doesn't swallow her up, but she's more convinced that it sits gnawing, persisting hungrily, like a baby sparrow waiting for food. If it was just Jenny eating she'd remember what food tastes like, what she's eaten. But she doesn't remember and she always feels light, almost buoyant. The black hole gets fed and is happy, not yet swallowing Jenny, just swallowing her memory of anything that enters her mouth.

She used to remember eating, when she was six. Even, she thinks, when she was seven. That was probably when she hated Brussels sprouts too. But something changed. Something dark and shadowy that made the black hole grow.

Sometimes—Jenny shudders and looks at the book's pictures of Jupiter and Saturn. Sometimes the black hole burps or something. Late at night, when she sleeps, she almost remembers what she has eaten. The tastes and textures come back, and the fear. A fear that chokes her throat and slides warm and heavily like slime into her belly. The bad things that enter her mouth. She awakes shivering and shaking but never remembers what scared her. She's kind of happy to have the black hole. If it wasn't for the black hole Jenny thinks she would be afraid more than just in her dreams. It does kind of make her special, too.

After homework and watching some TV Jenny burrows deep under her fuzzy blanket and dreams of puppies and windmills. The black hole keeps the bad tastes away.

Jenny's up, dressed in a blue dress with sailing ships on it and ready for breakfast while Dean still stumbles about in his room. Yawning, she says, "Morning, Momma."

"Morning," Momma smiles.

Jenny pours puffed wheat cereal into a bowl and milk on top. She spoons up mouthfuls and watches Momma sip coffee while wrapping blueberry muffins up in foil. Momma's dressed in a dark green skirt and jacket, ready for work and looks cool, for an adult. She puts a brown bag beside Jenny, and the muffins.

"Here's your lunch, Jen, and..."

"Jenny."

Momma sighs. "Jenny. And here's some muffins I'd like you to drop off to Mrs. Kreiger's after school."

Jenny feels the black hole in her. It seems to spin, rubbing against her insides, making her queasy. "Why can't Dean do it?"

"Because he has a baseball game after school."

"I don't like Mrs. Kreiger. I don't want to go." The black hole has already eaten all her breakfast. She can only remember she had cereal from seeing the box on the table.

Momma kneels down and looks into Jenny's eyes. "I know poor Mrs. Kreiger may be boring and old to you, but with Mr. Kreiger dying a year ago she's had very few people to talk to. She gets very lonely and a few muffins and a smile won't hurt you." She stands and pats Jenny's shoulder and is already walking toward the door with her briefcase.

Jenny's sniffing, trying not to cry. Why can't the black hole swallow her tears? But she knows it's because they don't enter her mouth. "She makes me eat yucky things."

"Like what, Jen?" her mother asks distractedly while fishing in her purse for her keys and balancing a mug of coffee and the briefcase.

"Jenny!" she almost screams. "It's Jenny."

"All right. Calm down. You're in a bad mood this morning." Momma stares at Jenny, one hand on the door. "What food is it you don't like?"

Jenny shrinks in on herself, shoulders hunching. "I don't know," she whispers. "I don't know." The black hole has chewed up her memory.

Momma looks at her watch and is already half out the door. "I have to go, dear. Look, if you don't like it just tell Mrs. Kreiger, no thank you. You don't have to stay long but be polite and give her the muffins."

Did Momma even hear her, she wonders?

Jenny trudges to school, knowing Momma does this whenever Daddy's out of town, Dean's playing a game, or Momma has to work late. Momma may want to be nice to Mrs. Kreiger but she also uses her to look after Jenny when no one's at home. Jenny hates it and would rather spend the time over at Kris's house playing with her dolls.

Jenny's day passes and she forgets about the muffins until she's putting her books back into her purple pack and encounters the crinkly foil. She thinks, *I could throw them away but Momma would find out and be so disappointed.*

Resignedly, feeling the black hole spin hungrily inside her Jenny walks up to Mrs. Kreiger's house. She's sitting on her porch reading a book as Jenny approaches. Her dress is a worn brown and she doesn't look lonely or poorly to Jenny at all. Her hair is thick and wavy, and silver, and her square chin is still strong if wrinkly.

She spots Jenny and puts down the book. "Well, well, Jen. Nice to see you. Come on up, I won't bite." She smiles from bright white and crooked teeth.

Jenny stands at the bottom of the steps looking up from under lidded eyes. "My mother sent something for you."

Mrs. Kreiger's standing and stretching. Jenny lowers her eyes and rummages in her pack, pulling out the muffins and holding them out to her. She stares at the tulips.

Mrs. Kreiger grins again and says, "Well, don't just stand there. Bring 'em in and we'll have some juice." She turns and enters the cool darkness of the house leaving Jenny no choice but to follow.

Jenny thumps her pack up the steps behind her. She stands just inside the door, smelling roses and mustiness. Mrs. Kreiger walks into the living room with a jug of lemonade and two glasses. She glances at Jenny but goes back to her kitchen for a plate of the muffins, their fat purplish berries looking like bruises.

Mrs. Kreiger comes back and pulls Jenny into the house, shutting the door behind her. "Come on in to the living room, Jen Jen, and tell me what you've been up to."

The living room is filled with shadows that seem to creep across the floor. Jenny swallows, dry-mouthed and sits on the edge of the old, worn burgundy sofa, as far from the old woman as she can. It rubs coarsely against her bare legs. Mrs. Kreiger pours her a glass of lemonade and all she can think of is pee. Mrs. Krieger passes her the muffins and she takes part of one hoping she will move away. Jenny bites into the muffin to avoid looking at Mrs. Kreiger and recognizes Momma's cooking. She tries to hold onto that thought, that comforting familiarity. She takes a sip of lemonade and it is only lemonade.

Mrs. Kreiger is asking about her family and she answers but wonders, *Why am I afraid? The food is okay. I wish I could remember*. The black hole seems to be bouncing around, banging her stomach so it flutters, and at her heart so that it beats hard.

"Well, Jen, would you like to see my parrot? Perhaps we can get her to whistle a tune."

Mrs. Krieger looks at her expectantly and she nods shyly. Mrs. Kreiger leads the way into the adjoining room. A big overstuffed chair rests near the cage that is on a high stand. The wires of brass curve gracefully together. The blue and green parrot cocks its head and whistles saying, "Hello, hello."

Jenny smiles.

"Here," Mrs. Kreiger's hands grab her about the waist and stand her on the chair. "This way you can see eye to eye with Flora."

Jenny thinks Flora is the most beautiful bird she's ever seen and watches its movements. Mrs. Kreiger talks about Flora and where she was born in the jungles. She talks about what they eat and how old the birds become.

Jenny is so rapt in the bird and what Mrs. Kreiger is saying that she doesn't notice the wrinkled hand rubbing her bare legs at first. She tries to move away but the springy cushion of the chair makes her wobble. Mrs. Kreiger steadies her with the other hand and both touch her in ways she doesn't like. She can feel the black hole beginning to spin faster and faster in her stomach. It tries to swallow the fear that seems to bubble from her heart, her heart that beats like too many drums, but the fear is too large. It is making her shake.

Jenny pushes at the hands and says, "Don't. I don't like that."

"Shh, my Jen." Mrs. Kreiger smoothes her hair and presses Jenny into her body, nearly suffocating her. "You are so pretty, so young. It doesn't hurt to touch you. It doesn't hurt to hold you."

Mrs. Kreiger's working at her own skirt pulling it up and rubbing between her legs. "I won't hurt you. I have a lollipop...a candy for you. You'd like to lick my candy, wouldn't you, Jen."

"No," she shakes her head. "No, I don't want to. I—I have a black hole." And she can feel it pushing inside her, hungry for more, pushing in her throat, making her feel like throwing up.

She's somehow off the chair and standing on the floor but her head is at Mrs. Kreiger's waist. Mrs. Krieger's sitting on the edge of the chair and she's holding Jenny's head. "It won't hurt you. Just lick at my candy." She pushes Jenny's head toward her spread legs. Jenny struggles, her lips pressed firmly together. The food that tastes bad. The bad food. She's trying to force it on Jenny and Jenny doesn't want it, is scared. The black hole will take away the memory but Jenny doesn't want to touch her candy. She whimpers.

"Come on, Jen Jen," she breathes. "It's nice. It will feel good and make me happy. You want to make me happy, don't you?"

No, she doesn't and the black hole reaches up through the tunnel of her stomach and throat causing her to gag and gasp. Mrs. Kreiger tries to pull Jenny closer and Jenny feels the pull of the black hole. Jenny opens her mouth to scream but the black hole is there.

It sucks and swallows Mrs. Kreiger's legs and the skirt puckers as it goes into her mouth. Jenny watches, helpless, frozen. It's as if Mrs. Kreiger is a plastic bag with all the air being squeezed out. She starts to crinkle and shrivel as her eyes grow wide. She tries to pry herself from Jenny's mouth as the black hole swallows her chest, her arms. She compresses, falling in on herself. A thin wail comes out of the cartoonish face just before the black hole consumes it.

Jenny shakes, gasping in air. She gags and throws up but only liquid and half-chewed blueberries splatter the carpet. Flora shrieks from the cage, flapping wings, and seeds and feathers shower to the floor. No Mrs. Kreiger. Jenny looks about, dismayed. The bad food. Mrs. Kreiger was the bad food and the black hole has taken care of her. Jenny knows that she will not have to visit her any longer and goes to gather her pack.

She looks back at Flora and opens the cage and the window. Flora would starve otherwise and Jenny doesn't want that to happen. She quickly leaves, shutting the door behind her and runs all the way home, reciting the times tables in her head.

She can't think to do her homework and goes to bed without eating, feeling a queasiness in the black hole. The next morning Jenny barely touches breakfast before she goes to school. But school is the same. She feels heavy, bloated and senses the black hole churning now. Jenny remembers the half piece of toast she nibbled at breakfast and knows now what Mrs. Kreiger had done to her on each trip to her shadowy house. She now knows all that's gone into her mouth; the tastes, the textures. Jenny runs from the class and vomits.

She goes home early, ignoring the birds and flowers. By dinner she is hungry, a rumbling that challenges the black hole's churning. Silently she sits to eat the shepherd's pie that Momma has cooked. Momma watches quietly but Jenny doesn't look at her. The meal sits in her stomach like clammy lumps and seems to roll about. Jenny rushes to the bathroom and throws up. Momma follows her in as she gags over the toilet. "You poor thing. I'll put you to bed and we'll get you some broth."

"I don't feel t—too good."

Momma runs her hand over Jenny's brow, frowning. "You don't seem to have a fever but I think you better go straight to bed."

Jenny doesn't object and let's Momma wrap her in a flannel nightie too warm for the summer night. Momma sits holding her hand until she drifts away into sleep.

Jenny floats above a large black hole, suns and stars twinkling about her. The black hole is darker than the surrounding night and bulges as if something is trying to get out, and she hears Mrs. Kreiger's voice. "My Jen Jen, you take good care of me. You licked more of me than ever before. I'm in you now."

Jenny awakes shaking and whimpering, and tries to avoid sleep. But waking is not much better. The black hole is expanding. It makes her arms tingle and her head throb. Mrs. Kreiger was too much for it. The poisons in the woman are infecting the black hole and it grows and throbs like a large boil.

The next day and the day after Jenny tries to eat. Broths, soft eggs, juices, but nothing stays down. The black hole has taken all the room in her stomach, and constantly pushes on her throat causing everything to spew from her. Even the good tastes won't stay.

Momma sits on her bed on the third day and looks worried. "Jenny, I have to take you to the doctor. You're not getting any better. I should have listened when you said Mrs. Kreiger fed you bad food. I've tried to reach her but she doesn't answer the phone or her door. Do you recall what she gave you last, if you ate anything when over at her place?"

Jenny clears her throat and says, "I told you, Momma. There's a black hole inside me and it swallowed Mrs. Kreiger."

Momma doesn't say anything but leaves her room. She can hear Momma talking quietly on the phone.

Jenny goes for tests and more tests and this doctor and that doctor talk to her. They poke and prod and take blood. They never get near the black hole that makes it hard for Jenny to think these days. Finally, someone asks about the black hole and Mrs. Kreiger and she tries to tell them everything that she remembers. It is all she remembers now and her brain feels bruised and swollen.

Several days pass, unnoticed to Jenny. She has trouble forming words. Even her tongue feels thick, infected with the black hole. The blackness seeps into everything and muffles her. At last it is covering her, keeping her away from the memories. The hurt and fear are moving away, distant.

Back in the doctor's office Jenny is vaguely aware of words reaching her through the thick congealed coldness of the black hole. Like jelly. She wishes distractedly that they could remove it and Mrs. Kreiger from within her.

"Mrs. Cardston, most of the tests show that Jenny is suffering from malnourishment."

"You say most of the tests. What do the others show?"

"She's suffering from anorexia and what is looking to be a form of psychosis that will need further testing and therapy. As you now know, this Mrs. Kreiger, that the police are still searching for, seems to have sexually abused her."

Jenny hears Momma's cries and her choked, "What does this mean?" Jenny doesn't respond. She is muffled, cold.

"It's affecting her mind and only time and therapy will be able to help her."

Jenny doesn't feel the arms wrap around her. She doesn't feel or think of Mrs. Kreiger. Jenny has a black hole in her head.

TIN HOUSE

by
Michael Skeet

Michael Skeet's first short story was published in 1986, and since then he has appeared
in a number of Canadian and U.S. anthologies, and won awards both for his writing and
editing. He is married to Lorna Toolis, head
of the Merril Collection of the Toronto Public
Library, one of the world's greatest repositor-
ies of speculative writing. His story, "Tin
House," was inspired by a real building lo-
cated in a central Toronto neighborhood.

You've passed this house dozens of times before without noticing it. There's no particular reason for seeing it today except maybe that you're in no hurry to reach Front Street and your meeting. Designing test data is the thing you like least about your job, and so you let yourself be distracted as you walk past the rambling old house on Huron.

There are plenty of houses like this in Chinatown. It seems not so much to have been built as accreted onto its site, a room here and a room there, in a variety of what could only generously be called architectural styles. Its age is disguised by grime, but if it were human it would surely be collecting a pension by now. Its windows are carefully barred, even the tiny circular pane that lets light into the second floor.

What has finally caught your eye, though, as you walk past this morning, is the wall that runs perpendicular to the street.

The white paint has fallen away to reveal an undercoat the color of old, dried blood. The contrast between the dirty white and faded cranberry beneath it reveals something else: this wall is neither brick nor stucco nor siding. It appears to be made of square panels.

Curiosity overcomes the embarrassment of being caught in someone else's yard, and you walk up to the house, running a tentative finger over one of the panels.

You feel the nubbly, crusty grit of rusting metal.

Strange, you think. But further inspection confirms it: the panels are actually metal. You've never come across anything like this before.

Sure, you've seen aluminum siding. You've even heard of buildings with stamped tin ceilings. But metal plates? Was this because some long-ago builder got a deal he couldn't refuse? Smiling, you turn to go, pleased that your curiosity has been repaid. Now you've got a story to tell before the meeting.

You're beginning to turn your mind back to the test-data problem when motion draws you back to the house. A piece of paper is emerging from under the door and onto the stoop. You flush, sure you've been caught and hoping you won't be forced into any humiliating explanations for your trespass. But no one opens the door; nobody arrives to peer out at you through the windows. Most of the windows offer views of nothing but blinds or heavy drapes behind their streaked and spattered panes, but behind one window the blinds are kinked, giving you a narrow portal to the inside. When you look there doesn't appear to beanything at all behind the window. You can't quite tell whether you're just looking at an empty room, or whether you're actually looking at emptiness itself. Suddenly you're colder than to-day's weather warrants.

Though you're suddenly conscious of time drawing closer to the meeting, you walk to the door and pick up the piece of paper anyway.

You read one word. "Help" is what the note says.

Now you're feeling uneasy. The sun disappears behind clouds, and the skin on your arms puckers into gooseflesh in the suddenly cool breeze. Then the sun's back out, and you get a grip on yourself. If someone really needs help, and you are the one who provides it, think how good you'll feel. Giving money to the homeless has nothing on this. So what if you're a couple of minutes late for your meeting? That's a small price to pay for a chance to be the hero. You knock on the door.

The sound booms out. The door isn't wood, it's metal. So is the frame, under its fragmenting coat of white. What's more, the brick you thought made up the other walls turns out to be a facade molded onto vinyl or arborite or something like that, laid in sheets over the real walls. Drawing back the edge of one of those sheets from where it abuts the door frame, you uncover more rusted plating. The entire house appears to be walled in metal.

Toronto's always been about as safe as big cities get; why on earth would someone feel the need to armor a house with metal? Even the three little pigs, you remember, were eventually satisfied with brick. What, you wonder, would a tin-plated house be meant to keep out?

Your thoughts return to the note. Somebody clearly saw you looking at the house, and that somebody, for whatever reason, can't get out on their own. The note is hand-printed in haphazard, thin pencil-strokes. An elderly shut-in, perhaps?

The easiest thing to do would be to call the police. But you're in Chinatown, and you read somewhere that people here are reluctant to involve the police in personal affairs. Short of walking down to the divisional headquarters a kilometre east on Dundas, how would you contact the cops? Easier to just stick your head in and see if there really is a problem. If the door's locked, even easier to just walk away.

The door opens — reluctantly, unoiled hinges whining about the miserable lives they lead, but it does open. You step in; a sniff of dry, dusty air scratches at the back of your throat, forcing a brief, barking cough. There's a short hallway ahead of you, and a second door at the end of it. No other exits between you and the second door, so why is it there? An airlock, maybe? To keep out the cold, you decide. As you step toward the second door, you hear a thin click behind you. Turning, you see that the outside door has closed itself. The hinges made no noise this time.

When you try the handle to the outside door, it turns loosely, refusing to engage the bolt.

You've been tricked — or worse. You curse as loudly as you can, but your voice seems to be sucked into the cheap paint on the walls; this hallway is, acoustically, as dead as a whole gross of doornails. When another round of curses accomplishes nothing more than to bring on more coughing, you shrug your shoulders and turn from the outside door to the one at the other end of the hall.

Like its companion, this door is metal. Unlike the other, this one opens as soon as you try it. You're beginning to wonder whether these doors were actually meant to keep anything out, but with little choice you step through the doorway and into the house.

You find yourself standing in a small room. The air is, if anything, even more dry than that in the entry. Your nose twitches as your soft tissues begin to shrink, and the flat smell of old dust is everywhere.

Something isn't quite right about the way the room looks. It's a second before you realize that the light is wrong. It's too bright, too... even. There's no light source other than the window, and the window is blocked by drawn blinds. Yet the light is bright enough that you can see clearly, and diffuse enough that no discernible shadows are cast by the shrouded furniture-shapes in whose midst you're standing. Your eyes begin to widen as you realize that some of the blinds in front of the window are kinked. You're in the room into which you were looking, from outside, just a moment ago. None of these shapes was here then.

There's undoubtedly a rational explanation for all of this. But you'd glady forego logic if you could only be on the other side of that heavily barred window right now. You're not, though; and someone in here still needs help. You turn away from the window and are about to call out to whoever wrote you the note when your hand brushes one of the shrouds covering the furniture. It falls away in a cloud of dust, and the chair it covered is revealed.

The chair is made of bones.

Even as you scream, part of your mind is calculating the size of the bones and confirming that they're human, femurs making the frame, and tibiae and fibulae forming the seat and back. You fly back as quickly as you can, never looking away from the chair, which gleams in the strange light.

The inner door opens willingly enough, but the outer door still refuses to work. You pound on it anyway, until your hands ache, and scream until the dust reduces you to helpless coughing that leads to gagging and retching. The need to regain control of your breathing forces you to tamp down the fear, at least to the point where you can think. However you're going to get out, it won't be this way.

"Up here."

The voice is faint, but you hear it clearly. "Where are you?" you ask.

"Upstairs. Come up here fast. Please."

You think you can hear anguish in the voice, but you really can't be sure. You can't be sure of anything in this place."What is going on in here?" you ask.

"I'll tell you when you find me," the voice says. "But come up here quickly. The dust — "

"It is pretty bad," you begin; but then you turn to look for a staircase and you see what the voice has really been talking about.

Above the skeletal chair a cloud of fine dust has been coalescing. You don't see any apparent movement, but the dust is still forming itself into a coherent shape. In the strange subdued light it almost seems to be glowing, as the shape becomes more recognizably humanoid. Soon, a glowing skull is grinning at you. It might even be pretty, viewed from any safe vantage-point.

You spot the stairs ahead of you and to your left, and as you move toward them the dust-shape moves as well. You begin to run, but the dust moves faster and you are scarcely on the stairs before the dust is on you.

It wraps itself around you, a gritty, spectral cloak. Even as it disperses to encompass you, the dust-thing seems almost to be pulling at you, tugging you downward as its individual components work their way into your soft tissues. Your eyes sting as bitter tears begin to flow; your nose and throat scratch; you collapse to your hands and knees on the stairs as coughing overtakes you. You cough so hard you can't even lift your hands to try to brush the dust away. You cough so hard your head begins to pound and your neck aches with it. You desperately want to stop, but each time you manage to suck in fresh lungsfull of air the vicious, tickling scratching begins in your throat again and once again your head is snapping back and forth as you cough.

Come upstairs, the voice says. There might be safety upstairs. One hand on the bannister, you begin to pull yourself up the stairs. Grit stings your palms and knuckles as the dust insinuates itself between your hands and the wood. You don't dare let go, because while the tugging of the dust-thing is gentle it is insistent, and you are sure that to let go is to be dragged back downstairs, where suffocation is probably the least painful thing that will happen.

In spite of the agony in your throat and lungs, and the pain in your hands, you can see the top of the stairs approaching. The dust-thing is tugging more insistently now, but now that you know what it wants you are all the more determined to deny it, and you continue to struggle upward. Then, suddenly, there is a blast of cold air and the dust is gone.

On your hands and knees at the top of the stairs you cough and cough and cough and then you are vomiting, spewing up clots of yellow, ropy phlegm that seem to glitter for a second as they land on the stairs. Below, the dust-thing reassembles itself and grins at you, and from time to time as you regain your breath it seems to be gesturing to you, commanding you to come back down into its kingdom. As you get unsteadily to your feet you understand at last why this building — if that is what it truly is — has been clad in metal. It is not to keep anything out, but to keep the dust — or whatever force animates it — in.

You find the source of the voice in a small room at the front of the house. High in the far wall is the barred, circular window you saw when you were still safe, ignorant and outside. Slumped below that window is, presumably, the person you're here to help. The young, scrawny body is so emaciated you can't even guess at the person's sex. The gaunt face and short, dark hair provide no clue either. The ugly, blackened wound on one bare leg tells you why she/he didn't come to the stairs to help you.

"You the one who's been talking to me?" you ask. He/she nods.

"What's your name?"

"Chris," is the reply. An androgynous name to go with the androgynous voice and body.

You decide that until you learn differently, you'll think of Chris as male. "How long have you been here, Chris?"

"I don't really know," he says. "A couple of weeks, I think."

You find that hard to believe. Chris is dressed in a t-shirt and cut-off jeans, hardly appropriate wear for the end of March. Dressed like that, it's more likely he's been trapped here since late last summer. But can that be possible? There's a bucket of water and a cracked old teacup beside him, and a stained, yellowed porcelain sink at the far end of the room; you know that, with water, people can survive without food for some time.

You try to think back to stories of missing children, but that's not the sort of thing that normally occupies your mind.

"What happened to you?" you ask. "How did you get trapped here?"

"I was just fooling around," Chris says. "Me and some friends. We were going up Huron, trying back doors to see if any were unlocked. This one was. I came in — and then the door slammed shut behind me and I couldn't get it open again. I don't even know if my friends saw me coming in here. Then when that dust started diving down my throat I freaked. I fell down the stairs — and it was like sliding on sandpaper." He looks down at his leg, and a shiver rattles through him. "I'm afraid it's infected or something. I can hardly stand up, it hurts so bad."

You look at the raw, bleeding knuckles of your right hand, and the scrape on your left palm, and you understand his pain.

Something nags at you, though.

"How did you get that note to me?" you ask, suddenly suspicious. Something about his story isn't ringing true.

"I didn't," he says. "I put it out there when I first tried to get out the front door and found that it didn't work either. I was afraid it had blown away or something, because nobody came for such a long time."

You stare at Chris for a long second. How can you match what he's just said with what your own eyes saw a few minutes ago, when the paper slid out from under the door? And how long ago was that, anyway? You look down at your watch. Suddenly you find it easier to believe Chris's story.

Your watch is running backward.

"Okay," you say. "How do we get you out of here? I've tried the front door and it doesn't work for me, either. Could we work these bars free? The outside of the house is all rusted; maybe the screws holding the bars in are old, too."

"I tried that," Chris says, "before my leg got sore. I couldn't even break the glass."

You're tempted to curse again, but that defence mechanism that keeps adults from swearing around children kicks in, and you kick at the bare linoleum floor instead. "Why doesn't the dust come up here?" you ask.

"I don't know. Something to do with the stairs, maybe. Or maybe it's magic. I haven't gone downstairs to find out since my leg started to hurt."

You think back to your own experience on the stairs. "Maybe it's something as simple as air pressure," you say. "I felt a breeze near the top of the stairs."

"Yeah," Chris says. "I think there must be a vent in the top of the roof or something, because sometimes I can feel the air moving too. I don't know where the vent might be, though."

"I'll go look," you say.

"Listen," Chris says; "the one thing I do know is — "

You don't hear the rest. Fired by the thought that there might be an opening in the top of this metal-clad hell, you rush out of the room.

Five minutes later (you think; by your watch you've been gone thirty seconds in total, not counting the time the second-hand spent moving backward) you're back. There is no vent visible in the ceilings of any of the small rooms on this floor. The only fresh air you've felt is coming from a tiny floor vent, and while that air is cool and scented with the peculiar damp, vegetable-smell of Chinatown in the morning, you're no closer to guessing where it's coming from.

"Listen, mister," says Chris as you step through the doorway. "If you've got an idea of how we can get to one of the doors down there, I think I know how to get the outside door open."

What? Has this kid been holding out on you? "Wait a minute," you say. "You said before that you couldn't get out."

"When I first came in, yeah. But I think I figured it out. I tried to tell you a minute ago, but you didn't listen."

"You can tell me now."

"No."

Anger coalesces like the dust cloud, emerging from your mouth in a shout. "What the hell do you mean, 'no'? Tell me!"

Tears flow, and as he blubbers you suddenly realize just how young Chris really is. The kid can't be more than twelve, he's nearly starved to death, and you're screaming at him like a drill sergeant. "I'm sorry," you mumble. "I just want to get out, that's all."

"I don't want you to leave me here!" Chris cries. "How can I trust you unless I don't tell you how to get out until you've helped me get downstairs?"

Okay. You both need each other, then. It's only appropriate, you suppose. Humans are supposed to be social, cooperative animals.

"I'll help you. You don't have to tell me yet."

Time to try another idea. Unzipping your jacket, you leave the room and walk back to the end of the landing. Cautiously, you step onto the stairs. Below, the dust begins to sparkle and coalesce. Unwilling to trust your watch, you count steamboats until the skull-headed shape is fully formed and moving to the bottom of the stairs. You take another step down, removing your jacket as you do so. The dust-thing begins to move up the stairs.

Flapping your jacked rapidly, you create your own air-pressure differential. The dust-thing explodes into glittering micro-fragments that shoot back into the middle of the main-floor room. You stop flapping, and again you count until the dust has reformed itself. Then, hoping it isn't clever enough to think of a countermeasure in the time you're going to give it, you rush back to Chris's room.

"Take off your t-shirt," you say. He looks puzzled — but he's stopped crying. "We're going to make our own breeze," you say. Tying your jacket around your waist by the sleeves, you walk over to Chris and, as gently as possible, pick him up. It's surprisingly easy to do.

"I'm going to put you on my shoulders," you say. "It's up to you to stay there, though, and you can't use your hands. You're going to have to use those to flap that t-shirt for all you're worth when we get down the stairs."

You don't give Chris a chance to reply; he barely has time to duck as you go through the doorway, untying your jacket and gripping it by the collar as you go. You have to do this quickly, before you have time to think about how simplistically stupid you're being. At the top of the stairs you pause. "Take a deep breath," you say, "and hold it. Just in case." Then you start down the stairs, and as soon as the dust begins to move toward you, you both flap like idiots.

Stupid it may be, but it works. You don't feel any scratching at all, and then you're through the first door, ducking down as you go through. Laughing with relief, you sink to your knees and help Chris off your shoulders. "That was almost too easy," you say. "Now let's get this door open and get out of here."

You look up, and your stomach shrinks into a cold, stony lump at the expression on Chris's face. "You were lying about the door," you say. "Weren't you? You don't know how to open it."

He looks like he's going to cry again. "I do so know," he says. "But — "

"But what?"

"The only way to get the outside door to open is for someone to close the inner door — from the inside."

"What a load of crap," you say. "If you don't know how to get us out, just say so. How could you have 'figured out' something that would mean one of us would have to stay inside when the other one—" You stop, realizing the truth.

Chris doesn't look like he's going to cry anymore. "Of course I didn't figure it out, man. I learned it the same way you're learning it: from the person who was in here before me. That's how this damned place works. One has to come in before another can get out."

"You suckered me." Taken in by a twelve-year-old con artist. That makes you feel just great. "Well, what if I decide I don't want to play that game?"

"Then we both have to stay here until we can get someone else to come in. If it even works that way." Chris will probably die before then, you realize. Then you'll still be stuck here, but with his ghost to keep you company. He's staring at you now, with eyes that are small and dark and far too cold for a kid his age.

You turn away from those eyes. But you can't turn away from the inexorable logic of the situation. After all, you had to be prepared to take some kind of a risk just sticking your head in here. Being late was a small price to pay, you thought. Well, the price has gone up, but it still has to be paid. Your reasons for paying have changed a little, too. Before, all you cared about was a good feeling. Now you can save a life, even if it is just a punk would-be burglar. This house, you decide, is all about sacrifice. You look at him. His leg is in really bad shape. And you're an idiot. "If I help you to leave, do you promise you'll send help?"

"I'll do anything I can." Chris doesn't sound like a twelve-year-old. But who knows what's happened to his mind if he's been trapped in here since last summer, knowing that his only way out was to do what he's just done?

You sigh, and step back through the inner door. You can almost hear the dust chuckling. "Remember," you say as you close the door. "You promised."

"Thanks, man." The door clicks shut. For a mad second, you try to open the inner door, but the handle just spins. When the door does open, the hallway is empty and the outer door is closed again.

You sit down on the floor, trying not to cry and wondering how long you'll be here. At least you're pretty sure you can get back upstairs without the dust getting into you again. And maybe, being mobile and determined, you can find another way out of here before help comes. Maybe.

You take your notepad and pen from the inner pocket of your jacket, and start to write a note. Your note is detailed; you're in the information business, after all, and you pride yourself on being thorough. You include everything you know about the dust-thing, and the doors — and when you're finished, you crumple the note and put it into your pocket.

It's occurred to you to wonder: if you had known, from the outset, what was waiting for you in here, would you have opened the door at all?

The note you eventually slide under the door contains just a single word.

HORROR STORY

by
Robert Boyczuk

Robert Boyczuk confides: "I originally wrote
this story at the Clarion West Workshop in
1993 during the week when Lucius Shepard
was our instructor. As part of his critique, he
rewrote a page and a half in his own inimita-
ble style. Three years later, after selling a
number of other stories, I tried to do what I
had previously thought impossible: to rewrite
the entire piece in the same voice that Lucius
had used in his original revision. Much to my
delight, no one has yet been able to pick out
the part he wrote."

The third murder happened at a dumpy motel on Lakeshore Boulevard, just off the Gardiner Expressway. The Lakeview Inn. A real hole, peeling paint and pigeon shit everywhere. Meyers sat hunched in his car, parked behind two cruisers, staring at the scene through the curve of his windshield. The motel was a way station for the down and out, for transients, junkies, prostitutes and their johns—rooms to let by the week, day or hour. Meyers was familiar with its water-stained walls, its florid, torn curtains, its grey, sway-backed mattresses. When he'd worked vice, he'd been here on at least half a dozen calls. Bright yellow tape, snapping in late autumn gusts, closed the entrance way. The uniforms had sealed off the parking lot even though it was empty. Leaves scudded across the cracked asphalt. Through the big plate-glass window of the office he could see the sad-eyed, East Indian woman who worked the front desk. She was flanked by a couple of detectives, pads open, scribbling impassively as she talked.

Christ, how could this be happening?

I knew, Meyers wanted to tell them. *I knew the call was coming.* But what could he have said? That this morning, while scrambling eggs for Sarah, he'd seen the killer outside his kitchen window? No, not seen. Not clearly, anyway. More a silhouette flitting between houses, an indistinct, half-formed image, flat mask for a face with only the eyes clear, two tiny pinpricks of ruby light, blazing points that pulsed with the rhythm of his own heartbeat.

Twice before he'd seen the shadow, each time just before the call had come. This morning had been the third.

There was no fucking way he could tell them. *A shadow?* they'd ask in disbelief, then laugh. *You saw a shadow?* And the Staff Inspector would call it stress, and replace him with someone who could no more help the case than Meyers could help seeing his shadow. Perhaps if had explained earlier, in the beginning....

Shit, no. Even then they'd have figured he was nuts. He couldn't have told them about the dark figure that stalked the edges of his world, that lurked just outside the periphery of his vision. Nor about the file folder he carried with him all the time now, that sat on the passenger seat of his car. A folder he'd pulled from the dust-grimed filing cabinet in his basement when he'd first understood the pattern. Christ almighty! He stared at the folder. It had been an exercise. Just a fucking exercise!

Meyers' hands trembled; a trickle of perspiration ran down his temple, clung to the edge of his jaw.

Even the Scotch didn't seem to be helping. He had dawdled, let the others leave the Operations Room before him, telling them he had to make a quick call, that he'd meet them at the Lakeview; and when they'd all gone, he pulled the mickey from his desk drawer, taken a stiff pull on it, then slipped it into his pocket. Now the smokey bottle weighed heavily in his hand again, its stubby, black cap atop the folder on the passenger seat. Ducking so the cops in the office couldn't see him, he took another slug, screwed the cap back on, then tossed it into the glove compartment, snapping the door shut with his elbow. He wiped the sleeve of his overcoat across his mouth and climbed from the car.

Halfway along the boxy, white-washed block of rooms, a door stood open; figures swam through the murkiness inside, a uniform standing watch outside. Meyers ducked under the police tape, walked unsteadily across the lot. He nodded brusquely at the officer, sucked in a big breath and plunged inside the room.

Luckas' bulky form loomed up, blocked the view. He held a half-eaten cinnamon roll in his left hand; a coffee steamed in his right. "About time you got here."

At first Meyers couldn't see anything. Then, as his eyes adjusted to the dim light, he saw either end of the bed, Luckas' girth still blocking its middle. A pair of arms and legs was all he could see, the body spreadeagled by black straps wound around wrists and ankles, the straps secured to the four thick wooden feet of the bed. A leather jacket, jeans, and a pair of ragged underwear had been neatly laid out on a chair near the head of the bed. Leather biker boots sat on the floor at the foot of the bed. On the far wall, the words, *Once upon a time* had been painted in blood. Meyers throat tightened.

"Thought we'd have to send someone out to look for you," Luckas smirked.

Meyers brushed past him.

Like the others, this victim had been splayed like a pinned insect. Two lines had been neatly incised at the top of his chest, and wadded, blood-soaked kleenex had been stuffed inside to distend the skin below the incisions into the shape of small breasts. He had been emasculated, his penis and scrotum cut away, a crude vagina formed and the flaps of skin held in place by several large safety pins. The sheets beneath him were black with dried blood. His thin, parted lips had been slathered with bright red lipstick, and, beneath his open eyes, exaggerated dark circles had been painted in mascara that gave him a plaintive, questioning look, sad and bewildered, as if he couldn't quite believe what he'd become. His eyes seemed to stare at Meyers, asking him, *Why? Why did you do this to me?*

Christ. The bitch had done it again. Something inside Meyers crumpled like a tissue crisped by a flame. He felt the blood drain from his face.

"No signs of struggle," Luckas said. He took a big bite out of his roll, a thick line of cream bleeding onto his chin. He nodded towards the wall.

No shit, Meyers thought. No fucking shit. Stun guns don't leave marks. But he couldn't tell them about the 40,000 volt gun; not yet. They'd think it was too fucking weird that he knew. They'd just have to figure it out themselves. Forensics would pick it up eventually. Wouldn't they?

"Put on your gloves. You've been elected to baggie detail," Luckas said, grinning. He put his coffee down on an end table, pulled an extra-large, zip-lock baggie from the pocket of his rumpled jacket and shoved it at Meyers. "You can begin with the garbage pail in the washroom. That's where his balls are. Oh, and look before you pour yourself a drink," Luckas said stuffing the bag in Meyers' hand. "His dick is in a dixie cup by the sink."

But then, Meyers already knew that, didn't he? That was the way he'd written it.

Alone. Everyone else had gone home long ago.

The lights of the Operations Room at Metro Headquarters burnt brightly, painfully. Meyers turned on every one of them when he'd felt the darkness pressing against the window panes like a slavering beast. Against the utter black, the unnatural brilliance dazzled him, made his head spin. Meyers snatched his glass from the desk, Scotch slopping over the side and watering his hand. It was his fourth—no fifth. He took a big swig, let the warmth of the liquid wash down his gullet, quell his jangling nerves, blunt the glare of the lights. Then his hand fell, the thick bottom of the glass clacking loudly against desktop, making him jump. He released the glass, watched it wobble for a second, then settle.

Two folders lay on his desk.

One was old, shedding fibres along its edges, its cover stained, dog-eared. The other folder was new, unmarked, drawn from the supply cabinet that afternoon.

Meyers opened the fresh one. He stared at the white sheets, filled with crisp, orderly lines of black type. The crime scene report he'd written earlier today. Clean, neat, methodical. The murder reduced to simple, comprehensible facts:

Arriving at the scene at 10:45 a.m., I found the victim, subsequently identified as Ronald Kurt Aikmen, in room 12 at the Lakeview Inn. The subject sustained numerous sharp force injuries, including massive incisions in his pelvis and chest. Coagulated and dried blood stained the bed and surrounding carpet, principally near the pelvis of the victim. Cordura straps had been looped around the wrists and ankles of the decedent and secured to the feet of the bed. The victim was naked with the exception of a leather vest. Lividity was fixed and rigor mortis was fully established. To the right of the bed, a flannel shirt, leather jacket, and jeans had been neatly arranged on a chair...

He poured himself another shot, a smaller one; he threw it back. The tremor in his hand seemed to diminish infinitesimally. Goddamn if he couldn't have used this earlier, when he'd had to bag that guy's nuts.

Meyers slapped the folder closed. The bottle clicked against his glass as he poured himself a double this time. A moment later the burning liquid curled into his throat. Yeah. That seemed to do the trick.

He fingered the other folder; its cover was filled with scribbles, names and phone numbers, cryptic notes made to himself that no longer made sense, and the name of a recommended restaurant to which he'd never had the chance to go. It was an exercise he'd done at the seminar in Pennsylvania, nearly seven years ago. Something he'd almost forgotten, stuck in a filing cabinet in his basement, along with miscellany of his life: tax returns, receipts, warranties and bills, birth and marriage certificates, the deed to his house, a yellowing envelope containing his only citation in an otherwise undistinguished career at Metro.

He flicked the folder open.

Inside were several sheets with his cramped handwriting, all in pencil. On its index tab he'd written the name *VICKI* in large, dramatic letters, then underlined the name twice. It had been his project, an exercise in creating a psychological profile for a serial killer. While the other cops at the workshop had struggled to imagine a killer, his had flowed easily, naturally. But then, he'd always liked that sort of thing, making stuff up. Like the stories he'd woven for Sarah soon after they started dating. At first he'd thought it was kind of weird, the way she'd insisted, late at night when they were settled into the pocket of warmth beneath the quilt, that he tell her a story. But, much to his surprise, he found he had a talent for storytelling. For imagining things he'd never seen.

Vicki is a white female, in her early to mid-thirties; she keeps herself in good shape. Personal appearance is very important to her. Parts of her residence, however, are disordered. She has split into half a dozen distinct personalities, all with different and sometimes conflicting needs (though bits of each leak through into the other's life). Two personalities dominate, one meticulous and organized, who keeps an immaculate home, a woman who has no close friends but many acquaintances, and seems to be searching for stability—and is possi-

bly even married; the other a careless, often slovenly, thrill seeker, insensible to threat and oblivious to danger, though acutely aware of her other half's attitudes towards her—and often resentful of them. When living this second aspect of her personality, she frequents local bars, strikes up conversations with complete strangers, takes them to their homes or hotel rooms.

Vicki is the only daughter in a family of men. From an early age she was raped repeatedly by her father and brothers, suffering severe beatings in the process. What Vicki remembers of the women in her family is unflattering: she sees her mother as an ineffectual, withdrawn woman who suffered similar abuse at the hands of the male members of the family, and slipped into alcoholic or drug induced stupors to numb her pain. Most importantly, perhaps, Vicki came to see her mother as a passive, non-threatening, creature. From this stems her desire to remake the people in her world into equally non-threatening entities...

Meyers' teacher at the FBI's road school had dismissed these preliminary notes as contradictory, an unlikely blend of psychological traits. Too clever, he had called Meyers' work, designed only to fool his fellow students, and of little use in real life. There was simply not enough information available on women serial killers to justify his portrait.

Vicki. Meyers could see her clearly in his mind's eye, just as he had all those years ago. Short cropped blonde hair. A severe, narrow face. Grey, washed out eyes, flat and lifeless, shoulders stooped and withdrawn, begging to be ignored, left alone. Except... except when she hunted; then her eyes shone, glittered like chips of ice, cold and dark and predatory. As they did now in his imagination. She smiled at him, a sly mocking thing that made him shudder.

No! He slammed a fist down on the desk. You're not real! I made you up! He shook his head, trying to dislodge the picture of her, but only succeeded in making the room spin.

Christ, he thought, panicky, staring at the sheet. Christ almighty! Sweat rolled down his temple, collected in the small of his back. He pulled his hand from atop the page, leaving a dark palm print in its centre. An absurd notion occurred to him: he wondered if perhaps no serial killer, not a single one, had ever existed except in their files, that it was the fact of the files that had given them shape and meaning and life.

Swallowing, he turned the pages, lifting the pieces of paper like he'd have lifted the sheet from a corpse in the morgue, until he came to the descriptions. His mock crime scene reports. The third one began,

The victim, an unidentified white male, approximate age 30, was discovered in room 3A of the Sandylot Hotel by the chambermaid. The decedent was naked with the exception of a leather vest. Cordura straps had been used to bind the subject to the bed. Minor bruising was observed on the victim's upper right shoulder and two large sharp force injuries were evident on the victim's upper chest and lower pelvis. A leather jacket, jeans and boots had been arranged neatly on a chair to the right of the bed...

There were still three more reports left in the folder. They were only supposed to write two reports, but Meyers had enjoyed the assignment so much he'd written six. *Six.* Meyers' stomach felt like a knot being pulled tight. He grabbed the mickey, turned it upside down over his glass, and was rewarded with only a thin trickle, two, maybe three, drops. Empty. Goddamn empty.

The bottle banged into Meyers' wastepaper basket, spun the pail until it fell to its side flinging its contents onto the floor, spilling rubbish everywhere.

In his head, Meyers heard the echo of Vicki's mocking laughter.

Sarah was in bed when Meyers got home.

Swaying only slightly, he tiptoed into the room. Close now, he could see she breathed deeply, regularly. Her clothes were scattered about the room, and, weaving between bed and dresser, he picked them up, one by one, a silk blouse and a linen skirt in a pile near the closet, a serge jacket thrown carelessly across the foot of the bed, one arm brushing the floor. Her clothes were expensive, impeccable, beautiful. Like she was. In her late thirties, and she could still turn heads. Meyers placed each item carefully on a hangar and smoothed it, his fingers thick and coarse against the fine material.

"David?" Her voice weighted by sleep. She stirred, propped herself up on an elbow, blonde hair spilling over her shoulders and across her small, perfect breasts. In the cross-thatched shadows of their room her face was hidden, her expression veiled, unknowable. Meyers stepped over to the bed and gently brushed back her hair until he could see the pale oval of her face. But in the dark it wasn't the face he remembered, its lines and edges were different, deeper, hardened. The face of a stranger. How long since he had last looked at it closely?

"You've been drinking." She pushed his hands away, like she was disgusted. "Dammit, David," she said, her voice tired, resigned. "You're going to kill yourself."

"Just a quick one. After work."

She drew her lips into a tight line; her eyes narrowed. She looks pissed, more pissed than usual. "I waited an hour." Her voice was cool, not angry, more detached than anything, as if her words belonged to a different scene, a different couple. "Where were you?" she asked, staring at the sheets, the wall, the open closet, anything but him.

Then it hit him. *La Piazza*. Her favourite restaurant on Bloor. Christ, how could he have forgotten? He was supposed to have met her there for lunch. Then drive her to the garage where they were going to pick up her old Tercel. He'd forgotten all about it when the call on the latest victim had come in that morning.

"Sorry." He dropped numbly onto the edge of the bed, moving his hand towards her again, but she continued to recede. "Work, you know—"

"Shit, David! I had to take a cab to the garage, and I didn't have enough money with me to pay for the work. They had to replace the whole bumper. They almost wouldn't let me have the car." She pulled herself into a sitting position, away from him, crossing arms over her breasts. "I had to promise them you'd come by tomorrow with the rest of it."

"Don't worry. I'll take care of it. Tomorrow."

She frowned, but said nothing.

"We had another one today."

She stiffened, and her voice sounded strained, not frightened exactly, but tense, breathless, as if she was struggling to control it. "You know I don't like hearing about these things."

She thought his work gruesome. At home, she skipped past the stories of murder and mayhem in the papers, flicked the remote whenever they came on the news. But the Scotch had loosened his tongue.

"Just south of here. Along the Lakeshore."

Pulling up her legs, she wrapped her arms around her shins, flattening her breasts. "David, please—"

"The Lakeview Motel. You must know it." Meyers stared at the curve of her muscled calf. "You jog past it all the time."

Her eyes darkened. "Jesus. What did you have to tell me that for? You know I hate hearing about these things!" She shuddered.

"No reason to worry. You're safe." Reaching up, he placed his hands on her arms. Cool. Her skin was cool, like that of a fresh corpse. He began rubbing her arms, trying to put some warmth back in them, but she shrugged free of his grip, edged backwards. He let his hands drop to the bed. "She's only interested in men."

"She?"

Meyers panicked; he pushed off of the bed, staggered over to the dresser, clutched it for support. Christ. What the fuck was he thinking? He hadn't told anyone yet. They were only beginning to suspect. But no one had seriously suggested the killer was a woman yet. "He? She?" He tried to shrug nonchalantly. "Whoever."

"You said *she*. A woman."

"I did?" Meyers lowered his head, swallowed. He decide to bite the bullet. "Yeah. I think so, anyway." He shrugged. "It would answer a lot of questions."

Sarah nodded gravely in the dark; she seemed infinitely distant. A mystery deeper than any of the ones he confronted every day. If only he could apply the same methods to his own life...

Christ, yes! Why hadn't he thought of it before? He was an investigator, a problem solver, a simple fact that had somehow eluded him before. It was only a matter of finding the proper clues to untangle Sarah's motivation, to understand what needed to be done to keep them from drifting even further apart, to repair the damage time and indifference had done. A strange optimism flushed him, a crazy hope. "Listen," Meyers said in a sudden rush, stumbling back towards the bed. "Let's go away, huh?" His words were quick, excited, his hands extended. "When all of this is over. I'll take some time. We'll go away somewhere nice. What do you think?" Meyers meant it, really meant it this time, though he was not sure how to say it convincingly, how to make the words sound real instead of like the drivel that came out of the telvision. Jesus, he hadn't told her a story in years. Even though he knew she loved them. When had that all stopped? Why had it stopped? He couldn't remember. It had just faded, disappeared without a trace. But he'd make up for it. Had to make up for it.

He reached out, thinking he might tell her about the folder he'd pulled from the filing cabinet in the basement, about the shadows. About his monster. But she jerked back reflexively, eyes wide, surprising him. Could she smell his fear, sense in her own groping way the weight of his responsibility, the guilt leaking out from around his edges. "Sarah?"

She blinked, pulled the sheets up around her, then looked away. "You know I hate to hear about this stuff."

His heart, thumping expectantly an instant ago, withered. He let his hands fall to his sides. It was too late for stories. It was too for anything. How could he have believed that he might unburden himself to her? Silence had grown too strong a habit between them, become too much part of their lives. He was alone in this. Turning, he walked to the door, paused, hand on the jamb. "I've got some reports to go over."

She nodded distantly, but he could see she wasn't really listening, hadn't really listened to him in years. Some actions had no motivation that could be understood; like random, pointless, murders, some feelings couldn't be solved.

Three days later the shadows gathered again.

Meyers stared out the fourth floor hallway window by the vending machines, the coins in his hand forgotten, his attention focussed on the small square opposite the station. Not a square, really, more an interruption in the face of abutted office towers, an indentation in which a few low-slung concrete benches had been scattered around two large, ugly concrete planters. The space was empty, the awnings of an adjacent bar trembling in the breeze, the day bright and relentless, casting sharp dark lines that sliced the world into strange, distended planes. Beneath the arching branches of a denuded oak, in its shadows, blackness in the form of a human shape uncoiled, twisting and turning like a grub in black earth.

Meyers stomach flip-flopped; his coins clattered to the floor.

The shadow solidified like an egg hardening in a frying pan; colours sprang up along the thing's edges, ran along it like spikes of flame. Clamping his jaw shut and fighting a rising panic, Meyers willed it to still, to cease its restless stirring. The tendons in his neck tightened with his concentration.

His efforts were having an effect. The shadow's growth slowed, became sluggish, then stopped. He felt the tug of it against his will, fighting to take on shape. Vicki's shape. But, if the thing didn't grow, neither did it shrink. A standoff. Sweat collected on his brow, ran down along his temples; he trembled. If only he could hang on, he might yet drive it back into the recesses from which it sprang.

"DTs got you?"

The words jolted Meyers. A hand clasped his shoulder, making him jerk like he'd been shocked. He blinked rapidly, his eyes suddenly watering as if they stung. His attention wavered then dissolved, his eyes cutting to Luckas who had spoken, then back to the tree. But in the moment of his lapse, the shadow had completed its metamorphosis. A woman stood there, wrapped in a long coat blacker than the deepest shadows. Her face was shaded by the broad brim of a hat, but her head was angled towards him. Two crimson points for eyes, watching him. She waved. The bitch waved!

Meyers' shoved past Luckas, ran towards the stairwell.

"Asshole." Luckas' word pursued Meyers as he took the steps two at a time. He broke out into the bitter fall light of the day and loped heedlessly across the street, ignoring the squeal of tires and the angry honks.

Gone. She'd fled. The square was deserted.

Meyers looked up and down the canyon of office towers. Nothing. Not a Goddamned thing. A few pedestrians strolling in the distance, carrying shopping bags, office workers in suits but no overcoats hustling from heated building to heated building, an older man walking a terrier. And doors. Dozen of doors, any one of which she could have slipped through.

"Fuck!" The shout burst from him; several people glanced over, then looked away quickly, hurrying past, and Meyers was suddenly aware he was standing there in the square, jacketless, his shoulder harness visible for all to see.

She was gone. And there was nothing he could do but return to the Operations Room and wait for the next call. This time it would be a security guard, a deserted office building, and common hardware-store string in large, crude stitches in place of safety pins.

The call came early the next morning.

"Rise and shine, asshole," Luckas said when Meyers picked the phone up, the big man taking obvious delight in waking Meyers. But Meyers was up, had been up most of the night, sitting at the dining room table with his file spread out before him. In a way it was preferable to contemplating the insuperable barrier of Sarah's back. "We got another one. The night watchman in the Hunter-Thompson Building. Fifth floor washroom. Jesus, doesn't this guy ever sleep?"

Half listening to Luckas, Meyers lifted a sheet of paper. *The fourth victim, the security guard at Dominion Securities*, began the report, *was found the day after the previous murder.*

He crumpled the page in his fist, let it fall to the floor. The phone was back in its cradle, but Meyers couldn't remember hanging it up. The Hunter-Thompson Building. He'd been in the building a few times, the last time maybe two years ago. To pick up Sarah who'd been working as a copy editor for a trade publication, something to do with concrete. Had she worked on the fifth floor? He couldn't remember. Christ, he'd even used the washroom there, once.

Half an hour later, Meyers' heart was hammering, his pulse pounding in his neck, as he walked through the glassed-in lobby of the building. But even when he stepped off the elevator on the fifth floor, he couldn't be sure if this was where Sarah had worked; if it was, the partitions had been changed, the furniture moved. He followed a trail of police tape to the washroom.

"You look like shit," Luckas said. He half-leaned, half-sat against a long vanity with four sinks, flipping idly through a pad filled with scribbles. "The photographer's not here yet."

Meyers ignored him; instead his eyes flicked over the scene, the smashed mirrors, the smears of blood over the tiled floor, the guard's feet sticking out from the last stall, the metal trash can with the mess spilling out of its flap. A fucking mess. He took another step into the room and glass ground loudly under the soles of his shoes.

"Lucked out this time," Luckas said, grinning.

"What?" Meyers blinked stupidly. He'd been trying to remember if the mirror had been on this side of the washroom he'd used. Christ, all these places looked the same.

"We maybe got a witness," Luckas said tapping his pad with a thick forefinger. "A cleaning lady. She said she saw someone leaving just as she was coming in for her shift. A *woman*."

Meyers heart froze; he stared at Luckas, every atom in his body seemed to quiver, every sense intensified, painfully aware of the buzz of the fluorescent lights, of the intermittent drip from the closest tap.

"Can you fuckin' believe it? A broad's been doing this." Luckas shook his head ruefully. "The cleaning lady didn't get a good look at her face. Short, pale, thin. Orange, spiky hair. Carrying a black case. Leather dress and jacket, she said."

Christ Jesus. It wasn't Vicki. Not the Vicki he'd described, anyway. He'd never imagined her with the hair or the leather skirt and jacket.

"Oh, and she said some weird shit about her eyes, like they glowed or something." Luckas snorted.

Meyers' stomach fluttered, like he'd hit a dip on a rollercoaster.

Luckas flipped his pad closed. With his free hand he pulled something from his pocket, flicked his wrist. The thing shot across the washroom, struck Meyers squarely in the chest and dropped to the floor between his feet. A pair of latex gloves in a plastic package. "Come on," Luckas said cheerfully. "Let's get to work."

Eleven p.m. and Sarah wasn't home.

Meyers sat in the wingback chair by the door, a small bottle of scotch balanced on its arm, rolling his glass with the tips of his fingers, back and forth, watching the amber liquid pitch first one way then the other.

His tongue tingled from too many drinks.

Something was buzzing inside Meyers' head. He tried to rub it away by pressing the glass of Scotch against it, but the glass felt hot, scalding hot against his temple, and he dropped it, liquor and ice splashing the papers scattered at his feet and going all over the rug. He knew he should clean it up, Sarah would go nuts, her favorite rug. He slid down out of the chair and gingerly touched the glass. Cool, now. He needed a rag, but was too drunk to want to get up again; he shrugged out of his shirt, began blotting up the liquor, bunching ice cubes in the folds. The thing in his head was still angry at him, like a wasp on a hot summer's day bumping into the windowpane. How could he fucking work with this shit going on? He pressed the damp of his shirt to his forehead, felt the chill go deep, breathed fumes of Scotch. There, that was all right, that was the ticket. He glanced up, hearing a click from somewhere in the house, some mechanism, the furnace, the water heater, switching on. Shadows everywhere, closing in on the lamplit oval where he was sitting; but when they felt the pressure of his stare, they oozed back several inches, like frightened oil.

The report. He had to see his report again. Dropping his shirt, he moved the strewn pages around, sheet sliding on sheet, mixing them even more. Then he spotted it, the one he wanted, a brown streak on its upper right corner, smudges of chocolate from a candy bar he'd been eating when he first wrote it years ago. He snatched it up, stuck it in front of his face. It was hard to read, his tiny crabbed handwriting swimming like an army of spiders across the sheet.

The fifth victim is a salesman on his bi-annual trip to Toronto. His body was discovered in the bathtub of his room in the Sutton Place Hotel...

He thought about Sarah alone in the house all day, his filing cabinet collecting dust in the basement. Bored, she might have noticed it one day, pulled open the drawer searching for something, anything....

Jesus, what was he thinking?

Sarah was nothing like Vicki. Was she? He'd met her parents several times, and they were both normal, stable people, not like the parents of the killer in his profile.

Unless....

A vague memory drifted through his mind like the snatches of a half-remembered song. A late night shortly after he'd met Sarah, before she'd given up drinking, two or three bottles of wine into the evening and a slurred recollection about her childhood, about her...step-parents? Had she called them that? Or was he imagining it, constructing and reconstructing the memory as he had the killer in his file, as they did now in the Operations Room, piecing the portrait together bit by bit until it matched his own?

No! Not Sarah! Christ, he was a cop. He'd been trained to identify the signs, would have recognized such darkness long ago, seen it for what it was. And have helped her. He was always willing to help, wasn't he? He shook his head to clear away the creeping fog.

But what that left him with was, a ghost, a phantom. A paper killer.

Where are you, Sarah? he wondered.

On hands and knees, his glass cradled in one fist, he crawled back to the chair and the bottle of Scotch miraculously still balanced on its arm.

"David?"

Meyers opened his eyes, and the light made his head throb; his mouth was dry, filled with the gummy residue of Scotch. He sat in the wingback chair, something hard pressed between the arm of the chair and his thigh. A glass. His empty glass.

"David, I'm leaving."

He lifted his head, and a spike of pain shot through his neck, blazed in his skull. Colors danced madly before him; the radio blared loudly in the background. Who had left it on? "What?" he croaked; everything was too dazzling, too loud, a hash, and he couldn't make it settle into any kind of sense.

"I didn't want to sneak off. I wanted you to know."

His eyes snapped into focus. Sarah stood by the open door, a look of disgust on her face. Her gaze wandered over the scattered sheets, the stained carpet, the wadded mass of his shirt. "I'll pick up the rest of my things later," she said. Bending, she lifted her suitcase. Then, she was gone, vanished, like she'd never been there in the first place. He hadn't seen her turn, walk out the door, but she wasn't there.

Meyers heaved himself to his feet, staggered forward, crashing into the doorframe, his head spinning, the muscles in his legs rubbery and unwilling. His vision blurred, then cleared, in time to see Sarah climb into her Toyota. The new front bumper glinted blackly against the fading red paint of the car's exterior. Meyers blinked, looked through the windshield. Behind Sarah, in the back seat, a shadow rose, like someone sitting up, but it was a silhouette, an emptiness darker than tar, its only clear feature two pupilless, glowing ovals in the centre of her face, eyes that expressionless red colour you'd sometimes get in pictures taken with a flash. Eyes staring blankly at Meyers. Asking...asking for what? Christ, he thought, trembling uncontrollably. Christ almighty.

The engine started, and the headlights flared in the night, blinding him, making him raise his arm across his eyes.

"Sarah! No! Stop!"

Her car backed out, its lights raking the front of the house as it swung into the road.

Meyers stumbled back into the house, crashed through the bedroom, the hallway closet, the kitchen, until he found his jacket on the back of a chair. He rifled the pockets, looking for his keys. Not there. He began his frantic search again, tearing through the house, his head throbbing, his heart hammering, his stomach heaving. But the keys weren't anywhere.

By the time he found them dangling from the ignition of his car, it was too late, she'd been gone nearly five minutes and there was no hope of catching her.

The phone in the Operations Room trilled, and Meyers jumped a little, just as he had every time it rang that morning.

He felt like shit. His head throbbed unmercifully; he shivered, sweat peppering his forehead, running freely beneath his arms. It rang again, and Meyers shuddered. Standing in front of the corkboard, he pretended to study the sheets of paper tacked to the board, the psychological profile of the killer. Behind him, he heard a sigh, the creak of leather shoes, the click of the receiver being lifted.

"Yeah?" Luckas' rough voice, sounding bored. "Yeah, okay. I got it. We'll be right there." The sound of the receiver being dropped back into its cradle.

"Number five," Luckas announced to the room.

Meyers turned with the others, watched Luckas shake his head; he looked pissed, like this time he'd been insulted personally. "The Erskine Hotel," he said gruffly. "Jesus, can you believe the balls?"

The Erskine Hotel. A block away. Only a block.

Meyers knew the place, because once he'd spent a weekend there with Sarah. Just for the hell of it. *Let's be good to ourselves*, she'd said, giggling. She'd always been that way, impulsive where Meyers was methodical. It was one of the things he had loved about her. Her impetuousness. He'd capitulated, gave in to her whim. They'd taken the Oriental Suite, complete with Japanese teak furniture, hinged, painted screens, a hot tub with woven mats next to it, and a king-size water bed with an ornate headboard. They'd ordered champagne. Sitting across from him in the tub, he'd thought it would be fun to watch the soft-core porno movies on the tv, but she'd shaken her head, then said, "Tell me a story."

And in the midst of swirling jets of heated water, with the inspiration of the implausible setting and the wine coursing through his veins, Meyers had told her stories, one after another, as if they would never end...

The body had been carved up in the same way as the others. But this time it had been dumped in the hot tub, an empty champagne bottle and two shattered glasses beneath it. Around the tub the killer had arranged two black lacquered screens, their panels filled with the pink cherry blossom trees, long-necked cranes, and incomprehensible Japanese ideographs.

What was happening?

Meyers barely managed to stagger through the day. Three times he'd slipped away to call everyone he could think of: Sarah's parents, her few friends, the fitness club to which she belonged, even the people at the store where she'd worked last year during the Christmas holidays. But no one had heard from her. Or if they had, they weren't telling him. When he spoke to her mother, he tried to sound calm, as if this was nothing more than a small spat. But when she began to flip out, Meyers told her that he was sure Sarah was all right. Knew that she was fine. For an instant he thought about telling her. But Christ, what could he say, that he was worried her daughter had been kidnapped by a shadow? He made reassuring noises, promised to call her her the moment he heard anything, made her promise the same thing. And in all this he lost his nerve to ask her about Sarah's past, to confirm or refute his hazy, alcohol-laden recollection of what she'd said about her adoption.

At six p.m. they finished with the scene, and Meyers stepped from the Hotel into an overcast day, dark, snarled clouds blotting out the lowering sun.

Jesus, he was tired. He hadn't slept well in days, not at all in the last twenty-six hours. He felt giddy, light-headed. People hurried past, clutching their coats tightly around them, holding their hats firmly on their heads against an bitter, blustering wind. Meyers moved forward, travelling on a wave of numbing energy, an enervated momentum that pushed at his back like a large, insistent hand, driving him ahead, across the street to Headquarters and the underground parking lot. He found himself in his car, his hands clutched tightly on the wheel to keep them from shaking.

Where now?

Home. He'd go home.

But without Sarah, the word *home*, the whole concept, seemed empty, pointless. Repellant. His stomach churned apprehensively. Bad idea. Maybe he'd just drive around for a while, to get his bearings. To calm down. Stop somewhere for a quick one. A drop to help him think things through. His mouth watered. Yeah, that was what he needed. Sarah would understand, wouldn't she? How could she fault him for doing what he had to? He imagined the sting of Scotch sliding down his throat, its perfume seeping into his brain, blunting the edges of his jagged world. He fumbled for the keys he'd dropped on the passenger's seat, stuck them in the ignition, pulled the car out of the lot.

He drove through two intersections; at the third, the light went yellow. He pulled up to the crosswalk just as the first drops of rain pattered onto his windshield. Then it began pissing down, sluicing off his windshield in tiny streams that blurred the outside world. Meyers starcd out, unseeing, into the wash of colours. A patch of red across the street snagged his attention.

Red like Sarah's car.

He flicked on his wipers, forced his eyes to focus.

On the opposite side of the intersection, idling at the stoplights, was a Tercel, its front bumper too new for the rest of the car, its driver an outline.

The shadow.

Christ Jesus! Meyers' heart stuttered, stalled.

It was her. Alone in Sarah's car.

The figure was sitting upright, clearly visible, dead black where there should have been some detail, some hint of colour, of flesh, but there was only absolute, undifferentiated black. And two tiny red glimmers for eyes.

As the light went green and the Tercel pulled away, Meyers spun his steering wheel around—then stomped on his brakes to keep from tee-ing into a beige Bonneville that trundled into the intersection behind the Toyota, drifting past like it was moving in slow motion. By the time he managed to pull a u-turn, the Tercel was two blocks ahead. Meyers hit the gas, swung around the Bonneville, just making the next light, and closed on the Tercel, his breath coming hard, but beginning to get a grip, to think coherently, to feel a strong, gleeful confidence. No way she was going to lose him now. He'd cuff her, beat her, blow holes in her if he had to, whatever it took to make her return Sarah. Panic tightened his chest when he realized he left his gun behind. No, no, wait. The glove compartment. He'd stuck it there that morning. He punched open the compartment, kccping an eye on the Tercel, and groped inside it, felt weighted leather, the familiar grip. Fucking A! He was down with it this time.

A block ahead, the Tercel sped up and turned right. Maybe she'd spotted him. Shit! Meyers swung after her, cutting across the apron of a gas station with a big painted sign out front proclaiming NO AIR, some guy in a greasy coverall cursing at him, and sped along a residential street, houses here and there among the clusters of low-rise apartments, and every fifty feet or so a diseased-looking sapling planted on the narrow mcdian. The Tercel was still a block ahead, and before Meyers could cut much of the distance, it turned again. By the time he rounded the corner, it had pulled ahead nearly two blocks, separated from him by three cars. He slammed his hand against the steering wheel in frustration, so hard pain spiked his wrist, and he leadfooted the gas, blowing through a stop sign.

They were in some kind of industrial park.

Ahead, the Tercel's right taillight flashed once, then it disappeared, unhurriedly, around the corner. Meyers honked, roared past a white sedan, his wheels squealing as he took the corner and—

—tromped on his brakes.

A dead end.

A short street lined with squat, red-brick buildings, concrete stairs leading up to metal doors, narrow margins on which cars had been parked haphazardly under NO PARKING signs, crammed in between dented, green dumpsters. And at the very end, facing him, a bar, a glaring neon sign low along its front, parts burnt out, others flickering and buzzing angrily, red in a border of white: *Vicki's Place*. The Tercel was parked under the sign, jammed between two other cars, the door on its driver's side open. Meyers thought about the last crime scene report he'd written for his project, about the final victim, a bartender.

His stomach went cold. Lifting his foot off the brake, he let his car roll forward, fat drops of rain thumping on the roof and splattering on his windshield. He angled in behind the Toyota, blocking it.

Meyers switched off the engine, climbed out of his car into the downpour. Shoulders hunched against the rain, he sidled up to the bar's entrance, a blistered wooden door, and listened. Nothing but the staccato pattering of rain. Cautiously, he pushed the door open. It swung inward easily.

Just inside was a small foyer with flimsy, plywood walls. He stepped in, paused, hand on the inner door. He sniffed the air, a whiff of something underneath the smell of stale beer and urine, something trickling past him that, at first, he couldn't quite place, a familiar smell. Sarah's perfume. Christ Jesus, Sarah's perfume! Pushing open the door, he stumbled into the gloom of the bar.

The room was long and narrow, the wall on the left covered in a burgundy wallpaper that had faded to the colour of dried blood, beneath which were scattered half a dozen small round tables and plastic chairs with splayed legs. On the other side was a long mahogany bar, the only clear illumination in the entire room coming from its far end, a small table lamp, its porcelain base cracked and its shade askew, sitting on the polished surface of the bar where it curved back towards the wall. The place was deserted, except—except for the far corner, where a lone woman sat at a small table, legs crossed, a cigarette dangling from her fingers, its smoke curling away into the hovering shadows.

She lifted her hand, took a drag. The tip of the cigarette glowed bright red and her eyes blazed too, burning intensely for an instant, then diminishing with the cigarette's retreating glow as she lowered her hand. "I've been waiting for you, David," she said, smiling, smoke sliding listlessly from between her lips. Her face was pale, bloodless, her teeth small and sharp and perfect.

Christ Almighty, it was her. Vicki. But not as he'd imagined her, as he'd written her. She'd changed. Remade herself. Cropped and colored her mousy hair into a spiky orange tangle; exaggerated her soft, unassuming features with dramatic, uneven slashes of ruddy blush, green eye shadow and black lip gloss; replaced her baggy, shapeless clothes with a skin-tight leather skirt and zippered vinyl vest, a leather biker's jacket hanging from the back of her chair. And she held herself with none of the uncertainty and fear he'd imagined for her, but with the sort of corrupt assurance Meyers had seen in the countless punks he'd busted. She beckoned to an empty chair next to her.

Meyers' head spun. This couldn't be real, couldn't be happening. He closed his eyes and opened them. But the bitch was still there, still smiling. Christ, what was he doing here? Sarah. He was here for Sarah. But his legs trembled, failed him, as if they'd developed a life of their own, as if the only way they would work was if he turned and let them carry him out of this fucking bar as far and as fast they could.

"Sarah sends her regards."

Rage suffused Meyers; he staggered forward, came to a swaying halt in front of the table, his fists bunched. Behind the woman, the shadows seemed to stir themselves in response, thickened like a congealing gravy, closing in. He ignored them.

"Sarah," Meyers sputtered, his voice rough, almost unintelligible; his face burnt like it had been splashed with acid. Here, near the table, an overpowering smell curled into his nostrils, sweet and sickly and nauseating all at once, made his throat constrict and his gorge rise. The coppery smell of blood.

"Ah, that got your attention." She laughed lightly, carelessly, like a child.

Back by the wall Meyers caught sight of a body on the floor, arms and legs splayed. The blood in his own body stilled, froze in his veins. He stared, but shadows clung to it like a thousand dark spider webs, cocooning it, making it impossible to see with any clarity.

"Don't worry," Vicki said cheerfully, nodding at the figure. "The bartender. Looks like it's self-serve for the next little while." She laughed again.

"Answer my question!"

"Sarah's safe." Leaning forward, she stubbed out her cigarette in a chipped ashtray and Meyers caught the rising scent of Sarah's perfume. "Or is for now. As long as you treat me right."

The anger drained from Meyers; despair filled the space it had vacated. How did you fight a shadow, a phantom? He felt helpless before her, as helpless as he had in his disintegrating marriage. He went limp, collapsing into the empty chair, cupping his head in his hands. "What... what do you want from me?" His words were choked.

A glass scraped across the table. He looked up. Two fingers of Scotch in a dirty tumbler in front of him. He hadn't noticed it before. He stared at her. And suddenly noticed something he hadn't seen before. She looked like Sarah. Christ, he'd never realized, even when he'd pictured her years ago. But Sarah was there, in the shape of her mouth, the lift of cheekbones. And he was too, Vicki's eyes identical to those that stared back at Meyers from the mirror every morning. It was like he was looking at their child.

"I need a small favor, David. It's nothing really. Something you've done before...."

Something he'd done before? Meyers gaped at her, at the cold, dead flesh cloaking the monster. His monster.

Uncrossing her legs, she reached into the pocket of her jacket, the leather of her skirt creaking as she shifted. "Here."

She dropped a pencil in front of him, smoothed out a folded piece of paper next to it. It was blank. She stood and her heels ticked across the linoleum, stopped behind him. He felt her lean over his shoulder, could hear her breathing, only it wasn't the breath of a slight woman, but ragged and huge, in and out, in and out, like an enormous, shuddering bellows; moist air licked the side of his face in warm, nauseating waves. In it he could smell the beast, her distinctive reek, the stink of the putrid organs she had carved like trophies from corpses—and the dust from his file, laced with the stench of his own fear and uncertainty, of long sleepless nights, of unhappiness, anger and failure. The room heaved beneath him, began a long, slow, lazy spin.

Reaching past him, she dragged the glass of Scotch closer, until the odor of the alcohol rose into his nostrils, merging with the stench, became so twisted, one in the other, that it was impossible to separate the two smells. She worked the pencil into the cold claw his fingers had become. In a voice that could have been Sarah's, she whispered, "Tell me a story."